TO FOLLOW THE GODDESS

A Novel By

Linda Cargill

Cheops Books
Charlottesville, Virginia

TO FOLLOW THE GODDESS

A Novel By

Linda Cargill

Published by Cheops Books,
    977 Seminole Trail, Suite 179,
    Charlottesville, VA 22901

Cover art by ©Karen Bognar
Cover Design by Deborah Chappell

Copyright©1991 by Linda Cargill

All rights reserved. No part of this book may be reproduced or transmitted in any form or by any means, electronic or mechanical, including photocopying, recording or by any information storage and retrieval system, without prior permission in writing from the Publisher, except for the inclusion of brief quotations in a review.

Library of Congress Cataloging in Publication Data
Cargill, Linda
To Follow The Goddess
1. Helen (Greek Mythology) —
Fiction. 2. Trojan War — Fiction. I. Title.
PS3553.A676T6 January, 1991. 90-083559
ISBN 0-9627258-7-0: $9.95 Softcover

Printed In The United States Of America

To Gary Cargill — only he knows why.

Acknowledgments

Many people were helpful during the writing of this book. But I would especially like to acknowledge the generous support of my grandmother, Doris B. Lappe. Also special thanks to Jim Barnes of the Jefferson-Madison Regional Library in Charlottesville, Virginia for his tireless assistance during the research of this book. To my eleventh grade teacher Arthur Tosh for first instilling in me a love of history. To Steven Toby who helped with the naval lore. To my father who served as a first reader. And to my mother and Sharon who designed and sewed together a Mycenaean costume.

I

The Bull Covers The Sun

A black bull charged across the face of the sun and consumed it until only a halo could escape. Then the Goddess of Heaven passed, and it was daylight again.

Old as I am now I can still remember the day the sky went black in Sparta. I had just turned sixteen summers in the moon of the first grape harvest when about midday the sun disappeared. No one could remember such an omen before. Only the memories of our singers went back so far. They sang of a time when my people, the Achaeans, sailed across the Great Sea to Hellas from the north many ages ago and conquered the empire of the Dorians. Then too the Great Mother of Heaven had taken away our light and given us a sign that all was not well.

And indeed all was not well. I have said it was the season of the harvest, and the grapes perished in a plague of locusts. The Dorians of Sparta, our commoners, ate dogs and cats. Disease spread like canker on the vines. I saw many cases of bleeding gums, skin sores, and the black tongue when the people flocked to my mother to be healed. And they came to her like children wailing because she, my mother, Queen Leda of Sparta, was their Goddess on Earth, and the Goddess of Heaven had turned her back on them.

They despaired that the hot season was unremitting, and no rains or cooling winds blessed our valley. The Eurotas River dried to a trickle, and only the mountaintops of Parnon and Taygetos reminded us that there was such a thing as greenery or snow. Even the frogs came belly up.

No grain issued from the temple or palace storerooms to ease their want. That grain was marked for the soldiers. All the able-bodied men in Sparta had gone with my father, King Tyndareus, and my kinsmen, Prince Agamemnon and Prince Menelaus, to lay siege to Mycenae. It was a time of war as well as a time of want.

At the time the shadow fell across our city I was giving audience to the poor women of Sparta who had no figs or olives to eat. When my mother was occupied with other duties, I, Helen, Throne Princess of Sparta, acted as Goddess on Earth to these people. Yet She of Heaven had not touched me, and it was all ritual to me.

I was curtained in a corner of the court of the megaron which is open to the sky. (Excuse me, those of you who are my age and remember when such palaces were common sights, but I am writing for a posterity who may forget since no more palaces of the Achaeans stand.) A slave girl passing by carrying a jar of olive oil to one of the storerooms chanced to look up. It had been getting darker and darker as if a storm were coming on and it was about to rain. She screamed and dropped the jar. Her hands flew to her eyes, as she fell to the floor writhing in pain. I ran to her and laid my hands on her to bring her comfort. "I'm blind!" she cried. "I cannot see anything."

I stared in horror at the sight in the pool of spilled olive oil. "Cast your eyes downward!" I ordered the women. "Do not dare to look upon the naked face of Heaven." I knew this sight was meant for me alone, and I felt the pain in my heart. I must watch in the pool as much as I wanted to shut my eyes and hide my head. The

Goddess of Heaven was stretching her hand across the sun and grasping it in her palm. Now it was as dark as night.

One of the village crones, robed all in black with only her nose protruding from the hood, fell on her face and cried, "Oh, Great Mother, you who were first and created all, even Zeus, forgive us!" She crawled along the floor, groping, and grasped the hem of my robe.

"It will pass," I promised with a confidence I did not feel. "The Goddess does not mean her people to die." Everywhere around me slave women, eunuchs, and villagers ran screaming for the light that they might see their hands in front of their faces.

"I swear I shall never leave Sparta again without your permission," I prayed to her who could see into the hearts of every one of her children and was not to be deceived or cheated of her due. I had broken one of the great taboos: neither the Queen of Sparta nor the Throne Princess ever leave the city or her shrines. That is to take all hope away from the people and abandon them to the powers of darkness.

"The Goddess is returning!" I said. Slowly she uncovered her face. It went from night to dusk to evening until finally noon was restored. The sun shone just as it always had. But the slave girl's eyesight never came back.

"Go in peace," I said, touching the bowed heads of the village women with my fingertips. I hoped they did not feel the trembling in my hands.

I had to find the Queen, my mother. She would need me and would probably scold me for keeping her waiting. I forgot to fasten my veil, not fearing that a man might see me. All would be too preoccupied with their fates to notice.

To Follow The Goddess

I hurried to the Shrine of Heaven in the Queen's apartments. My father had long ago ordered it barricaded shut, for my mother was a great sorceress, and he feared her spells. But she had never paid attention to what my father wanted. Now I knew why.

On the hearth a fire roared red against the sky. The hands of my mother and her priestesses, dressed in their starched skirts with formal flounces, were joined as they formed a long snake undulating, twisting, and darting, now flirting with, now turning their backs on the flames. Now of a sudden they jumped towards it, now they leapt away. They stuck their bellies painted with red snakes inward towards the flames, shook their hips, and the snakes seemed to hiss. Eunuchs sat apart keeping beat on their drums. When the beat stopped so did the dancers, and they tossed clay images of animals into the flames to appease the wrath of the Goddess of Heaven.

My mother wheeled around and caught my eye. Two fires burned in hers. Her naked breasts heaved and glittered in their spear points, for she had painted her nipples gold in the forbidden style of Old Crete. I thought she would burst the tight lacing of her waistband in anger.

As she approached nearer, the crow's feet about her eyes seemed to deepen into grooves. I could see the stretch marks on her breasts from nursing my sister Clytaemnestra and me. But although she was old there was nothing soft about her. "We must all come to the Goddess as naked as we were born from her," she said.

I blushed and stepped into a side room alight with candles. I was surrounded on every wall by frescoes of priestesses in procession to the Goddess of Heaven, bringing her offerings. I tried to forget my modesty and shut my eyes as I bared myself to the waist. Unguent vases sat neatly on a shelf. The paint was beyond me, for I had not the art of it and cursed myself for not learning it when I had the chance.

My mother lifted her eyebrows when I returned. Only then did I realize I was clutching my breasts in my hands and slumping my shoulders in embarrassment. She was still not sure of me, and who could blame her? I had always been my father's daughter. I was the first to admit it.

When I was a little girl and had nothing else to do I sometimes watched my mother rehearse the ancient dance steps, so I now knew enough to keep up. At the beat I too stopped and threw clay figurines of animals into the fire, all creatures of the Goddess. In the old days of Crete we would have sacrificed real goats, sheep, horses, and pigs, but my father and his father had long ago forbidden it, wanting to keep the power of the women under tight rein. Even though at a time like this the Goddess might miss the smell of blood about her altar, I was glad the animals could live.

The sanctuary of the Mother of Heaven is paved with unpolished stone. We danced until I felt the sores and blisters on my feet. "You will punish me, won't you, Almighty One, for neglecting you?" I thought.

But the dancing did little good. All around us, even in this secluded spot, we could hardly hear ourselves sing for the moaning and wailing. Women and children ran about tearing their hair and beating their chests even though the light had returned to the sky. "Oi-moi! Ai-ai!" echoed from the very walls. It got so that none of us could concentrate on the dance, and every priestess except my mother missed a step. Only when we heard the serving women throwing themselves out windows onto the acropolis beneath did my mother hold up her hand. Something must be done to keep the people from going mad with despair, and she was their Goddess on Earth.

"Helen, Heaven is not appeased," she glared at me with no mercy.

All the priestesses stared at me in fright and whispered. I could see nothing but a thousand black eyes dancing in the flames, all closing in on me. No matter if the responsibility for it could bring her death when my father returned home. No matter what else anyone could say about Queen Leda, no one could deny that she was dedicated to the old religion.

"Would you desert us again in the people's hour of need?" she taunted me. "Would you have our blood on your hands?"

"No, but...but...you ask too much," I found my tongue. My hands were creeping slowly upward to cover my breasts.

"But you brought down heaven's wrath on our heads," she insisted. My escapade, unfortunately, was well known. As was its cause.

"Yes," I acknowledged it freely, holding my head high.

"Menelaus," she spat, "is more important to you than all of Sparta. I see it now. It was foretold. My daughter will be Queen here, and under her Sparta will be no more."

To be cursed by the Goddess on Earth was no light matter even to her daughter. But I remembered who I was and said, "A private word with you, if you please, Your Highness."

"You may go," she scowled at her priestesses as if challenging them to deny her authority.

My mother wanted me to agree to the Sacred Marriage. If this forbidden ceremony were to take place in Sparta for the first time in many ages it would prove a curse to me. If you know anything of my story, you have heard that I have a reputation for beauty as men perceive it. My disappointed suitors as well as any beggar or sailor from kingdoms around could come to me that night in the temple and demand my maidenhead. The blood I shed would appease the Goddess of Heaven, and she would again allow the crops to grow. And I would have paid one hundred times over for my crime. I would also be lucky to survive.

"Perhaps you are no longer a virgin. Is that what you mean?" my mother accused me. "What happened in Mycenae?"

"I am still a maid," I answered, blushing hotly.

She threw up her hands, and I saw her gold nails as if for the first time. "For this traitor who would desert Sparta in her need so he can gain power, wealth, and kingship? That is all men think of. They have forgotten the people. To remember is the duty of the Queen."

"Menelaus would not gain power for himself — "

"Don't be a fool. If his brother captures Mycenae, he will take you and through you Sparta."

"I don't believe you. And even if I did, I would rather die than break faith with him."

"Better to die with dignity now than die the slow death."

I was aghast, but they say madness comes from the gods. "What is your meaning?"

"I was like you once, all doe eyes. I fancied Tyndareus your father when I married him. I watched him change from a caring man into a tyrant. The people became pawns to him. He would make even me a prisoner to his designs. The old truth still holds. Such is the nature of men. We must bring back the rule of the Queen." Her eyes were luminous and bright as if she had just seen a vision from the heavens.

For many cycles of the seasons my parents had barely nodded to each other except on state occasions or during the Festival of Light, the Festival of Sowing, or the Feast of the Harvest Moon. This was easy enough since they lived in separate wings of the palace and had separate entourages, duties, and functions. But this shocked me. "You speak treason!" I said.

"As long ago your father's Achaeans brought treason to this land, dethroning the Mother of Heaven and giving the scepter to their Sky God Zeus. I will take back what is Hers — and mine!"

I had forgotten that her blood was all Cretan. My father had sent for her when she was a girl as often the Achaean lords do to justify their right to rule the people. Crete was the land where the Mother of Heaven was born, and aeons ago she ruled all Hellas. Our Dorian common folk still hold by her religion, all that is now left of her empire. Being my father's daughter it was easy to forget, at least in those days, that I too had Cretan blood.

"I could never raise a hand against my father, you know that," I said.

"But you could raise one against the Mother of All?"

I reined in my temper which threatened to outstrip me. "I think you want the same power you accuse the men of wanting." With that I changed my outfit and took my leave.

I ran straight up the grand staircase to my chamber in the women's quarters. My maid Atossa was waiting for me. "Look, Princess," she said, leaping forward as eager as a tit or nuthatch when she saw me. "The sun is shining brightly again." She stepped out onto my balcony, slipped off her veil, and bathed her tiny, heart-shaped face in the sunlight, running her fingers through her long, black hair. Atossa seemed so excited and vibrant that she was like a ray of light herself, pure and innocent. I often thought what a contrast her petiteness must present to my tallness, for I was the tallest woman in Sparta.

I barely had a chance to join her on the balcony when there was a knock. Two men wearing long white robes bordered with rosettes stood before me — armed. In those days I had never seen a eunuch carry a sword, although now it would hardly surprise me.

I thought of my mother. The eunuchs stared at me in astonishment and hid their faces in their hands. Only then did I remember to fasten my veil. In more settled times it was death for any man outside my father and my honorary brothers to look upon my face or my mother's. I did not want to bring anyone to an untimely end.

They slipped past me, grabbed Atossa by the arms, and dragged her away. Her eyes bulged from her face, and her mouth opened in a strangled scream.

I ran after them, knowing I was safe because no man dared touch me. "Stop!" I commanded.

They dared not move.

"On whose authority have you arrested my maid?"

They bowed their heads as they answered, as I knew they would, "The Queen's." Sweat had started on their foreheads, and I could smell their fear.

"On what charge?"

They replied, "We hear and obey the Goddess on Earth."

The Queen had never approved of my closeness to Atossa, for she thought I should whisper my secrets to her instead. Atossa knew it. Weeping, her eyes rimmed with red, she said, "Don't worry about me, Princess. Look to yourself."

I remembered the hot nights we used to hide ourselves under the sheets, giggle, and trade our secrets. The tooth gnawed at my vitals. I willed this not to happen. It was me against my mother. I could not afford to lose my head.

My father had taken most of his soldiers with him to the siege of Mycenae to reclaim Agamemnon's right to rule that city, but he had left behind a skeleton force of the palace guard to man the watchtower at the propylon gate of the palace. Their job was to spy down upon all who entered and left. Others manned the walls far down on the slope, looking for an attack from without, not from within the fortress.

I knew a way to the watchtower that was not much frequented by others. A careless maid had dropped an oil lamp, and a fire had blackened the halls. They awaited the builder's adz and saw.

I looked right and left at the foot of the tower. From above I could hear the sound of harsh, masculine voices. The stairs were worn by the tramp of boots. No woman was allowed here, not even to serve food and drink. That had to be left at the base of the stairs.

The guards crossed their spears at the top of the stairway. They would not let me pass even though they could tell by my saffron robes who I was. They merely averted their gazes.

"The Queen has armed her eunuchs and priests. She is planning to shed blood, I know it," I spilled out breathlessly. It was treason for anyone but my father to command them. Yet I knew my father's mind in this.

They bade me wait while they consulted their commander. The captain of the guards appeared, averting his gaze in an instant. "Please tell me more, Princess," he said, trying to cover the gruff ways of the soldier with the tone of a courtier.

"You must hurry to the secret shrine in the Queen's hall. Even now it may be too late."

I could see his ambition warring with his caution. If it became known that I had commanded him he would lose his place and his life. But if he had found out what the Queen was planning through a Palace grapevine, he would get all the credit for shrewdness. And, of course, if she carried off a palace revolution without his knowing about it, he would certainly lose his head.

"Give me the time it takes for a cock to crow," I said. "I will go ahead of you and remonstrate with her. Follow and storm the shrine by surprise." In those days I was more impetuous than wise.

To this day, some two generations later, I can remember that scene as if I just dreamed it. I expected to find my mother interrogating Atossa about my doings, perhaps even taking a whip to her. After all, Atossa was a slave, a prisoner of war taken from the land of Hesperia in the west. No one but I could care very much what happened to her.

When I pushed open the door I met a sight that made me giddy. On two hastily constructed wooden altars next to the fire lay Atossa and a young male slave of Menelaus's whom he left behind when he went to Mycenae. They were both stripped naked, bound, tied, and gagged. Their wrists were bloodied where the rope frayed and bit into them. Their eyes were open wide but stared at nothing, so they must have been given the drink of oblivion to make them senseless.

In a deep hush a crowd of priestesses and eunuchs stood in a circle, their eyes fixed on what my mother was holding. Her hand was raised, clutching the Tooth of the

Goddess. On its ancient bronze blade passed down from Queen to Queen of Sparta was carved the head of a terrible beast: the face of a bull, the eyes of a fox, and the tusks of an elephant. Around it coiled a snake of gold. Its hilt was all rubies, the color of blood.

Just as I screamed, in stormed my father's guards. But when they saw what Queen Leda was about, they too froze as if turned to pillars of stone. Swords clattered to the floor. They too had seen the darkness at noon and were afraid. None of us had ever beheld anything like this ceremony in our lifetimes. It was the Sacrifice of the Return to the Goddess to be performed only in times when the very life of the state depended upon it, a last plea to the Goddess to preserve our world.

This was Queen Leda's supreme moment. Her eyes glowed red as she spoke in a low, commanding voice that emanated from the bowels of the earth and made the ground tremble. The voice we heard was that of the Goddess of Heaven who was also Persephone, Goddess of the Underworld: "They must return to the Mother of All from whence they came."

One guard dared to step forward to stop her, remembering his oath of allegiance to his lord. But my mother cast upon him the Evil Eye and made the sign for cursing, pointing her finger towards the earth. He threw his hands over his face and fell moaning to the floor. Everyone was powerless against her. The guard could not speak although his mouth opened and shut in spasms as he writhed about on the floor.

The Queen again raised her hand to strike. The shadow was upon me. For a second I was suspended between one world and another over a yawning precipice. Atossa would surely die, while I would at least have a chance. She was my only friend. "Stop!" I heard my voice.

"I consent to the Sacred Marriage."

Although as I write Atossa has been dead for over a generation as men reckon it and I have long since forgiven her, there came a time when I regretted my decision to spare her life. I have said she was my best friend. She never wavered from saying she was, but in time her treachery grew so great I would have wrung her neck with my hands. Only my pride spared me the deed.

But the next morning we were as close as we had ever been. Her gratitude was so great there was nothing she would not do for me. She even offered to dress in my robes and take my place in the temple on the appointed night.

"That would only cheat the Goddess of her due, and I am already in her bad graces," I said. "If it were discovered, the people would tear us apart." The Achaeans might be able to steal a peasant's land, his money, and even sell his children into slavery, but we could not take what was already dedicated to the Goddess. "But you can try to get to Mycenae," I said. On two papyri I had scribbled notes, one for my father and one for Menelaus.

Even then I think she was a little in awe of Menelaus. "Mistress," she said, hanging her head, "I could not presume to speak to the lords of the land."

I said, "Here," and handed her ten pieces of gold. "Find a guard who will accompany you and do your speaking for you." We embraced and said our good-byes, fearing that we might meet next only in the Land of the Shades.

On the appointed day they anointed me with scented oils. I donned my best scarlet robe trimmed in gold.

Weeping, my women came for me at nightfall and led me with torches down the darkened hallways which could not be lit until I passed. Even still I saw out of the corner of my eye men peeking from behind curtains to catch sight of me, for this is the only time in the life of a princess when she walks without a veil. My hair hung about my shoulders.

My litter awaited me outside the propylon gate for the trip to the Mountain Shrine. A wind was stirring the dust for the first time in two full moons. The breeze's coolness prickled my skin and made it stand up on end in anticipation. All my women left off their keening and gaped at the sky. Their mouths opened wide when the first crash shook the earth, light streaked across the sky, and the rains came.

I held out my hands and reveled in the warm wetness. The earth smelled clean once more, but I might never see her in her morning newness. The Goddess of Heaven was pleased with my sacrifice. My heart was glad for my people.

Yet, as the curtains closed around me and I was alone again, my face was covered with tears. The shrine where I might end my life tonight was the one I had gone to that day eight cycles of the seasons ago when I first met Menelaus.

I saw him dressed in brown homespun with scars all over his face. Agamemnon was slung over his shoulders, hanging limp, for his arm dripped blood where a mountain lion had gored him. Menelaus carried his brother as easily as Hercules carried the slain Nemean lion. When Menelaus told me later that his Uncle Thyestes had just killed their father Atreus and chased them out of Mycenae, I knew who was the brother who had kept them alive in the mountains.

Now I might never see Menelaus more.

It was not as far to the Mountain Shrine as I had remembered, but then I had always been eager to meet Menelaus there. In procession we progressed up to the door. My priestesses touched their palms to my cheeks and bowed to me, for I had to enter alone. I pressed my palms together and made the sign for peace. Though I could not take a torch to light my way, I did not stumble where I had trod countless times ere this. The night might be oppressive in its sultry dampness, but I shivered, and the stone felt cold beneath my feet.

I unpinned my robe and let it crumple around my feet. I kicked it aside like the old skin the House Snake molts in season when it is reborn into the new life. Somewhere in all the blackness swirling around me was the Goddess. I wished she would come to me swiftly and claim me for her own. What did it feel like when she sucked the soul in and spat it out again?

No sound but the rain without thunder....

After awhile I thought I heard a muffled scream. The priestesses would not dare make a sound at a sacred moment such as this, or they would have their tongues cut out. Then, footsteps were coming towards me. The hollow clunking of stiffened leather against the rough stone floor. Whoever this peasant be, he sounded confident. Not a moment of hesitation. I conjured up all sorts of visions of the terrible wretch who was coming to claim me as his bride for the night, of his friends who might come after. For a generation he would be able to boast that he took the Queen of Sparta to bed with him, and he probably a drunken sailor who on any other occasion would not be able to gaze even at my foot.

But I had been born to my part. I stepped forward to meet him, conquering the desire of a woman to hide herself at such a moment. When the footsteps stopped and

I could almost feel his breath as he stood before me, I said, "I give myself to you in the name of the Goddess." Now I had only to shut my eyes and allow him to do as he would with me.

I found myself grabbed by the shoulders and raised half off the floor. "Helen, do you realize what you have done?"

I opened my mouth, but some god robbed me of speech. I struggled and finally croaked, "Menelaus!" For an instant I felt numb, and then I was possessed by such joy that my spirit nearly flew out of my body. I tried to embrace him, but he held me firm.

He said in scorn, "We return home after two cycles of the seasons of hard fighting in Mycenae and a successful campaign with many good tidings to find a revolution brewing and you in the very center of it! You have spat on all our laws and broken all the taboos. And you very nearly gave the right to the kingship to the first comer."

"But don't you see? The Goddess has been merciful. She has brought you to me. You are the first comer," I kept trying to reach out to him. To feel him in my arms again would be blessed whether he was angry at me or not. My whole being seemed to yearn towards him. I could feel the tension in his muscles, the strain it took to keep me at arm's length. I felt he longed to be reunited with me again for the first time in many moons, for at Mycenae my father had sent me away without seeing him. But his anger held firm.

He shoved me away from him. "Wrap my cloak about your shameful nakedness and see that your face is well-hooded. I will not have my men hooting at you," he said, hurling his cloak at my feet. He was a man who meant what he said, and I obeyed to keep the peace.

He picked me up and strode out of the temple. I put

my arms around his neck and laid my head on his chest, resting at last from my long travail. No matter what he said I felt safe with his strong arms about me. "Not even the Goddess of Heaven can touch me here," I thought. "But what happened to him in Mycenae?" I wondered. "He sounds so serious for one who is only eighteen cycles of the seasons."

The sight that greeted my eyes stopped up my joy and changed it to weeping. There on the rain-cooled ground in the torchlight lay all my priestesses with their throats slit, dying or dead. Blood welled up through the slits in their windpipes, gurgling bubbles and choking them as they tried to groan. Fresh from the march back from Mycenae soldiers stood over them, their swords still bloodied from the deed. An army of bronze. Their gazes were lowered so that they could not look upon my shame. Only the hooded figure of Atossa stood there to greet me, still among the living. She must have reached Menelaus in time.

"I consented to this!" I thought. "My women trusted me, and I led them to slaughter." The Goddess was not pleased with my sacrifice or with me. She had spat me out without tasting me.

"But Menelaus!" I turned to him. "How could you have ordered such a deed? This is not like you."

He looked stunned himself, and I followed the direction of his gaze. There astride his horse sat his brother Agamemnon, now High King of Mycenae. "These sluts deserved no better," he boasted.

"How little he has changed!" I thought with hatred. I glared at this huge, hulking figure of a man crowned with a mass of red hair that he had always said was a mark of divine birth.

"Was this necessary, brother?" Menelaus asked.

"They were traitors!" he said. Some of his soldiers were eyeing him with fear, some with admiration.

"So this is what it takes to be High King of Mycenae!" I thought. "A murderer! Long live the King of Men!"

Menelaus would never contradict his elder brother, the chosen of their father Atreus. He had sworn allegiance to him from the time he could talk, and even if he no longer admired him, his honor would never let him speak. I could feel Menelaus's hands trembling as he said, "So be it!"

When his hands had regained their steadiness he thrust me up onto his horse in front of him. "And my mother?" I hardly dared to whisper, already knowing.

"The King has ordered her walled up in a cave in the hillside with food and water. If she dies, it will be her Goddess's doing."

Fate slapped me in the face, and I began to cry like a babe — all gray-skinned, wrinkled, and covered with blood — newborn into the world. I had no love for my mother, but she had died the death of a traitress. In that instant I was no longer Throne Princess but became Goddess on Earth. All who dared gaped at me as if I were suddenly transformed before their eyes. Menelaus had to tie my hands in front of me. I was his captive and a traitress too by virtue of my office.

No one ever knew what happened to Queen Leda. The villagers to this day are afraid to go near the cave. They say on rainy nights they can see her. And to this day whenever there is thunder in the skies, I hear her voice.

II

I Defy The Goddess

There was a time when nothing came between my father King Tyndareus and me. That time was now ending, and nothing could I do about it. We became enemies at sunrise when the women who survived took me outside into the stream naked and threw rice over my head.

When I was about eight cycles of the seasons my twin brothers Castor and Pollux died in battle. They were the jewels of my father's kingdom. I knew he was grieving alone so I sneaked down from the women's quarters and came to him in the king's private court, open to the sky. I put my hand into his.

"Let me show you something," I said through my tears.

He seemed surprised but was in a docile mood and could be led. "Look," I said. "I saw it from my window." I pointed up into the heavens. "Do you see those two bright stars, bigger than all the rest and seeming side by side? They are almost like twins. My brothers' souls have flown up there and found a home. Every night they can say hello to us." I wore on my finger a ring of the magic gray metal that fell from the sky, thinking they had sent it to me. It possessed a certain sheen of its own.

He caught my thought, "Oh, my little Helen, the

gods have left you to comfort me in my old age." He buried his face in my hair and kissed me. "You shall have to make do for the two of them."

And he kept his word. From that day he brooked no words of disapproval from my mother but treated me as much as possible as if I were a son and not a daughter. He helped me deny my destiny as long as possible. He let me conceal myself behind curtains as he met with the Council of Nobles and asked me later what I thought of heavy matters of state. He knew I often took riding lessons from Menelaus, and though women were not allowed to ride he winked at it.

Once he said to me, "Sometimes I wonder if Zeus the Father sent me Menelaus and Agamemnon to be my sons and soothe my heart, poor orphans that they were. But especially Menelaus I do trust."

Even in later years when I used to meet Menelaus in the mountains so that we could be alone, I think my father suspected. But again, he was certain that Menelaus would not break the Seal of the Goddess and draw her wrath down upon the kingdom. There was no other man he would have trusted so. Tyndareus reprimanded me occasionally for forgetting to fasten my veil, but that was about as far as it went. He loved me, though before he came to the Kingdom of Darkness, he had cause to rue my birth.

I thought on those early days in the sunrises that followed my mother's passage to the beyond. For the first time my father ordered me confined to my rooms while he and Menelaus decided upon my fate. Agamemnon left Sparta for Mycenae as soon as he discovered that my sister Clytaemnestra had eloped with the King of Pisa the hot season before. She did not love Agamemnon and wanted to escape him.

Soon the word went out by herald and by proclamation that the kingship of Sparta was a prize to be won, and I was the booty. All the chivalry of Hellas who were not wed were invited.

The unthinkable had happened. Menelaus had refused my hand which my father had offered him. Atossa, who had been serving wine at the time, overheard Menelaus say he feared I might prove "as treacherous as Queen Leda". She told me he sat there with his shoulders squared and let my father's entreaties bounce off him like rocks aimed at the shield. No matter how my father urged upon him that it "was no light thing to turn down a kingship" he said he would return to Mycenae where his brother Agamemnon needed him. Agamemnon had always come first with Menelaus. Blood was stronger than love.

No logic would prevail with him. He seemed not to care that my father must abdicate. Tyndareus no longer possessed the Queen who gave his rule legitimacy, and my husband must succeed since my brothers were dead. Menelaus did not care that Sparta needed a strong King. Troy was levying a tariff on all our ships that sailed up her coast or passed Asia Minor in search of bronze. If our bronze stores fell short, we could no longer defend ourselves. So great was his revulsion at my deed that he could turn his back on what Priam and his sons Paris and Hector were planning.

"He must be bitter indeed," I said to Atossa, "if he can turn me away whom he has sought so long to win." Atossa, sweet thing that she was, knelt on the floor and lay her head on my lap. I stroked her long black hair and dried her tears. She was the younger, and I had always taken care of her, so thought nothing strange of it that the mistress should succor the maid. I fancied her my daughter who was not yet born.

"I am accustomed to my freedom," I told her. "So

I will not bestow my hand according to the luck of the athletic contests nor the richness of the bride-gifts. I can't help following my nature in what I do now."

"But, mistress, you may already be in danger of your life!" she clutched my robe. "Don't tempt the Fates." Her eyes were two luminous tears.

I put my hand over her mouth. "Lend me your robes," I whispered. The maids were allowed to come and go to bring me my meals, and it was about time for the midday repast. Men were not permitted in the kitchen, and no guard would follow me on such a mundane task. Only then did I thank the lawgivers that women must be veiled, for I could pass as a serving woman.

But I was far too tall to imitate Atossa's mincing step. I would have to stoop over and pretend I was an old crone with a rounded back. Nor could I show even a woman my face. People who had never seen me before inevitably recognized me for who I was. Once, gazing into a mirror, I asked Atossa why this was so.

Atossa had said, "Princess, yours is the face the people see in their own minds when they think of the Goddess."

I have never understood what she meant by this, just because I was well-featured. No mortal could ape a goddess. But when they beheld my face for the first time men and women alike acted as if this were true.

Most of the palace consisted of dark, internecine passageways that threaded their way around the state rooms like the meshes in a spider's web. Not all of these were lighted by balconies, windows, open courts, or light wells. An occasional torch was stationed in the wall, usually at a guard post. I glided past these nameless faces. To judge by the phalanx of guards stationed in the lobby next to the king's study I could tell my father and Menelaus

I Defy The Goddess

were meeting there. There I hoped they remained until I escaped.

Through hall after hall I wended my way into the old wing of the palace. The soft clay under my feet was grooved from hard use during the rule of many houses of Kings and had been replaced again and again. In the center of the open court was a huge hearth with leaping flames that sizzled and sparked with the smell of burning olive oil and the juices of the lamb being turned on the spit. Around the fire were gathered with stooped shoulders the female denizens of the place, condemned to toil their lives here with barely a glimpse of the world of trees and flowers. Their eyes were half-closed from the smoke. I wondered if they could see in the dark like moles. Not even the Goddess on Earth had ever visited them.

I hurried to the waiting block where the maidservants stand. Soon one old gnome asked me, "What will you have?"

I replied in the Dorian dialect, the language of the common people, which I had learned from Atossa: "A luncheon for the King."

The gnome was at once surprised, "Only one woman for such a large order!"

A convenient lie sprang to my tongue: "A luncheon snack. The King conducts business." The gnome soon handed me a tray with two goblets, a pitcher of wine, and pickled lamb wrapped in grape leaves, which was a favorite of my father's.

As soon as I was out of sight I poured the wine into a skin and fastened it to my girdle under my veils. With the food I did likewise. I would have one day's head start, no more.

It was a novel sensation to see the guards glancing at me indifferently instead of averting their eyes as I wove my way in and out of the halls, stooped over and halting. Even in my sadness I could enjoy the freedom in it. I was truly like the invisible Goddess walking freely among men with no man suspecting unless I should will it.

There was enough of the gambler's blood in me to take a desperate chance where the stakes were so high that I could lose my life. But my life was not worth much without Menelaus. If he thought better of his decision, he would come and find me, for he would surely know where I was — only he. But twice since that day have I taken bigger risks. The first time I lost and started a war, the second I won and ended it.

I emerged from the palace and was immediately swallowed up in a crowd of chattering palace women smelling of every scent in nature but their own. They giggled and jangled the bracelets on their wrists, trying to while away the time. I pushed through these idlers until I stood in front of the group. The creaking wheels of a donkey cart fast approached the propylon gate. Bouncing up and down in her seat was the fat old washerwoman, waving "hello" to everyone who crowded around her cart with sacks of dirty laundry. In the bustle I pretended to consult her about my mistress's garments.

"Hide yourself in my wagon," she whispered.
"I knew I could count on you."

I had befriended her, even as a little girl, and she had sneaked me out of the palace to watch her doing washing in the river, although on no account would she let me help her. She imagined I was the Princess's maid, for I never let her see my face.

So we drove the old rickety cart down the acropolis and out the walls, down the hill towards Sparta and the Eurotas River. She gossiped with me the whole way, cherry-cheeked and laughing. "Quite a scare we had the other day, wasn't it?" she said.

"Yes," I said. "But the new Queen promises all will be well."

I exchanged clothes with her, trading her rags for my palace finery. In the marketplace, in the farmer's dialect, I haggled and bargained for a good horse, paying for it with a silver bracelet with ax and bull's-head charms.

Lakonia is the region of Hellas most famed for its horses, and it is so even to this day. No one can call himself a man unless he owns at least one of these fabulous beasts. In other regions of Hellas fathers give dowries of oxen or goats for their daughters. But around Sparta, it is often horses. And this horse was in no way an inferior specimen. He was sleek of limb and a shining brown in the sun like the newly washed earth after a storm.

Neither Menelaus nor the Goddess seemed to want me. I could belong to myself, just like an ordinary person. So I climbed the mountains. First I passed the reeds and oleanders that grew thickly on the banks of the Eurotas. Then I made my way through the olive groves on the lower slopes which were beginning to feel the touch of the season of changing leaves. Billy goats looked quizzically at me, trying their horns on each other while goatherds milked the she-goats.

Higher I climbed into the foothills. I surprised a group of wives beating their laundry in a mountain spring, which had renewed itself since the last rain. They laughed and hailed me from under their brown hoods. I saluted them in their language.

Now the path was so steep that my horse was breathing heavily, and we moved at an ant's pace. We were past the line where the poplars grew and were now surrounded by a forest of firs. Overhead swooped the vultures with the sharply curved beaks, harbingers of the

Goddess of Death. Down I peered into the dizzy chasm of sheer rock where the people of Sparta were wont to throw their deformed babies who could not live. I could imagine the bleached white bones staring up at me.

Where I was headed I would be even more alone. I could see it ahead every time I came to a clearing — Mt. Ilios, the highest peak in the Taygetos Mountains. Its snowcap could dazzle even from this distance. Ever since I was a girl it had fascinated me, and I had always longed to go there. I had often told Menelaus of it, and now I wanted to see if he would remember — and if he did, if he would care.

If he repented of his recent mood, he must come to find me. The Menelaus of old before the siege of Mycenae would not be able to help himself no matter how he cursed me. That Menelaus would be too embarrassed not to do it alone. It was my only chance to speak to him in privacy.

I stopped at the stream for the night and watered the horse. Then I set about collecting fallen branches to build a fire, for the nights were becoming chilly at this height. You may wonder how a Princess of the royal blood would know how to build a fire. I had watched Menelaus do it many times when we ate our luncheon in the woods. But there was no way I knew how to imitate his hunting feats. I had my "King's snack" for tonight and had discovered that it contained enough dried figs, nuts, and cheese for seven sunsets if I did not indulge myself.

After that time if he had not come I would either have to return home in disgrace and failure or proceed to the kingdom of Pisa where my sister Clytaemnestra was Queen. There I could claim sanctuary at the altar of the Goddess of Pisa. No man could force me to marry him then. But that would condemn my Spartan people to perpetual night, and I had sworn when the sun disappeared from the sky that I would never again leave Sparta. Being Goddess on Earth was a terrible burden.

So I waited, hoped, and prayed, and did much weeping besides. At night I slept with my arms around the horse's neck for company. I even dreamed that the horse was transformed into Menelaus, who would vanish whenever I woke. But on the third night it seemed colder than usual, and I opened my eyes early in the morning to a light blanket of snow covering the ground. It was far too early in the season for this, but then on the mountain frost came early, and snow was no stranger as it was in the valley. Yet I could not help feeling as I shivered that some god was against me. Or perhaps the Goddess herself was still angry.

I fell to my knees in tears and prayed aloud, "Oh, Artemis, Mother of the Mountains, I beg of you, be not wroth with me! I would gladly have given myself to you, but I was prevented." I then recalled all too clearly that it was Menelaus who stopped me and his brother who ordered my priestesses slain. Those maidens belonged to the Goddess.

Suddenly as clearly as if it were happening in front of me I saw a vision. My skin prickled, and I felt a coolness. I had never felt this power before. I saw Menelaus riding into the mountains disguised in the skins of a goatherd. At once he was attacked by a band of hooded men. He brandished his sword, but he was outnumbered. He was lying on the ground wounded, and I saw his blood red against the snow. "Helen!" he said. "Helen!" across the blackness of my mind. He was drawing me down the mountain in his great need, and I must go to succor him.

I leaped onto my horse and headed back, alarm thudding in my chest, hoping to overtake whatever fate was in store for my best beloved and to turn it back. Even if he did not care for me anymore, I could not help but care for him.

Late in the evening I reached the lower slopes where the snow had already melted. I heard voices in the clearing. I tethered my horse to a poplar, took off my sandals, and tiptoed silently to where I could see. In the leaping shadows of the fire sat a band of lawless mountain brigands wearing lion and bear pelts tied around their loins and shoulders. They feasted and drank as they roasted a wild boar whose blood dripped into the flames and made them crackle and spit. They passed around a skin of wine which each one grabbed in laughter from his fellow. Wine dribbled down their chins.

To one side roped to a boulder sat my Prince bound hand and foot. I recognized him despite his disguise of a hooded cloak of skins. Around his arm was tied a white cloth soaked with blood. So he had been wounded!

My feelings were so mixed that I fell to my knees overcome. He had followed me! The Menelaus I knew before Mycenae was still alive. Yet now I had brought him to this impasse for my sake.

One of the brigands with a long, hooked nose who wore a string of gold coins and lions' teeth around his neck — he must have been their leader — tossed a bone at Menelaus and said to him, "For the last time tell us who you are. You must be a wealthy noble carrying a sword like this." This brigand with the visage of a vulture brandished Menelaus's battle sword in his face. This was the sword bearing the double lions of Mycenae on its hilt which Menelaus had brought with him from his native city when he first came to live in Sparta. "You might yet live if your relatives will send us a ransom," he said.

"For the last time, no. I would not bring such shame upon them, fool."

"You must be a brave man to speak such words," the brigand pointed Menelaus's sword at his throat.

"I hope I am not of such quality as to shame my ancestry," Menelaus said. His dark eyes flashed, but the rest of his countenance he held as expressionless as a rock. His quality was obvious by his light skin and blond hair. He could not be one of the people.

The brigand said, "You can dream on it until tomorrow morning."

Yes, he was brave, honorable, and true, and that is why I loved him so. I who had to creep around, play tricks, and devise schemes revered one who was unbendable. Also, he was wise. He knew that once they received the ransom Tyndareus would surely send, they would kill him.

I crept silently back into the woods like a wounded animal and kneeled on the ground of newly fallen leaves. For even though the hot season had lingered overlong, the season of falling leaves had begun with a vengeance ever since the rain. As evening came on, the breezes quickened, and they were cool.

"Goddess," I whispered aloud, "spare me his life. If I must be your Goddess on Earth, I must needs have him by my side." I trembled because I dared bargain with her.

The leaves rustled all around, their hollow, scratchy sound like so many ghosts of the unburied. My skin prickled, stood up on end, and I shivered with cold and fright. The rustling became louder and louder. All at once I heard the wind speak, and I knew it was the Goddess. At last I was her chosen vessel, and I knew what it meant to be in the Presence.

"Helen," she hissed very low like a snake among the leaves, "if you be child of my womb, you will put this son of man from you. He has displeased me. His blood calls out to him, and his allegiance is to the House of Atreus and his accursed brother Agamemnon."

"No," I dared to beg, "ask me anything else!"

"Very well then. Choose. But choose wisely," she seemed to enter into me and speak in the beating of my heart. "If you sacrifice this hateful son of Atreus up to me this day, you will live long and prosper peacefully in Sparta alongside a husband of my choosing. He will come to you along with the other suitors, but you will know him at once. He is the wisest among the Achaeans, and he respects me. He will bring you peace, and one day will be the same as the next until you die, which for mortals is an uncounted blessing.

"But," she warned, "if you will have me grant you the boon of your lord's life, you must pay for it more dearly than woman ever paid. You and your King, and yeah even your children, and your children's children will curse you for it, and even all Hellas. Your very name will become a byword among the Peoples of the Great Sea for ages to come for trouble and strife. You will be beholden to me, and I will do with you as I choose."

"Lady, forgive me," I wept, "but I would choose him over my life. He is dearest to me of all mortals. Lady...."

She left like a great wind being sucked out of me. I felt shaky with amazement and drained of all strength. But when I was empty of her, I had a plan.

That night all of the brigands but two rode off to raid a nearby village. I crept into the camp and cut Menelaus's ropes with my knife. He did not seem the least surprised to see me and did not spare me a glance. He put me aside behind a tree for safety and grabbed his sword from the sleeping brigand leader.

"Arise, thou son of a piggish whore," he said, "and

I Defy The Goddess

defend yourself." Another would have slit his throat while he slept, but not Menelaus. Both robbers awoke and jumped to their feet. "Before you die, know the quality of the man who was your captive and tremble. I am Prince Menelaus, son of King Atreus, brother of King Agamemnon, the High King of Mycenae, and kinsman to King Tyndareus of Sparta. Surely some god has plotted your downfall."

Menelaus made short work of one robber, but the chief was something of a King himself and found his own sword. The robber chief had lived by his wits for too long not to try to bargain now, but Menelaus would take only the straight road to death or glory. They began to circle now one way and now the other. It seemed like some kind of dance to me, in time to the beats of my heart. If no one takes a chance with his life, he cannot hope to win a victory. Menelaus lunged at his breast. The robber was taken by surprise, but with the instincts of a cornered animal he parried the blow at the last moment. I could see he was using all his strength as he threw Menelaus back.

Menelaus was not at all disconcerted. He was merely biding his time like the lion who waits for his victim to tire before moving in for the kill. The robber saw this too and grew frightened. He started hacking away desperately at Menelaus before his own courage and strength gave out. Menelaus merely stepped back, to the side, or parried his blows.

Sweat poured down the robber's face. He looked like one who had seen his fate. The life went out of him. He fought on but without a will. Menelaus feinted to the right and then lunged to the left. The robber no longer had the strength to keep up, and the sword found its mark. He was dead before he knew it, and in that he was more lucky than he deserved.

Menelaus would not be impious. He did not have time to bury the dead, for the other brigands might return any moment. But he did kneel down and pour a handful of dirt over each of their heads. That way no man could say that the Mother had not come to them at the last to succor them and release their souls for the long voyage to the Underworld.

Without another moment lost we were on our horses and off. We could not go very fast. It was dark. He tied my horse to his, led me into a cave, and sat down beside me. We did not dare build a fire, though we could hear no sound but bats.

I was trembling, but I felt for his hand and found it. He yanked it away. "Menelaus," I whispered, "I am Goddess on Earth now." I remembered my bargain with the Goddess. "My first duty as Queen is to my people. Surely you can understand that, for as King it would be your first duty too. You have been in Mycenae, but surely it cannot have escaped your notice that the Spartans are starving. I must share their suffering and lave their wounds in any way I can," I tried to defend myself.

"Your first duty is to the King, to support him in any way you can. And to bear him legitimate issue," he said, "not to offer yourself to the first comer in an archaic ritual and then run off into the mountains so I must come chasing after you."

"Sh-h-h-h!" I said in fright. "The Goddess is already wroth with you for profaning her temple. Don't tempt her further. And you will have no kingdom to rule if everyone starves or rises in revolt to overthrow his masters. They have not forgotten that we are aliens in their land."

"The people will do worse than starve if the King of Sparta loses his place, and the Sea Peoples and the

I Defy The Goddess

Trojans come to raid, burn, and rape. Then all will return to chaos," he said.

"You know not the truth of what I am saying," I spoke. "You have been gone long." I felt tears coming at the gulf that was widening between us and was to widen in time until it stretched all the way across the Great Sea.

"I have been to war, killed many men, and know what a hard thing it is to be King. Before I was merely a boy."

"I suppose your brother showed you how?"

"He is a hard man but a better ruler of men than I," he said with loyalty.

I lay my head against his shoulder where I had so often found comfort in the past. He rose, took himself apart, and threw himself down on the floor of the cave as if to sleep. I could do nothing but follow the direction of his steps in the blackness. I stroked him gently with my hand from his forehead down his back. "Let us not speak," I whispered. "Let me soothe you." It brought me a pain that was almost physical to hurt him so. I felt as if I were being torn apart sinew by sinew. I wept to feel how his every muscle rebelled under my touch and tried to shake me off. I prayed to the Goddess and touched Menelaus as I laid my hands on my people to bring them peace.

I felt him start. He grabbed me by the hand and threw me over his side to land in front of him, almost knocking the breath from me. "My father had my adulterous mother put to death for less than this," he said under his breath and kissed me.

The blackness that kept us apart now enveloped us like night and hid our deeds both from the Goddess and from Zeus. Two cycles of the seasons had vanished. We contended with the other who could get closer. Our very lives seemed to depend on it. Just as in the past we forgot every scruple but one, the one we dared not break, the Seal of the Goddess. She had always stood between us there. I thought he had forgiven me, but then he said at the last, pushing me away with great effort, "My feeling for you is unchanged, you little fool, but still I can be no husband of yours. Honor forbids it."

III

Odysseus And The Suitors

On the first day of the Festival of the Choosing the great fire in the hall of the megaron was alight. Slaves in white robes stood around it, tossing herbs and incense into the maw of what seemed to be a living god in its terribleness and might. Now it would spark green, blue, red, or purple, and thus with a roar would it greet each suitor who presented himself to my father and Menelaus.

The King and the Prince, for Menelaus presided as my honorary brother, sat on thrones on a raised dais. The lion and griffin of Sparta guarded the throne against all pretenders who were not worthy of such dignity. They gazed down from the wall on each Prince or King from a less exalted kingdom who dared to claim my hand.

Each man would announce himself and return to his couch of gold to eat of the banquet from a table carved of a shiny black rock that was the gift of the Earth-shaker himself. Long ago when the kingdom was first founded the earth heaved and split. One of our mountains groaned, and spewed forth a fiery red flow. It hardened, and in reverence the earliest King of Tyndareus's line carved his treasures from it. He swore to keep them locked up and to use them only in times of great importance such as the occasion when the kingship passed from one generation to the next. If the choice fell upon the wrong man, it was said the Earth-shaker would show his displeasure. He would roar and destroy the kingdom, and the King's dignity would fall around his ears.

I sat behind a heavy silk curtain on the opposite side of the hall, well-shielded from the gazes of the men. Clutched in my hands was a wreath of ivy with which I must crown the next King of Sparta at the end of three days. All trusted that the Goddess would move me to the right choice. My father would pick himself except that he too greatly feared the Goddess, though he had been forced to wall my mother up in a cave.

A suitor who looked like a wrestler with arm muscles like the gnarled trunk of a tree strode up to the dais and did not even bow his head in respect. I stared in fright at the gashes and scars on his face which he proudly displayed. He put his hands on his waist and stood with his legs spread apart like the giant Atlas and glared around the room as if daring anyone to challenge his claim to the throne of Sparta. He cast his eyes my direction without shame or concealment, and they burned with lust. I shuddered and bowed my head. "Goddess," I said, "who is this creature?"

"I am Achilles, King of Argos..." he announced himself.

"Achilles!" I said to Atossa. "They say he is the strongest man in all Hellas since Hercules died."

Achilles clapped his hands and his Myrmidon slaves carried in a rolled up goatskin. They emptied it in front of Tyndareus's throne and out spilled a hoard of gold rings. Then another of jewelry in the Cretan mode with fine filigree work. Some of the jewelry looked so old it must have gone back generations.

"Goddess," I said, "I want no rich brute for my

husband." I thought of Menelaus. No matter how angry he got, he never dared lay a hand on me. The wife of this man would not be so lucky. He had no fear of the Goddess.

Suitor after suitor followed. Two young men contended with each other for pride of place and argued all the way up to the throne. I feared it would come to blows. They called themselves Diomedes and Ajax. They were smaller than Achilles but more wiry and sleek like two horses. I could imagine them running with the spear. Their slaves carried to the throne baskets of bulls' head rhyta and libation vessels of fine materials as their bride-gifts. As they were being presented they turned around and tried to peer at me like two youths who might die of curiosity.

"I will not take callow youths to bed," I thought. Again I could not help but stare at Menelaus. He was young but so old in his mind. He would not so far forget his dignity as to start a brawl in the megaron.

Menestheus, King of Athens, brought roll after roll of silks from the east. He dressed as if he carried his state treasury on his back. "But I cannot marry a suit of clothes with only stuffing for a brain," I thought indignantly. Menelaus never thought twice about the clothes he wore. He left that up to his slaves.

But choose one of these Kings or Princes I must since Menelaus had found me unworthy. "I would rather die," I said to Atossa.

"But, Highness, you have your Spartan people to think of."

"I know," I said. "That is the only reason I allowed Menelaus to bring me home from the mountains."

My father's face was growing more and more troubled as much as he tried to conceal it. He pulled at his long white beard and screwed up his brow the way he did when deep in thought. He had not counted on this, and could see disaster brewing. Usually the more important suitors would bring costly bride-gifts, the others humble fare. But this time every suitor outdid himself. These were proud men. All somehow believed they were favored to win the second richest kingdom in Hellas next to Mycenae. Indeed political conditions were as unsettled as Menelaus warned.

I tried to catch Menelaus's eye, but he evaded me. Menelaus sat beside Tyndareus as silent and aloof as an Olympian. His face was inscrutable. Yet he too did not miss the mood of the assembly. Not a muscle in his face twitched as his eyes went from one to the other of the suitors.

After I thought the ceremony was over, the last of the suitors stood up. All eyes went to him. He was short of stature and the most rough-featured man I had ever seen as if he lived all his life out of doors. The sun had darkened his skin and toughened it, although he was still obviously an Achaean and not one of the people. His hair was as dark as Atossa's, which was strange, and a few gray strands showed him to be older than all the rest.

As he approached the throne the crowd began to murmur aloud, "Look at his clothes! A northerner! A mere peasant King!"

Another said, "Look, he brings no bride-gift!"

He bowed his head graciously to both my father and to Menelaus and said, "And I, last of all, sue with only my humble self. The poverty of my Ithaca will not allow me to come bearing gifts," he said with the fluency of a polished courtier from the east, a man much experienced in the world and well-traveled, though he remained as rugged as the rock-bound land from which he came.

Achilles started the uproar. He pounded his goblet

on his dining table and shouted, "Throw the beggar out!"

That gave Diomedes and Ajax courage. Not to be outdone they cried, "Let's see him with a spear!" Menestheus of Athens merely sniffed and turned his head the other way.

Soon everyone was pounding on the tables. A few were even standing on their couches. Achilles towered over all and shouted over the din, "Who are you?"

This Ithacan turned to face his accuser and said with unruffled calm, "Odysseus."

The catcalling and hisses started anew. I heard charges of "pirate" being hurled at him. But he took advantage of the confusion to look at me. There was none of the lewdness or curiosity of the other suitors in his eyes. Instead he seemed to be trying to communicate something to me. He raised his eyebrows, and the Goddess put the idea in my head he wanted to speak with me.

I thought, "I must arrange to meet with this Odysseus." His bearing impressed me even if no one else, and I was indignant at his reception. Only then did I recall what the Goddess had said, "You will know him at once. He is the wisest among the Achaeans."

Menelaus was on his feet. "Son of Peleus," he addressed Achilles with a frown, "Odysseus is welcome."

The catcalling stopped. Achilles resumed his place, and the others followed. In such a way did Menelaus always command the Achaean host. There was such fairness and nobility in his manner, he was so far above them, that they did not dare to defy him.

My father exchanged whispers with Menelaus. Then he rose. "Suitors, you are all alike in honor. I fear you might take offense if I give preference to one or the other. I can accept none of your gifts. They are of too great a value."

The shouting broke out anew. Menelaus took to his feet and walked among them to quiet and remind them they were peers of Hellas. And this time Odysseus helped him. But there was no help for it. If one gift were accepted, they would all take to their swords.

The suitors were guests of honor, and my father entertained them as such. The maidservants brought in silver pitchers, poured water over their hands, and dried them with towels. Then each one was served the feast on his own table. His goblet was filled from the common wine bowl, and several sheep were slaughtered and roasted. The variety of fish in spiced sauces was past counting, for although Sparta was a landlocked city, her port of Gytheum was only a morning's journey by horse. And for the sweet course that followed all else, we enjoyed flaked pastries made with honey.

When I gave the orders assigning the maidservants to bathe and anoint the guests with oil before retiring, I made certain that Atossa would attend Odysseus. If he had a message for me he would send it by her. I could tell by his watchful eyes he would.

That night I merely pretended to retire. I could in no way get comfortable with so much on my mind. Atossa was gone long and did not return, and still did not return. It was unlike her. I was beginning to wonder if I dared go myself to see what happened (for there was no other handmaid I would trust with so delicate a mission) when she returned.

At least I thought it was she. She came and kneeled by my bed with a quiet step. Then she said in the deep Ithacan voice I remembered, "I can help you if you will help me."

For a moment of terror I clutched my sheepskin covers and wondered if I had mistaken what this Odysseus wanted. I found my voice, "Sir, you are mad! This is the bedchamber of the Goddess on Earth."

To deflower the Goddess on Earth was a crime that meant certain death. Menelaus, my nearest kinsman, would have to kill him.

He laughed lightly, and I was even more shocked. "Do you think I would rape you with the guards all about? Yes, I have seen to them. They are well-drugged."

My admiration of his cleverness soared. But I was still a little afraid of his boldness. I decided to try him further. "Why do you think I am in need of help?"

"It is my way when traveling to keep my ears open and my mouth shut."

"But surely I do not need your assistance in choosing a husband. So how else could you be of help to me?" I was not sure of my footing with this King of Ithaca and did not want to reveal more than I had to.

"It just so happens that you can assist me in obtaining a wife."

Now I was certain I had been mistaken. The others had been right. This man was an ill-mannered oaf. My ire was up, and I said, "Sir, you are the last of the suitors I would choose."

Again he dared to laugh. "Queen, you and I would be the oddest of matings! A goddess among women renowned for her beauty and a humble dwarf among men like myself, the daughter of one of the richest kings of Hellas and an obscure king from an island kingdom who had not even the money to advance a bride-gift. Besides, I have heard that you are already spoken for."

There was such irony in his voice I was certain I was being insulted. "Talk plainly," I said. "We Spartans have a tradition of saying our minds and knowing when enough said is enough."

"Very well," he said. "I no more fancy you for a wife than you do me for a husband. A wife must be chaste."

I leaped out of bed with the covers clutched around me. "I think you had better leave," I said. How dare he address me with such disrespect! He no more understood the Sacred Marriage than Menelaus did. But I did not love him as I did Menelaus, and I did not have to defend myself to him.

"As you wish," he said and headed for the door. "Tis a pity," he sighed. "I am the only one who can help you find your way to naming Menelaus your King."

I started. He really did know more than I imagined, and he never in Sparta before! "Wait," I said. "How do you — "

"I keep my eyes and ears open. It's obvious that's who Tyndareus favors as well, and you are your father's daughter. Besides, not even a man like Menelaus can hide his hurt pride from a keen and observing eye. Word of Sparta's troubles travels fast."

The man's shrewdness amazed me. "Sit down," I said. I managed to wrap my covers about me and light a lamp. "Why are you provoking me?" I asked.

Odysseus shrugged, "So you know who is in charge. I won't have you thinking you can wind me around your little finger as if I were Menelaus. The poor man is lovesick with your beauty."

So he answered insult with insult. "Menelaus is no woman's fool," I said.

"Will you deal with me or no?"

I calculated quickly. There was no use lying since he seemed to know everything anyway. "Very well, I admit that I would choose no one but Menelaus. But you are no friend of his. How can you help me?"

Odysseus had me where he wanted me, and then he

bargained, "First, since I could not possibly hope for the favor of the hand of a great lady like yourself, I do not particularly relish the idea of returning home empty-handed. My Ithacans would never forgive me for that. You are first cousin to the Lady Penelope, Icarius's daughter. And, more importantly, her father is Tyndareus's brother."

"Yes, King Icarius is my uncle. He brought Penelope here many years ago, and we were fast friends as girls. We have not seen each other since, but we still occasionally send messages at the times of the Festivals. You want me to persuade my father to use his influence to gain you Penelope as a bride?"

"Her virtue is as famous as your beauty," Odysseus said. "And I much prize humility and obedience in a wife."

"Sir, your sharp tongue does not advance your cause with me," I spat, piqued. I had done nothing to deserve this treatment, and yet I had to submit to it because I needed him. My fury mounted, and I began to dig my fingernails into my palms in frustration.

"On the contrary," he teased, "I think you admire my sharp tongue, or I would not use it. Even if I had really come here to court you instead of to ask a favor, I would do it no other way." He gazed at me in amusement.

He was right. His manner did make me respect his intelligence. Never before had I met anyone who could manipulate me. The knowledge made me blush. "This conversation must be ended soon," I said.

"First, pledge me your word of honor that we have an agreement. Then I will give you my advice."

"Very well, I pledge you my word."

But he was not satisfied until I swore an oath by the River Styx, the most terrible oath of all, and the one that could not be broken. Then he crept over to me and whispered his plan into my ear.

It bore the mark of a brilliant mind, just as the Goddess had promised. It was simple, but that was its genius. These suitors were full of hubris and would indeed behave as Odysseus said. "Go quickly," I said. "I will talk to my father at the first cock's crow."

When I met my father early the next morning, his eyes were brighter than they had been in a long time. "Well, child, what do you think?" he said immediately and recounted how Odysseus had been to see him already. I had a hard time concealing my surprise until I realized what Odysseus had long before thought of — I would have a hard time explaining to my father that Odysseus had been in conference with me in my bedchamber last night, for truly we had no other occasion to be alone.

Odysseus had left it to me to make up Tyndareus's mind. I took his arm and said, "Father, Penelope is just the sort of girl to appreciate so clever a husband. You know she could not lie to save herself." He hung on my words, for at his time of life he had little energy for prolonged conflict. Mycenae had sapped whatever he had left. And I honestly think he would do anything to gain Menelaus as a son-in-law.

It remained only to get Menelaus's consent, and of course that was the hard part. I convinced my father that I should speak to him first, and he arranged it.

I was nervous waiting alone in the King's study. The room was one of the largest in the palace, and I felt lost in it. Other than a few armchairs, a table, several rugs, and two or three vases there was nothing in it but me. If I spoke, the Goddess Echo would throw my voice from the dark wood paneling on the walls.

I paced about and stopped to look at myself in the mirror beside the Warrior and Chariot Fresco. My face betrayed my lack of sleep from spending half the night bargaining with Odysseus. I wondered why he disturbed me so much, and a voice seemed to answer from within that he was like me. We both tried to live by our wits, and the Goddess intended him for my husband. "But I could not love him as I do Menelaus," I protested. "He may be crafty, but he lacks Menelaus's nobility of soul."

I heard footsteps, and I could tell that it was Menelaus for my whole body responded at once. I spun about, and my heart began to throb as if it would burst. He looked at me sadly. He acted as if this were an unpleasant duty for him as he advanced into the room.

I thought, "If I come right out and tell him Odysseus's plan he will resist. I shall have to soften the ground first."

"Today is the athletic contest, and tomorrow the Choosing Ceremony," I said, casting my eyes downward. "Unless you will change your mind, I must pick one of the suitors. The choice is an indifferent one for me. As my honorary brother, who would you have me choose?"

"Helen, you know this is not kind," he said, turning away from me and walking to the table. He put both his hands astride it and bowed his head in deep grief.

"What if I told you I inclined towards Achilles?" I bit my tongue, and it smarted. Smart it must, for I must persist in my strategy.

He pushed away from the table and strode down the room until he stood in front of the fresco of the bulls. "I would say the man is a pompous bull, chafing at the bit for a fight. No sooner would he be King than he would declare war the next day on his neighbors. Sparta does not need wars right now."

"But it is important for a King to be a good fighter. You have said as much yourself," I was cruel so that later I could be kind.

"Yes, but a King also needs sound judgment."

"What think you of Ajax?" I said. "He and Diomedes put on quite a regal display yesterday."

"Helen, this is no joking matter," he gritted his teeth as if in pain.

"And Menestheus," I said in a shrill voice as I tried to fight back my tears, "certainly he dresses like a King."

He stopped pacing like a caged lion and turned on me. He grabbed my arms and shook me. "Better it would be for us both if you did not have so smart a tongue."

"Perhaps I shall choose Odysseus," I said, for I could tell yesterday that Menelaus was beginning to respect the man, though it was against his training to do so.

Menelaus looked at me in anger. "I had to welcome him as the duties of guest-friendship dictate, but the man is not honest. I don't know why he dared come here. Everyone knows he is some sort of pirate King up there in Ithaca."

I gasped, and we both spun about to face the door at the same moment. In walked Odysseus with as much calmness as if he were entering his own dining hall. Quickly I flashed "Not yet!" with my eyes, but he ignored me. I had not yet learned that it was hopeless to dictate the moves of Odysseus.

Menelaus stepped in front of me, for I did not have my veil fastened. "What do you mean by intruding upon our private conversation?" he challenged Odysseus.

I blushed as I realized that Odysseus had probably been listening at the door all along, carefully choosing his moment.

"You must be King, Menelaus. You are the only one who can save Hellas from a civil war. And that would be no smart thing right now with the Sea Peoples and Troy threatening us on every side."

"This is none of your business. You are a guest in this house," Menelaus said.

I held onto his arm and pleaded, "Menelaus, listen. My father has sent him."

Menelaus glanced at me as if he wondered what I was up to now. "Very well, if Tyndareus has sent you, but he has told me nothing of this."

At that moment Tyndareus followed Odysseus into the room. "I knew you would be too stubborn to listen," Tyndareus said. "Hear this man out, for he has our good at heart."

Odysseus explained to Menelaus just as he had to my father and me, "You no doubt have noticed how all Helen's suitors are ready to set upon one another as soon as they have reason to suspect one of them is preferred?"

"Yes," Menelaus said. "They do not show their breeding in this."

"Well," Odysseus continued, "the way I see it you are the only one who can prevent disaster. Remember how they all listened to you when you chided them and did not resent you for it?"

"Yes, but that was only the duty of any host and the response of any guest," Menelaus said.

"Menelaus," I said, "surely no man of your humility has yet graced your high station."

"That's exactly the point," Odysseus said. "They do not resent you because they sense you are too far above them. And you certainly outrank every man here. As brother to the High King of Mycenae as well as Tyndareus's foster son, you are the only one they would respect being placed over them."

"My brother outranks them, but I have no place, no kingdom," Menelaus said, correct to a fault.

I stamped my foot in impatience.

Tyndareus put his arm around Menelaus's shoulders, "My dear son, you have only to consent, and all shall be yours."

Odysseus continued, "Before the Ceremony of the Choosing Tyndareus will have the suitors take an oath of allegiance to defend Helen and whatever husband she shall choose against whomever contests the marriage. Each man will take it eagerly, imagining that he will be chosen. Then he will be too proud to be the first to break it when he loses, and too ashamed, I might add, when the choice falls on you, the more worthy one."

Menelaus looked as if he immediately appreciated the genius of this solution and seemed even more surprised that it could come from such a man as he imagined Odysseus to be.

"So it is your duty to put aside your doubts about the Queen and marry her," Odysseus concluded.

I did not thank Odysseus for his patronizing portrait of me and glared at him, but I could see in his eyes that it was his signal for me to speak.

I fell to my knees and grabbed Menelaus's hand as if I were a suppliant. "Do not hold it against Sparta that I am her Queen," I said.

He pulled me to my feet almost before I finished speaking and put me to one side, not listening. I should have known he would not be fooled by my show of humility. He knew me too well. Menelaus looked meaningfully at Tyndareus and Odysseus and said, "I shall reconsider."

A serving maid was coming with a letter.

Odysseus And The Suitors

Odysseus took it from her and presented it to Menelaus, saying, "From your brother." As my lord was reading it, I gazed in wonder at Odysseus. He met my inquisitive stare with a knowing grin. This Ithacan must have made a study of Menelaus to figure out that the key to his heart was his brother. And, he must have arranged this show well in advance, before he had anyone's consent.

I could not contain my impatience. "What does it say?" I asked Menelaus.

"Agamemnon orders me to be King of Sparta," he said, dazed. "He says that he can trust no one else to fill the post and to be his right-hand man."

"Good Goddess," I thought, "that I must owe this boon to Agamemnon!" But I remembered she had no sympathy for me in this and no love for the sons of Atreus.

That night there was more feasting, and the next day it was my turn to crown Menelaus the victor. On the chosen day the palace women prepared a banquet to surpass all banquets. I thought myself happy, but little did I realize that one more cloud must pass over my fortune that day.

It is a custom among the Achaeans to celebrate every solemn occasion with a sacrifice, "to take the omens" as it were and see if the gods approved of what they planned. I knew this, but I never suspected whom the choice would fall on. Tyndareus ordered a horse to be brought before him, the finest in the stables. An altar was erected, festooned with garlands of irises and wreaths of ivy. A sadness seemed to pass over the proceedings as the poor trusting beast was led all unsuspecting to the place appointed for his end. This was my horse, the one Menelaus had used to teach me to ride. He was now past his prime, but still magnificent. This just could not be.

"Mistress, are you all right?" Atossa was tugging at my robe. "You are turned white." She ran for water.

My hand was on the curtain of my tent, about to rip it across and stop the men myself, when I felt a cool breeze prickling my skin and the whisper of the Goddess: "Helen, I did make a contract with thee. I have given to you as husband the far-famed Menelaus against my will. I did warn you that your half would not be easy. But thus is fate when a mortal shall go against the gods. Another would I have given you as husband."

A hand grasped mine and pulled it back, almost wrenching my arm from its socket. "Fool, think what you are doing!" hissed Odysseus. "You could ruin it all." He had sneaked in the back of my tent. I could see the sweat of effort standing out on his brow, for he had run here to stop my folly, somehow sensing what my reaction would be.

I shall never know even to this day why I was not more shocked to find him there. Perhaps I had already gotten used to him appearing in the oddest of places, but I do not think it was that — at least not yet. Somehow, I knew he understood. "No," I protested, "it's not fair the horse should suffer for my sake. He has done nothing." I cried and tried to break free from his hold. But his grasp was much more powerful than mine.

It was then that they slit my horse's throat. I heard his whinnying protests as he thrashed about on the ground, and the life went out of him. A deep groan welled up from my stomach. Odysseus clasped his hand over my mouth and drew me over to his shoulder where I sobbed with a will.

He held me and tried to quiet me. I could feel the roughness of his dark beard with many gray hairs against my head. "The horse was lucky," he said. "Unlike us mortals he had no vision of his own end haunting him all the days of his life and slowing his step. His agony was but a moment, and now he is with the gods. Better to die now, since die we all must, than wait until old age had crippled him and dimmed his eyesight. Think of it that way," he said as if explaining life to a child. I suppose I was but a child to him. "I know how you feel, for I have a dog named Argos at home of whom I am very fond. I wish such an end for him," he said with a sensitivity I was surprised to discover in the wily Odysseus. "But I must go now," he said. "I will be missed. For I must take the oath too. Dry your eyes," he raised my veil and helped me. "You must still crown the King."

"Yes, I suppose I must," I tried to smile. When he left as quickly and quietly as he came I felt a lingering emptiness. And such was the birth of our friendship which lasted many cycles of the seasons until he at last set sail from Ithaca never to be heard from again.

Atossa was waiting outside the tent and came in to me. "A strange man, a strange man," she shook her head. "One never knows what he will do next."

"No one can think as quickly as he," I said.

My father made a brief speech about the unsettled conditions in Hellas and how that called for a show of unity. A stable Sparta as a bulwark for the High King of Mycenae was the key to that. He asked for an oath to support his successor. Odysseus immediately stepped forward to second the motion. No one was going to let that pirate King from Ithaca seem more noble than he, and the rest stepped forward together in assent.

The suitors joined hands above the bloody sacrifice, each placing his right hand on top of the others. Each King echoed the one before him, striving to sound more forceful and louder than his predecessor.

On and on for the space of time it takes for sailors to hoist the sails of a ship went this roster of the Kings and Princes. Every speck of the soil of Hellas was represented. Menelaus spoke for his brother after he spoke for himself. Menelaus boasted of his brother's wealth and power as he would never do for himself, saying, "I, King Agamemnon, High King of Mycenae, son of Atreus, Lord over Corinth, Clenae, Orneae, Araethrea, Licyon, Hyperesia, Gonoessa, Pellene, Aegium, and Helice do swear...." And, representing his brother, he had the privilege of speaking last of all.

The word of a King or Prince was legally binding and needed no other confirmation. But, for the purposes of official record, the palace scribes of Sparta sat at a respectful distance, hurriedly scribbling down their very words on clay tablets. Later, at their leisure, they would transfer the sacred oaths onto scrolls of fine papyrus from Egypt and publish the alliance throughout the country to the far reaches of where our language was spoken.

I was more thickly veiled than usual for the ceremony. I wore my bridal clothes and the insignia of the Queen of Sparta. This occasion would represent the formal betrothal. Around my neck hung Queen Leda's necklace of tiny gold axes, stones, and blue rosettes, taken from her at the last as she was left in the cave.

Atossa exclaimed, "Why, mistress, you look like the Goddess indeed! So tall and stately, you tower over all mortal women."

But it seemed that a heavy weight was bearing me down to the earth as I parted the curtains and stepped out.

These Kings and Princes did not have to look at the ground as I approached them. They had the privilege of rank. I was unaccustomed to being stared at by a crowd of men in those days, although now when I go out I can hardly escape the stares and pointed fingers of those anxious to show me to their grandchildren.

    I had to reassure myself that they could see merely a veiled form and nothing of my face. Only my sandaled feet which peeked out from under my robe and my bejeweled fingers, laden with the gold rings of the Goddess, were visible. For in my hands I carried the wreath of victory.

    At first I had eyes only for my horse, lying there as if death had surprised him with his eyes open. Nor could I check my tears. I could not avoid going by his corpse, for it stood between me and the suitors. As I walked past him it seemed I left my girlhood behind, and a shadow passed over my heart that has never lifted to this day. I felt as if I were doing something very guilty that I could in no way atone for. His blood would be on my hands forever.

    Nearing the group of suitors, I looked up. In their eyes I saw wonder, astonishment, curiosity, and in all an eager anticipation that I should crown him. But could they not all peer into my soul and see my blood guiltiness? "Athena, Goddess of Wisdom..." I wept to myself, "guide my steps and give me strength." I felt as if there were a mist surrounding me, and I was hardly aware of what I was doing.

    Odysseus too was staring at me but not like the rest. He seemed oddly set apart, although he stood in the midst of them. I had the strange sensation of looking into a mirror as I gazed into his eyes. They looked puzzled as if taken by surprise by some alien presence. He was rooted to the spot, unable to move. It seemed he could look neither to the right nor to the left, but only straight ahead at me. My skin prickled with a coolness. I shivered and felt Her Presence.

    Then, at the last moment, with a supreme effort of

will, he shook off the spirit. He looked stern. With the slightest tilt of his head, he glanced back over his shoulder. At that instant I realized where I had been headed — straight for Odysseus!

I passed right by him and continued through the crowd which parted before me. I was numb with the shock of what had almost happened. I hurried on and placed the crown on Menelaus. He bowed his head slightly to receive it, for tall as I was he was taller. I was surprised that he seemed unaware anything had gone amiss. No one else had seen except we two and the Goddess. To this day, long after Odysseus has passed to the Other Shore, I often wonder if all the rest that followed from this ill-omened day could have been set aside if only we had not thwarted her will.

IV

The Wrath Of The Goddess

Even after Menelaus and I recited our vows by the fire in the throne room of the megaron, we could not be together. That first night and every succeeding night for the next two moons, my women draped shut every window and balcony in the women's quarters. No light must enter. And every night for two moons they took themselves downstairs to the storerooms to sleep on mats. No one could witness the deed of darkness that was to be performed in my bedchamber.

I myself lay in the darkness. When I heard Menelaus enter my room, I had to bite my tongue. I must not speak to him for fear of drawing the wrath of the Goddess down upon my husband and King. He was intent upon breaking her Seal.

To deceive her ministering spirits, my maids had even disguised me in the clothes of a peasant woman. I wore a plain cloth, a burlap, instead of my customary silks. Nor did I wear a beguiling scent.

I could feel the rough material of Menelaus's costume as he picked me up into his arms, for he too was disguised so that the Goddess would not think he was the King. He held me away from him as he swiftly took me to the place where my women were wont to sleep. There he performed the marital rites and spirited me back into my bed.

Every night for two moons this secrecy continued. Nor could we speak to each other by the light of day. Everyone in Sparta waited for a sign from the heavens. If the Goddess sent a plague or the Earth-shaker vented his anger, the marriage did not please the heavens. If nothing happened, it was well-omened and could continue.

I waited in agony, for the Goddess had not approved this union with the House of Atreus. She had promised me hardship and misfortune, and as my part of the bargain I had sworn I would endure it.

Yet it was our fate to become King and Queen at a time when our public duties set us at odds. I cannot help thinking the Goddess had a hand in it.

When our daughter Hermione was born Menelaus came to me with trouble on his face, enfolded my hands in his, and said, "Helen, I must ask your help."

When he explained to me what he had in mind I was aghast. This was worse than anything I could imagine. Surely my mother had spoken truly when she prophesied that I would be the Queen under whom Sparta came to naught. "But you will condemn our souls to eternal death," I said. "They will never be reborn but will return to dust when our bodies do."

"Better than for both body and soul to become dust before their time. Agamemnon has sent word that the Raiders have sacked Perati. The King of Perati listened to the Queen and would not profane the temples for bronze. He ran short of weapons and had to surrender. Nor did the Goddess come to his aid. Everyone knows that Zeus and Ares lend no succor to kings who are ruled by their wives."

This sounded like Agamemnon speaking indeed, a

King with little fear of the Goddess. "Menelaus," I said, touching his arm, "surely you understand that if I sanction this, the people will feel that there is nothing sacred left on earth?"

I looked into his gray eyes, and they were cold. His mind was hardened against the Goddess. Perhaps for the first time I was afraid of him. He would stop at nothing when he felt his honor as King at stake.

"And if I refuse?" I asked.

"Helen, I will give you plenty of time to think on this, but if you refuse...well, this is just too important. I will not allow it."

It would be a disgrace to be dragged from my rooms, so as soon as my confinement was over, I complied. But I let Menelaus see plainly that he had gone too far this time. Not a word would I address to him either in public or in private. I put on the regalia of my office. I would give him a good show if he insisted on one. Yes, even he would be impressed.

I had my maids bring me cask after cask of the jewelry that was passed from one Queen of Sparta to the next. I was determined to look like the Goddess whose arms the people weigh down with offerings of oil and honey. On my head I wore a gold circlet crown. It kept my veil of crimson silk in place over my coils of hair shaped like snakes that wound around my neck and shoulders. Suspended about my waist hung the chiefest of the treasures of Sparta — the skull of the last Minos of Crete dipped in gold. I would appear as Mistress of the Animals. And man would be not the least of my subjects. Let Menelaus look upon me and fear the power I have.

When the doors were thrown open I strode into the throne room of the megaron. I did not look either to the right or the left at the warriors. Not for me the rows upon rows of soldiers lined up brandishing their spears and sporting their bronze armor. I looked straight into Menelaus's eyes. He stood foremost among the companions and nobles of the palace and behind them the elite of the palace guard. As always he wore a simple tunic and leather leggings, functional and ready for action like all the Kings of our people.

With one swipe of my hand I wrenched the veil from my face. They stared in horror and fascination at my naked breasts protruding above my jacket bodice; they were tipped in gold. The men coughed nervously and looked away. I forced myself to meet their looks with all the courage I possessed. This was the forbidden dress of the Queens of Old Crete, the very one my mother donned for the Ceremony of the Return to the Goddess.

"Now he will send me back to my room, and the ceremony will be canceled," I thought in relief. My sacrifice of modesty had not been in vain. There could be no postponement of the ceremony, for the court astrologer had named this evening as the only time we dared to attempt such a dark deed.

The anger in Menelaus's eyes changed to one of cold intelligence. He had conquered his outrage and seen that my dress would give him more credibility with the people. I had miscalculated. I had not realized just how hard and determined events had made him. He was King first and husband second.

He stepped forward very correctly to take my arm, regaining his poise and making his face inscrutable. He was calling my bluff and making me go through with it. I looked towards him, but he would not meet my eye.

Like the Queens of old I would walk to the burying ground with my bare feet treading the dust. Let the earth give me strength. I went forward and thought of nothing but her power emanating upwards through my feet. As soon as we came through the acropolis gate, my skin prickled, and I felt her breeze. I heard her say for the first time since my marriage, "Well done, Helen. I am proud of you."

When the people saw me, the God of Speech deserted them. Never before in their lifetimes or their father's or father's father's had anyone seen the face of the Queen, the Goddess on Earth. All fell to their knees, and some lay prostrate on the ground rubbing their faces in the dirt. They wept tears of joy and poured handfuls of earth over their heads. It was the cold season. There were no flowers so the women cried out to me and threw dried kernels of corn over my head. The Goddess had appeared to them in her ancient glory. In this state I could take their babes from them, and they would gladly allow their sacrifice. I could lead them where I would, and Menelaus knew it.

Menelaus stopped at the edge of town and lifted me up on his shoulders. At first I did not know what to say, but Necessity gave life to my tongue. The Goddess would not desert me as long as I maintained my dignity. "My people," I said, warning Menelaus who they really looked to as their sovereign, even if Menelaus still held me in thrall, "the Goddess asks a great sacrifice of you this day. Never before in all the annals of the history of our people has such a desperate deed been necessary. The dead of Sparta, the ancient dead, rise up to me in my dreams and cry out to save her. Even they, who have given their lives for her safety once, are willing and ready to give their lives again. We need bronze to the very extremity, and we must take it wherever we can find it. The dead in the Royal Tomb have made known their wishes. We may open up the sepulchre and take their riches, take back what we have given to the Mother. The Mother loves her people and would not have them perish from the earth. The spirits of her dead will again march in our armies."

There were a few murmurings of dissent, but then they cheered me.

I knew I was no Goddess even if they did not. It was all I could do to keep back my tears and hope that no great harm would fall to them from my deed. There was always a guard at the Royal Tomb to keep away robbers, and now Menelaus was to play the brigand, to plunder the treasure of the Goddess. He was no better than the robber King we had encountered on the mountain. Worse, because it was his duty to protect the dead as well as the living. I thought, "My father would never sanction this," when I caught sight of my father marching in the procession. His face was ashen. When he met my eyes, he turned away in shame, but shame at my dress, not the deed.

"The men are all one in this," I thought. In measuring the distance between my father and me I knew I was Goddess on Earth.

Not far from the walls stood the great mountain tomb of my ancestors. Within its walls rested the bones of the House of Tyndareus. A great fire already blazed in front of the entrance. One of my priestesses, robed all in white, weeping, handed me a bowl of spices and scents that gave off their essence when burned. As the soldiers took down the wall of stones that blocked the entrance, I from time to time threw a handful of incense into the flames to sweeten the foul air from the inside. And the wind blew in our direction. The Goddess spoke her displeasure in no uncertain terms.

I looked around for the man who would perform the sacrifice, when Menelaus thrust the dagger into my hands. I closed my eyes. Scenes of my mother officiating at ceremonies flashed through my mind. Someday Hermione would have to look up to me and succeed me at these tasks.

The lamb's warm throat bleated under my hand as I felt for the place of the beating of its heart. I hardly dared trust myself to meet its gaze. Only the fear that if I did not I might miss and cause the poor victim to suffer more than necessary persuaded me.

Fear shone in its eyes, for even the dumb beast sensed its end. I stopped to stroke its head. It closed its eyes in relief and trust and nuzzled my hand with its nose. "Now!" my heart thudded, for I could bear it no longer. I quickly ended its life, and its life's blood poured into a bull's head rhyton below. But when I removed my hand its eyes stared up at me accusingly. The smell was foul, and that was a bad sign. I met Menelaus's eyes, but his were veiled and expressionless. I stepped back to Menelaus's side holding the rhyton. No longer could I restrain my tears. I had broken my trust with the lamb as I had with the Mother.

The torchbearers lighted the way as we processed into the tomb, the soldiers following. The dank gray stone rose higher and higher on either side as we traded dusk for darkness and fire. None of us dared to make a sound, for it was as quiet as I had ever imagined death would be. Suddenly the giant bronze doors appeared before us. An apparition. I looked questioningly at Menelaus, and he nodded without pity.

I thrust my stick into the rhyton of blood and marked the doors with an "X". The soldiers would pull them down and melt them into bronze for weapons. The doors fell back, glittering in the flames like a thousand stars.

"Whatever we find of gold, that too," Menelaus

whispered so that I only could hear. "Agamemnon needs to hire mercenaries to defend Hellas."

Against my will I strode forward. Who was this man at my side commanding me? His lips were closed tightly until they turned white, as he did when he was driving himself from necessity. I gaped at him, but the rest of his face was as impenetrable as the rocks of the circular chamber we were entering. The domed room thickened with dancing shadows. The earth beneath my feet changed to a rug of gold beaten and fashioned so thinly that it looked like silk cloth. There lay my twin brothers Castor and Pollux, Princes of Sparta and her chiefest glory.

I glanced around for my father, but he could not bear to look again upon his favorite sons. He feared to be haunted by the ghosts of these laughing and gay boys, bubbling over with spirits, and chafing at the bit to fight and prove their valor. They had picked me up and carried me around on their shoulders, and now they had dissolved to nothing but two skeletons, their hands still clasped as they had been in death, never to be parted more. Still they wore their armor of bronze in which they had died, and on their heads still gleamed twin circlets of gold. My father had wanted to show the shades what they could have been in life.

Everything was as we had lovingly laid it out nine cycles of the seasons ago when I was still a little girl stunned by the blow that cut off the House of Tyndareus. We had provided them with what they would need for their journey to the Underworld. Familiar bronze bowls for food, flasks of oil, combs and mirrors, all was still there with which they had sustained themselves until their flesh had dissolved and released their souls.

Their favorite swords had gone with them, melted down to set free their souls of metal for fighting demons.

Arrow shafts lay at their feet, a final tribute to valor from their companions. Leaving the last resting place, the companions had turned and shot arrows into the darkness to say good-bye.

Tears so blinded me that I nearly tripped over the bones of their horses who had gone to meet death with their masters. No one else was fit to ride them. A hand steadied me, and I stared up in the firelight into Menelaus's face. "A living soul is locked up within a statue," I thought, for only his eyes were alive to glare through me. Perhaps only I could read the tension there as his sympathy for me warred with his offended dignity, appalled by my costume.

I shivered and could hardly master my hand to make the red marks. It was then I spotted my doll. It was only a wooden, painted thing with black hair and eyes to look like one of the people, but it was my last tribute after all the family and kindred had showered over the dead their last gifts. No one had been able to stop me as I ran back through the darkness to place it there. Only now could I see that it rested between them.

Menelaus again thrust me to my feet and pointed me in the direction of the side chamber. I could see he was impatient to get this over with, for it had become distasteful to him. He swallowed hard. My feet balked. I could hear my brothers' voices howling in protest from the beyond. I took my stick, dipped it into the rhyton, and made a giant "X" on the wall of the tomb. "Take whatever you will," I shouted over the voices, but no one else seemed to hear them but me. "I shall have no more to do with this."

The ground moved underneath me. I felt a tremendous roar like a thunderstorm. The stone walls of the tomb shook. It was as if someone were pulling a rug out from underneath my feet, and I found myself in Menelaus's arms, my own clutched around his neck. "Forgive us, Goddess, forgive us," I prayed. We were running. Menelaus propelled me back through the long passage faster than I thought a man could run, almost as fast as my heart was beating.

Again a roar sounded, and rocks were wrenched asunder. Behind us in the tomb screaming rose. Everyone rushed for the fading light of day. We fell to the ground and rolled out of the tomb, dust enshrouding us. We tried to flee, but the Earth-shaker pulled us to our knees. The tomb that had stood for generations rocked on its foundations. The walls collapsed. The dome fell in, muffling the cries of those who had not had time to escape.

Practically the whole city had followed us to watch the ceremony. Now all Sparta ran about like wild maenads in the pell-mell rush to save their own lives. No direction was safe, for the Earth-shaker was everywhere just like the Mother's anger. She reminded us from whence we came and to whence we should return.

No matter that even from this distance we could see the city aflame from the toppled oil lamps and spreading cooking fires at the time of the evening meal, every person hurried to it. Injured men and women lay on the side of the road and cried out for help, lifting their arms, but anyone who was down was trampled to death. The people became a stream and then a river. The road was so choked it could contain no more. The swiftest pushed towards the center, and the weaker were thrust to the side in pools and eddies. Horses and carts crashed and foundered. People stabbed each other to steal a horse that could go nowhere in the press and which someone else would only murder him to take.

Menelaus had me on my feet and pulled me to high

ground. He tried to summon his guards with a wave of his hand. Those that were not killed acted as the rest and thought only of saving their own lives. He tried to let the people see him so they would take courage. No one looked. "The gods are not angry," he yelled. "It was fated, and even the gods must bow their heads to Necessity." But no one heard him. "Say something!" he turned to me in desperation. "Say anything!" I could see by his grief-stricken expression that he knew the Goddess was angry at him. But he was a brave man and took the responsibility upon his shoulders.

I could not speak but stood high on a rock and raised my arms in mute appeal. No one was looking my direction, so it did not matter. Now I realized that the Goddess had said, "I am proud of you," because she hoped by my costume to inspire me to my mother's deeds. I had disappointed her.

My husband was always a man not to waste time in useless regrets. He bowed to Necessity. He stole the cloaks of two dead guards. One hooded cloak he wrapped around me and the other around himself so that we should have the protection of anonymity. In case anyone recognized the King and tried to tear him apart for bringing this calamity upon the people he armed himself heavily.

He slapped me in the face and shook me to bring me to myself, for I could do nothing but gape around me and fall to my knees praying to the Mother not to let her wrath at me destroy the people. "Keep your legs moving and stay with me no matter what happens," he commanded. He took my hand and moved into the crowd.

To be a King among the Achaeans you must be strong and earn your title as well as inherit it. A man's fighting qualities were his manhood. So my husband had no trouble keeping up with the crowd, he who had crossed mountains in the cold season as a boy and who had seen battle. No one could push him aside. His shoulders were broad, and he could smash his way through the mob.

I was not as lucky. But he would not let me fall by the wayside. Our hands were as firmly welded together as two bronze swords melted in the fire. But to keep my arm from being wrenched from its socket he finally slung me over his shoulder.

We had to go through the city to get to the palace. The scene here was one of even greater confusion. As many were fleeing from the fire out of the city as were crowding into it to reach home, for even the wounded animal returns home to die, knowing no other place. Others wandered not going anywhere in particular. Children had lost parents, and parents had lost children. Dogs tried to save their masters. The yelping, barking, screaming, moaning, and howling were enough to deafen one.

One of the largest merchant's houses in town had collapsed into the main street so we had to take a back alley. It was so choked with smoke that we had to fall to the ground and crawl. Menelaus gripped the sides of the buildings that had managed to survive, and I followed his feet.

At the gates to the palace a mob was gathered brandishing sticks, clubs, knives, and their last remaining possessions if only a chair. They demanded to be let in. The palace, miraculously, was still standing, untouched, and whatever fires had been started were put out.

"The King!" they chanted. "The King!" They blamed his impiety for the shaking of the earth, and if they could lay hands on him would tear him apart. It would never occur to them to be angry with me for sanctioning the plunder. As far as they were concerned, I was not mortal, and a mere mortal dares not be wroth with the

The Wrath Of The Goddess

Goddess. Nor did they expect me to be rational or consistent. They adored the Goddess when she showered blessings upon them and feared her when calamity befell them. They blamed themselves, not me, for failing to understand my words. To them I was birth and death, harvest and famine, peace and war at once, and no man claimed to understand their causes.

Menelaus perceived that he dared not throw back the hood of his cloak and demand that the guard let us in. But he did manage to push us to the front of the crowd. I raised my face and let the guards look upon it without letting the people see. As I have said, even those who have never seen me before always recognize me for who I am.

A young member of the guards, a lieutenant to judge by the griffin insignia on his breast, stood only a handspan away from me. He stared at me boldly, grinned, and then tilted his head questioningly at Menelaus. I frowned at his presumption. He was asking me, if I did not misunderstand him, if I wanted him to save me and let the mob deal with the King. I did not have time then to wonder how the King had erred in allowing him to become part of his elite palace guard.

"I will permit these two to come in to see the King. They will carry your grievances to him" the lieutenant said, opening the gates just enough to put his hands on our shoulders and help us squeeze through.

V

Of War And Bronze

Menelaus ordered me to my chambers to be confined there until further notice. His anger at my show of power caused him not to come to see me at night for several days, but when he came he was more preoccupied than furious. The guards were putting out fires in the city and manning the gate in force to make sure the mob did not attack the palace. Menelaus was distributing grain from the palace and temple stores to the populace, for magically the palace and several temples still stood almost unscathed. He told me he had sent two runners to Mycenae to request reinforcements for his depleted army. Menelaus never wavered in his trust for his brother.

Agamemnon sent troops to Menelaus, and for the first time hired mercenaries roamed the streets of Sparta. When they were not keeping the people away from the palace, the mercenaries were busy digging out from the Earth-shaker's visit.

I should have guessed the word from Agamemnon meant only more trouble.

One morning I awoke to hear my women wailing. Menelaus had gone from my bed. I barely had time to throw my robes about me before Atossa came running in, her loose black hair flying about her face and her veil out of place. She threw herself to her knees before me and wept, "Please come and pray with us."

No sooner was I out of my room than my women were on their knees clutching at the hem of my skirt, tearing their hair and beating their chests just as they would at a funeral. Some were even running their nails down their cheeks and leaving red welts.

"Silence!" I ordered, but none complied. They just shook their heads and wept more loudly. I picked one girl up by her arms and made her stand on her feet and face me. "Give words to your grief," I said. She just wailed as if some god had bereft her of speech. I lost my temper and struck her face. She merely covered her face with her hands and sank back to her knees.

"If no one will tell me what has happened, I can do nothing," I said. "Where is my father?" I raised my voice above their sobbing.

At that their shrieks grew louder. It was just as I had feared. The scene at the burying ground and the Earth-shaker's visit had been too much for his old heart. "Atossa, come with me," I said as I felt my own knees sinking. She put her arms about me as we hobbled along supporting each other, two women crumpled up in grief.

I headed for his bedchamber in the old wing of the palace. That explained why Menelaus had left my bed so silently without so much as a kiss. He would be at Tyndareus's bedside to close his eyes as his loyal son. He wanted to spare me. But when I reached my father's bedchamber, two guards crossed spears to stop me.

"What is the meaning of this?" I asked. "Would you keep me from my father's deathbed?" But of course they were not allowed to speak to me anymore than they could look at me. It was easy to forget that they had no will of their own but were merely the instruments of the new King's will.

Atossa finally realized my mistake. She tugged at my robe and said, "Lady, it is not your father. He is with the King in the council chamber. But you are needed — "

I shook her off and ran. It must be bad news from Pisa. Perhaps my sister had died in childbirth or some similar horror. But why hadn't the women been summoned to their balcony to view the ambassador's reception in the throne room?

I tried to remember exactly how my sister had looked that day when she set out to be the King of Pisa's wife. Her brown hair falling around her shoulders, her eyes ablaze with love....

Guards again blocked my way into the council chamber. The door swung open, and out rushed a cohort of palace guards intent on some errand. They nearly ran right into me. I gasped as I recognized the young lieutenant wearing the griffin insignia. He seemed to have a crooked mouth, as if he were perpetually grinning at the world. It crossed my mind that he might be a new soldier my father had brought back from Mycenae.

The lieutenant did not seem surprised to see me. He smiled at me with his crooked grin and bowed in elaborate fashion. The other guards shrank back in terror at the presence of the Goddess on Earth. Most were the light-skinned Achaeans but they still had the fear of the Goddess in them.

"First to the shrine," the lieutenant barked to the other soldiers.

"But — but we men are not allowed to enter there," one of them protested in horror.

"You heard the King's orders," said the lieutenant in the tone of one who would march into the pit of Tartarus if he had determined upon it. "He specified every repository of bronze in the entire city. And shrines are not to be exempted."

In the time it takes for a man to go from sleeping to waking I realized what Menelaus was about. I was not allowed in the council chamber by long-standing tradition. But in that instant I forgot and slipped past the guards.

There sat my husband at the council table flanked by my father on the right. Menelaus was busily bent over a pile of documents to which he was affixing his gold seal of a lion interlocked with a griffin in mortal combat. To the right behind the King were his chief officers of the palace guard in gold-embroidered tunics and leather leggings tied at the knees, boasting the beards and long, ornamented hair that their calling allowed. To the left of the King stood deputies and representatives of the royal governors of the provinces of Laconia.

"I demand to know what is going on!" I strode up to the council table and confronted Menelaus.

Menelaus nearly dropped his seal. His lips parted in surprise, then pressed together in resolution. "We shall discuss it later," he said, hoping I would remember myself. His eyes flashed a warning.

The soldiers and representatives looked away in embarrassment, whispering. What King would allow himself to be questioned by a woman, even if that woman were his Queen?

But this matter was too serious to discuss later. "The altar of the Mother must not be profaned," I said. "That is sacrilege!" I glanced down and saw a letter before him marked with the double lions, seal of the Royal House of Mycenae. I knew it was useless to ask questions. Agamemnon was behind this. And where Agamemnon was concerned, Menelaus possessed no separate will.

I turned and left, remembering my dignity enough not to run. By the time I reached it, the soldiers were already plundering the palace shrine. All the bronze bowls, basins, jugs, flasks, bulls' head rhyta, daggers, lamps, and axes we kept in the storerooms were being dragged out and handed over to common foot soldiers. They stuffed them into sacks and carted them off. My priestesses were banging their heads against the walls and moaning, calling for the Mother to have mercy on them. Several of my eunuchs were lying in pools of their own blood, dying, martyrs to the cause of attempting to defend their shrine. They held their hands up to me as if I could stop the dastardly work at hand.

I could not believe it. I saw them carrying off the bronze bowls and saucers which the priestesses used to feed our House Snakes, which inhabit the walls and pipes of the palace as living emblems of the goodwill of the Goddess. If we did not present them with daily offerings of mice from the granaries they would desert our shrine and go elsewhere, and the Goddess would leave us too.

"Stop!" I ordered. The soldiers slowed their work and crept about with their heads hung low, but they continued their looting. "I am the Goddess on Earth in Sparta," I said. "I curse you. May the seed of your loins be dried up, and may your wives be cursed with barrenness from this day forth. May the sons of your house do you no honor and come to the darkness before their time."

They worked more and more slowly. Some were beginning to weep. I knew in my heart that I was not being fair. Many of these men had no authority. They were not officers but foot soldiers, despised members of the Dorian race with their dark skin, wearing their hair closely cropped and their faces shaven. They were the stolid, silent race that had borne so much from their Achaean overlords, and now had been ordered on pain of their lives to desecrate the shrine of the Mother in whom they deeply believed.

Indeed, it was trust in her that had kept them going these long generations of men.

The sarcastic lieutenant of the guards stepped up to me. He stared at me before casting his eyes to the ground as a matter of form only. I found him especially bold considering his years. He looked to be about Menelaus's age, for he was only starting a beard. Of course the light-skinned Achaeans began beards later than the Dorians. With his back turned to the others he whispered, "We are Queen's men, Your Highness, to a man. We want only to do your bidding if you should dare to complete what Queen Leda started. But for now we can hear and obey only the King." Then he stepped away and continued his work.

I did not have time then to ponder his strange and familiar manner and the boldness and confidence that would enable him to address a Queen without his tongue freezing to the roof of his mouth. None other had ever done so except the members of the highest circles of royalty. And to speak a name forbidden, that of my mother, and to commend treason and revolution to his betters, was an offense punishable by death.

But I did not have time to wonder more. They were carting the very image of the Goddess out of the shrine. The Mother of the World stared down at them with a look from beyond the grave, her arms outstretched and each hand holding a snake, and they dared not look back. She had stood at the very heart of the shrine since the palace was built. I threw my arms about her and screamed, "You are but mortal men! Touch her not."

Not even the bold lieutenant, it seemed, was prepared to use force on the Queen.

I had won a small victory. I called upon my eunuchs to help me put the Goddess back in place. But I could not prevent them from despoiling the rest of the shrine. Then I set the priestesses to dressing the wounds of the other eunuchs, lay my hands on each of them, and said my prayers.

In tears I followed the soldiers to the palace workshop and armory. I called upon the Mother to bless the souls of her sacred objects that were so soon to be released to come unto her. Menelaus, and through him Agamemnon, were tempting their fates to insult the Mother so. And I must bear part of the blame, for I had raised Menelaus to the Kingship of Sparta.

Fires were blazing in all of the forges. Heaps of bronze objects were lying about on the floor. There were ingots of copper from the state treasury, fresh from Sparta's trade ships that had endured the treacherous passage from Cyprus to bring them to the King. Now Menelaus would possess no reserve. I found my own toilet articles. While I was preoccupied defending the shrine, the soldiers had been busy pillaging the Queen's rooms and those of my ladies. Familiar mirrors stared back at me.

Soldiers melted down the objects as fast as they could hold them over the fires. As soon as the metal was malleable, they pounded and shaped it into instruments of war. Old chariots were being taken out of storage, creaking in protest. Their fittings, discolored and brittle with age, were pried and torn off and new fittings of bronze hammered on. Officers posed while new suits of armor were fitted on them. Axes were sharpened. Officers of the guard stood about trying out the new javelins, spears, swords, and daggers. They suddenly were the most important people in the city. Everything belonged to them.

The noise and heat deafened me. The close press of the soldiers left no room for me here.

I found my women huddled in my bedchamber,

clutching each other cheek to cheek. They seemed preoccupied staring out the window, their tears spent. Dull resignation hung from their faces. Cow-like, they had seen their masters and knew them. I would have none of this. "Go to your rooms and leave me in peace," I said. Then I caught sight of what they sorrowed over.

From my balcony I could see not only the acropolis and the walls encircling it but down into the city at the foot of the hills. Men at that distance seemed but ants. Yet I could tell that they were fanning out from the palace and going among the rubble where people were trying to rebuild their dwellings. With them came horses drawing carts. Crowds were gathering about the soldiers, and even at this height I could sense trouble.

Had Menelaus and Agamemnon gone mad? Were they attacking their own subjects? How could Menelaus do this to people from whom the Earth-shaker had just taken all? What need did the people have to fear the Sea Peoples and Troy if they were going to behave in this fashion?

"The Raiders landed at Lerna and sacked the city," said Menelaus, closing my door behind him. He looked exhausted as if he had not slept half the night. His cheeks sagged, and his eyelids drooped. His face was pallid in color, and he looked older than his nineteen cycles of the seasons. "The men of Lerna were killed to a man and all the women and children carted off as slaves."

He seemed to have forgotten about my intrusion into his council chamber, or perhaps he was too preoccupied with more important matters to care. The scandal of it would pass. He tried to take me in his arms and rest his head against my shoulder, but I pushed him away. I was furious with him. These were not the dead but living people he was robbing now, my people who looked to me.

"Helen," he grabbed me by the arms as if he still felt the agony of it, "the boys of Lerna over ten were made eunuchs. Women past childbearing age were raped and dismembered. We must prepare to defend ourselves, and all the bronze in the surrounding countryside will not be enough. We must send an equal share of what we collect to Mycenae."

"Agamemnon!" I said through my teeth.

"Lerna is just a day's journey from Mycenae, and Agamemnon just sent me word of it early this morning. That's why you didn't know."

I turned on him. "What? I would believe it if it were told of Agamemnon that he paid mercenaries to sack Lerna so he could blame it on the Sea Peoples. Then he could get all the scared princes of Hellas to send him unlawfully gotten booty."

"Helen, you overreach yourself!" he said sternly. "No matter what you think of him as a person, Agamemnon is the High King of Mycenae, the Atreidae, the elder son of Atreus."

"Who is King in Sparta — you or Agamemnon? Don't you care what you are doing to your people?" I said.

His brow began to darken. "You know this is a matter of life and death. If we do not fight back, we will have no city. Our people will be dead and I as well. You and our daughter will be taken captives. Is that what you want, for I tell you it is come to this!"

I could not bear the strain anymore. Perhaps what he said was true, but that could only mean I must choose between being Queen of Sparta and Goddess on Earth. The duties were clearly incompatible. I began to weep.

Now I did not have the strength to push him away, and he enfolded me in his arms. "Helen, Helen," he said, wiping the tears from my eyes with his kisses and nuzzling me close. His caresses came of themselves with no art, for Menelaus was incapable of it. Of the men I have known, he is the one whose feeling for me had the least of self in it. And the gods know, he never gained anything by taking me as wife. In fact, he lost all, as all the world knows. "I'm afraid I must ask for your help — again," he said.

I knew it before he asked. I had only to remain closeted in my chambers, and the people would tear the palace and Menelaus apart. My mother's work would be completed. I would bring back the rule of the Queen. "No," I said to the Goddess, "I cannot give you my lord's life. Ask me not for it."

"And what would you have of me?" I asked tiredly. "I have little power now that I have been stripped of my shrine."

"You have only to show yourself to the people, and they will be quieted. You are yourself your own best Goddess."

I saw Necessity. It had me fixed by its teeth and would not let me go. I dressed in my ceremonial robes and went out among the people. I was none too soon for the townsfolk were already gathering rocks. Some were hiding behind houses and tossing them at the palace guards. The guards were looking around for the perpetrators. They intended to make examples of them.

The people one by one caught sight of me. They stopped what they were doing and crowded about. Now these men, women, and children reached out, trying to grab the hem of my skirt.

Menelaus did not trust the people as I did and ordered his officers to form a ring around the Queen and point their swords at the people to keep them off. He himself stepped in front of me, challenging all comers. His hand was on his own sword hilt.

I could see that they would not be put off, not by the soldiers and perhaps not even by me. Hunger was their Necessity, and they turned to me for help. Menelaus lifted me on top of the litter, for he was the only man who could touch me. I held my hands out and spoke to the people: "Hear me, people of Sparta. Hellas has been attacked by Sea Raiders. We must collect all the bronze we have to melt down and make weapons. We must protect our city and the shrines of Our Lady of Sparta. Peacefully let the King's soldiers enter your homes and take what they must," I said. "Even at the palace we are melting all our bronze for weapons." I did not tell them of the fate of the chief shrine, for that would bring them to despair. "In return for your cooperation," my heart was moved, "the King will feed you from his own tables, and those at the palace will eat less themselves."

I looked at Menelaus, and he shook his head in assent. He would be just when he could.

The people called blessings on me, praising my name, and I felt their cries like so many knives of guilt going through my heart and draining my life's blood.

VI

A Visitor From Mycenae

I swore to the Goddess that I would never again allow myself to be kept in ignorance of what was transpiring in her kingdom. In secret I sent word to the lieutenant of the guards who had twice offered me his allegiance. I met with him whenever I could all during those next moons when I was carrying my twin sons Castor and Pollux the Younger, even when the discomfort was great.

"What is your name?" I asked him.

"Aegisthus," he smiled his crooked smile.

I shivered. I did not like the man, but there was no one else I could trust to inform me and not report back to Menelaus. He neglected to tell which Aegisthus he was, and in those days I saw no reason to question him.

"What is this I hear about Agamemnon?" I asked him. I had heard rumors, and Menelaus was trying to keep the truth from me.

This Aegisthus was as smooth as a serpent. Strange in so young a man and a mere lieutenant, he seemed to be practiced in courtier-like ways. A Mycenean. Perhaps he had been a favorite of Old King Thyestes before Agamemnon ousted him from Mycenae. And in one respect at least I did not know how close I came.

Aegisthus even remembered to approach me on his knees with his head bowed to the ground in the fashion of the old days when the Queen ruled.

"Rise," I ordered him. I would have none of my mother's ways.

But still there was the oddly familiar look in his eye, as if he thought himself more my equal than he should. "The Great King Agamemnon," he said sarcastically, "began a war to crush the invading Sea Peoples. His success made him bold. Now he attacks his loyal vassals, pretending that they are consorting with the Sea Peoples when there is no proof. I think he is merely ambitious for gold and bronze. They say Mycenae is magnificent beyond compare."

I had long believed Agamemnon capable of this and had even taunted Menelaus with it when I was out of temper. But the lieutenant was an underling, and I must be severe with him. "You speak lightly of the High King of Mycenae," I frowned, remembering to keep my voice low, for we were meeting in my chambers late at night. "Remember, he is my brother-in-law and honorary brother. Do you forfeit your life if what you tell me is a lie?"

"May I be swallowed up by the great Earth-shaker if I do not speak the truth," he said with conviction.

But even he could not warn me what was to happen next.

On a night when everything is still the Goddess Echo catches our voices and bounces them from hill to hill, playing tricks on us. Voices that are far sound close. I at first thought there was someone pounding on my chamber door one night less than a moon later at the end of the hot season. The palace was awakened by hollering at the gate.

I sat up in bed, then went to the balcony. A man was screaming in a country Dorian dialect, "Suppliants to the

Goddess! Open the gates. We beg sanctuary." The night was clear, and by the light of many stars I could see he was the driver of a covered wagon drawn by two horses.

"Mistress," said Atossa sleepily, stretching and yawning like a kitten awakening from a nap, "what is it?" Soon she saw the alarm in my face and sprang to her feet.

"Go in to the children," I told her. "Stay with them and do not leave them on any account. I am needed in the throne room."

The rights of the wandering stranger were sacred to Zeus. One had to take him in as a guest-friend, feast him as if he were kin, bathe him, and clothe him in raiment, the choicest of the household. In this way one honored Zeus and the gods, for they often wandered among men in disguise as beggars and travelers just to test a host's worthiness. One never knew.

I dressed to receive them. I had to don my ceremonial saffron robes. It took me awhile to prepare. By the time I arrived in the throne room, there was a dispute going on. The wagon driver in a plain brown burlap cloak and three shrouded and thickly veiled women stood before the throne, steadfastly refusing in the voice of the driver to reveal their identities to the King. In hurried whispers they consulted with each other. The taller of the veiled women seemed to give the orders, and the others obeyed her.

"No, King," the driver repeated. He shuffled about in the presence of so great a majesty, merely conveying the women's words with a bowed head. "We beg to be allowed to see the Queen. We will reveal our identities only to her."

I stood back and listened, not knowing what to make of the situation. Normally Menelaus would welcome them in the name of Sparta, and I would then greet them and give the orders for their comfort.

"The wanderer is sacred to Zeus," Menelaus said. "You have no reason to distrust me." He looked as if he had been hurried out of his bed as quickly as I had been, and sleep still hung heavily around his eyes.

When Menelaus frowned, the taller lady visibly reeled on her feet and looked as if she would fall. She clutched the hand of the driver for support. He steadied her with his hands with great reverence, and the two other women started to fuss about her. She broke free of their grasps and dashed out of the throne room like a pursued animal. So fast did she go, she did not see me.

Some inspiration told me to follow her. She seemed to know where she was going, which I found odd. How could that be unless she had been here before? Somehow I knew she was headed for the altar of the Goddess. She threw herself at the feet of the Great Goddess, suppliant-like.

"Sister?" I said before I knew my own thought.

She burst into tears and turned her face towards me slowly. Her veil was undone. Clytaemnestra now looked more like a thin wraith from another world, wasted half away. Her eyes were red and swollen from crying. Her cheeks were bruised and cut as if in mourning. The glossy brown hair I remembered so well had begun to gray although she was only ten cycles of the seasons older than my eighteen. No one could forget how beautiful she had been. By rights she should have been Goddess on Earth of Sparta, but there was need of an heiress to send to Pisa. Clytaemnestra loved him and begged to be allowed to go.

Clytaemnestra slowly stood up and held out her arms to me, arms like those of a skeleton. For a long time we did nothing but hold each other and rock back and forth, kissing each other's cheeks. She was so light I could nearly lift her from the ground.

"Promise me, no matter what happens, you won't let Agamemnon take me!" she said, breathing hard. She was so intent she dug her fingernails into my arm. Her eyes were wild.

"I swear I won't let him touch you," I said. I could only guess what he was up to now.

She was shaking convulsively. "He was in close pursuit. He will be here soon."

"Don't worry," I reassured her. "You know the rite of sanctuary was the first that the gods gave to man, the oldest sacred law of our people. By claiming it you have put yourself into divine hands above human reach and judgment...Sister, what has he done?"

She could do nothing but sob.

"Do you need aught, Your Highness?" Aegisthus said as if it were his right to interrupt such a private interview. He dared to stand in the doorway and gaze at us.

"This impertinence is too much!" I hissed. "What will the King say if he finds you here?" How I wished I could rid myself of this toad, but he had made himself too indispensable to me and he knew it.

"He will say nothing," Aegisthus said. "As you can see, I have brought my guards with me to protect our royal visitor. And we have brought her companions to join her." Two other women in veils and the mule driver rushed in to claim sanctuary.

In my anger I had not noticed how my sister was gazing at Aegisthus. "Who is this?" asked Clytaemnestra in a faraway voice.

"Aegisthus, Captain of the Guards," I said, for just yesterday Menelaus had advanced him. Now he too could boast a gold-embroidered tunic.

"Is he one of us?" she asked.

"Yes."

Aegisthus smiled at her, and their eyes held. For a moment my sister was lifted out of her sorrow. I think that to the very last, when she lay slain by the hand of her own son bleeding out her life in the palace in Mycenae with her dead lover by her side, I think that she never regretted throwing in her fate with Aegisthus. They were fashioned by the gods as a pair, each contesting with the other to see whose passion for revenge was the greater, each united in hatred for a single man.

Menelaus came in to the shrine straightway to greet his honorary sister and sister-in-law, and then Tyndareus from his wing to greet his daughter. She would not let Menelaus touch her, for she greatly feared his relationship to Agamemnon. At first she did not even trust her father, for he had once adopted the same man as his son.

Then trumpets sounded at the propylon gate. That could mean only one visitor.

Clytaemnestra clung to me and begged me not to leave her. "You are safe here with my women," I said. Indeed then I had no reason to doubt it. I had to go greet the High King and face him down, putting the fear of the Goddess into him.

Menelaus did not receive him sitting on his throne, for his brother outranked him. We stood on the dais and awaited his pleasure. He burst into the room like a ball of fire from the sky, his red hair streaming behind him. Menelaus's soldiers were drawn up in a line on either side of the Throne Room. Agamemnon hailed them and greeted many by name, remembering when they fought together before Mycenae. He slapped them on their backs and joked with them. I could see Menelaus hold himself more rigidly than before, for if Menelaus made a religion of dignity Agamemnon never thought he needed it. He was all in all to himself and assumed everyone else thought so too.

When he saw Menelaus, he called to him, "My brother!" and heaved himself up onto the dais. I noticed Agamemnon had put on much weight, and the breast of his purple tunic nearly ripped under the strain. Evidently being High King agreed with him.

With a laugh Agamemnon embraced his brother and kissed him five times on each cheek. My heart died within me for Menelaus.

I sensed what Agamemnon's next move was, and as he reached for me, I sidestepped his hands. I would not have him treat me, Goddess on Earth, like a kitchen wench, even if he were my honorary brother. I had put a stop to his little game, and he was taken aback. Anger glittered in his eyes, and he was a dangerous man when crossed. I remembered how he cut the throats of my priestesses. But he would not let a mere woman get the better of him and ignored me.

"Well, I've come to claim my blushing bride," he said, all smiles. He winked at Menelaus as if they, as men, understood these matters that were far beyond the comprehension of women.

"Come, brother," Menelaus said with gravity, "you and I well know that Clytaemnestra is married to King Tantalus of Pisa, one of your loyal vassals."

"A traitor!" he waved his hand, his face turning purple and ugly. "And he met a traitor's death. He was conspiring with the Sea Raiders." Now I knew why he was High King; men feared him as they could never fear my gentle husband.

Menelaus swallowed as he thought what a traitor's death was and straightened himself. Menelaus recovered himself and said, "Still, brother, you must needs set your sights elsewhere. Clytaemnestra is already spoken for. She has come suppliant to the altar of the Goddess and claimed her protection."

Agamemnon's eyes flashed, "I hope we understand each other. Surely you will not try to deny me this trinket of battle whom I have won in a fair fight?"

I could not bear it any longer, liar that he was. It was he who had conspired with the Sea Raiders. I said, "Widowed she has returned to the house of her father as is our custom. No one else may speak for her."

He grabbed me by the wrist and squeezed it. "Wench," he swore under his breath, "be thankful you are not my Queen!"

Menelaus's heavy hand landed on his brother's and removed it. I had never seen him oppose his brother's will before. Agamemnon was so shocked that he took one step backward. "Let us speak further in private," Menelaus's eyes were full of meaning. Perhaps he had guessed what was to come.

I, of course, was not invited to be privy to the discussion. Aegisthus was in charge of guarding the council chamber where Agamemnon, Menelaus, and Tyndareus met. He stationed me in a nearby storage room which had direct access to the council chamber.

The discussion had already begun, and I heard Agamemnon speaking, "Is it my fault if her only babe was a man-child? How could I rule Pisa with him as a thorn sticking in my foot? He would be the rallying point for any rebellion."

I said to myself, "So, he had her son torn from her arms! The beast probably had his skull crushed by battering him against the wall right in front of her eyes just to cow her. And he would have her go to his bed willingly after that...." I shut my eyes and prayed for Clytaemnestra.

The silence that followed Agamemnon's words lasted long. The longer, the heavier the condemnation it was. Soon Agamemnon could stand it no more. I could read Menelaus's and Tyndareus's faces by his words. "It was the hand of Fate, I tell you!" He blustered, pacing about the room, whining and offering excuses to hide the fact that he had acted rashly and out of anger.

Finally my father said, "I will go to my daughter and prepare her for her fate." His footsteps echoed across the stuccoed floor to the door. No one spoke. My father had just disowned Agamemnon in the only way he dared.

"Brother, this will never do," I could feel Menelaus's scowl piercing right through the High King. "I am beginning to wonder if there were really Sea Raiders in Pisa after all, or if you just invented them to satisfy your lust for power and a woman."

"Yes," I thought, "just as Aegisthus said."

Agamemnon laughed. His laugh grew bigger and louder. He slapped his thigh and fell down into his chair, rocking back and forth in mirth. Finally he summoned a slave girl to pour Menelaus and him a goblet of wine. He took such a slurp I could hear it from where I was, and pushed a goblet across the wooden table to his brother. "Here, brother, relax and take a sip," I could imagine him leaning back in his chair with his legs stretched out. "Your wits are addled. You speak as if my ambitions were a lamentable thing, and my vices deadly. I am a conqueror just as our father was, and I have need for recreation, women, and heirs. Now, you see, we are truthful with each other at last."

"Our father was a bloody tyrant, and you would become like him!" Menelaus had to restrain himself from shouting.

"And you were always our mother's boy," said

Agamemnon. "You drank the milk of womanliness at her bosom. And your wife came after her."

"And next you will be dragging women and children away from altars where they have claimed protection, hacking them up, and serving them for dinner even as our far-famed father did!" Menelaus said.

All Hellas would not forget how power-mad Atreus became in his later days. He would revenge himself upon his brother Thyestes for committing adultery with his Cretan wife Aerope. He slaughtered Thyestes's sons on the altar of Zeus where they had fled. Not being satisfied with that, he had them hacked into little pieces and served up in a stew to Thyestes. Thyestes called down a curse upon the House of Atreus, and when he later became King by murdering his brother, he showed no pity to Atreus's sons Agamemnon and Menelaus. They had to flee Mycenae for their lives.

"Brother, come now, I merely wish to marry Clytaemnestra, not serve her for dinner," Agamemnon's jest fell flat.

"I have ever tried to serve you for the greater good of Hellas," Menelaus clipped his words. "But as High King you should be wise, the first among equals. If you become drunk with ambition and want more than your fair share, how are you any better than the Trojans or the Sea Raiders?"

"I am your brother, son of Atreus!" Agamemnon answered glibly.

"But all the same, if you become tipsy, teeter, and fall, the earth will come crashing down and splinter into a thousand fragments, all at war with each other."

"Brother, I need you now more than ever," I could hear Agamemnon springing to his feet. He crossed the room to Menelaus. "You must be my right hand. I depend upon you because I trust you. Say anything you like to me, but don't turn away from me."

Menelaus remained silent.

"Besides, what choice have you?" Agamemnon said. "Unless, of course, you want to take up arms against me and split Hellas in two?"

Menelaus paced the room. I thought to myself, "If Hellas must split in two, it must. Anything but to serve this foul tyrant! It cannot be. Menelaus, you must see that!" I wanted to rush out of my hiding place and shake him.

Menelaus stopped. He said grimly, "We cannot have Atreus and Thyestes all over again."

"I thought you would see reason," Agamemnon clapped him on the shoulder.

Once Agamemnon left the room I debated whether to betray myself and try to make Menelaus see reason or whether to act alone to stop Agamemnon. But I had no need. Before I could make up my mind whether to stay and confront him or to flee, Menelaus opened the door and took my hands. I said as he drew me out, "Agamemnon's hubris is such that he would ride north even into Thessaly if he could and attack Mt. Olympus, home of the gods. He would be Zeus."

"I know my brother better than other men, but I hoped for better." The expression on Menelaus's face was so sad that I could feel his pain. I touched his cheek. He took my hand and kissed it.

I drew away. "Think of your sons. Next it will be Sparta that he will gobble up."

He stared through me and far away. "Better Agamemnon with all his faults than Priam and his sons. I must restrain him where I can, shame him if I cannot. But if I do not follow him I shall lose whatever little influence I have left."

"If you support him in his attack against the laws the gods have laid down you are doomed."

Menelaus said, "We all have been sacrificed in our own ways...Come, it is time to go." He led me by the hand out past the guards. I was too shaken to feel shocked that he would be so informal. It is an unwritten rule that the King and the Queen never touch in public.

There in the shrine Clytaemnestra lay face down on the stone floor before the Goddess. Her hair was spread out over the pavement in stark contrast. Her nails were red from her own blood as she clawed at her face. My father stood to one side with his head bowed, weeping. I had not missed him because of my own state of mind, but there Aegisthus kneeled beside the fallen Queen, trying to comfort her. For once the crooked smile had disappeared from his face.

"Where is Helen?" she wailed. "She promised me!"

I broke free of Menelaus's grasp and was at her side. She flung herself into my arms and clutched me so convulsively I could hardly breathe. "You must not let him take me," she sobbed. "I hate him! He is a monster."

"Sh-h-h-h-h-h!" I stroked her brown hair. "I know what he has done to you. I would stop him if I had an army at my command, but I have none."

"Brother," she turned her bloodied face towards Menelaus, "how have I offended you that you should leave me to die?" She crawled towards him on her hands and knees and grasped his legs suppliant-like.

"Here, take this," he removed the medallion of the lion and the griffin from around his neck and handed it to her. "If he offends you past bearing, send it to me, and I will remonstrate with him as best I can. But otherwise, try to yield to him and oppose him in nothing. Your opposition only fans the flames of his lust. Do it for your daughter Iphigenia if not for yourself."

I folded the weeping Iphigenia, the child of my sister's first marriage, in my arms, for she had concealed herself as one of the serving women. She was a trusting thing and no bigger than a bird at twelve.

A legion of Agamemnon's guards entered the room and fanned out on either side. Fearsome to look upon, they were men of bronze covered from head to legs in that gleaming metal. Tusked helmets of bronze that boasted plumes and cheek-pieces obscured their faces by torchlight. They held dress figure-of-eight shields and carried swords and daggers of several sizes. These were Agamemnon's elite troops, his bodyguard. They appeared to be the men of metal that sprang from the dragon's teeth sewn in the earth by Jason to fight alongside his Argonauts.

Agamemnon stepped into the shrine, and the priestesses of the Mother wailed, beat their chests, and scratched their faces. His very presence was pollution.

Menelaus knelt down as a King never does in public and took Clytaemnestra up into his arms. Menelaus slowly carried his sister-in-law over to his brother, and every step bespoke his strong disapproval. He stopped in front of Agamemnon and said, "I shall keep the Princess Iphigenia to rear in the house of her grandfather." It was a condition.

Agamemnon shrugged, "Very well, please yourself, brother. Keep her as a token of our goodwill."

"Bless you, bless you!" Clytaemnestra wept. "Brother, may you dwell in the Elysian Fields for this." As Menelaus handed her over to Agamemnon, she fainted dead away. Her mouth sagged open and her eyes stared into nothingness.

"Oh, my lady, save my mother!," wept Iphigenia. "This will kill her." Iphigenia was so distressed that she forgot her own danger and let her veil slip. Never had I seen skin so white — it was like the downy feathers of a swan — and her hair was the color of clouds on a sunny day. Agamemnon was eyeing her with a different kind of interest.

My skin prickled with coolness, and my anger knew no bounds. It was the voice of the Goddess commanding me, "This is my shrine, and you are its keeper." I rose to my feet and said in a voice greater than my own, "Son of Atreus!" I fixed my eyes upon the trespasser, "You may choose the long life or the short. Leave this woman with her father, and you may yet prosper in your own house. But take her one step beyond this door and beware the still wind that does not blow, beware the voice from heaven that only you shall not hear, and beware the silence at the feast that shall be your last."

The words welled up from some mysterious depth within me, and left me as tired as if the Earth-shaker had paid a visit. I was frightened myself, and I could see that Agamemnon was terrified, for it is no light thing to be cursed by the Goddess. He took several steps backward before he recovered himself. "See to this bitch of yours," he commanded Menelaus, "or she shall pay for her tongue!"

"Take one step towards her, and I shall no longer call you brother," Menelaus warned, his hand on his sword.

Agamemnon sensed that his brother could be pushed no farther. He turned and stomped out of the shrine, carrying his doom with him.

At the next dawn Agamemnon left the palace, taking Clytaemnestra. She walked beside him like a sleepwalker, as if she did not know where she was and had already become one of the shades in the Underworld.

In the days that followed his departure it was as if life had changed forever. He had brought a wind of bad omen with him, and it did nothing but storm. The heavens opened up, and the Eurotas overflowed its banks. We were confined indoors, and it seemed as if we did nothing but wait, and not just for the storm to abate.

We all sensed that something was about to happen, although we did not know what. Everyone was silent. There was nothing to say. Rules were strangely relaxed, and I could come and go as I wished in and out of the chambers of state. I did not need to resort to any of Aegisthus's strategems. Even the slaves seemed to be slow about their work with their ears perked up, listening. The nuthatches who flew to my balcony for bread stayed awhile and studied me.

The faraway, preoccupied mood that had settled upon Menelaus while Agamemnon was sojourning with us did not leave him. He stopped receiving petitioners, did not greet an ambassador, and called no council meetings. Once he met with his top officers of the guard. Aegisthus told me about it. He was restless and paced aimlessly about the palace with such an absorbed yet melancholy look on his face that the servants feared to interrupt him. Even Hermione, her father's favorite, shied away from him, and the twins, who were usually of a sunny disposition, were frequently foul of temper, especially in their father's presence.

It was hard for me to be angry at him. My suffering was hardly comparable to his. Once when I approached to

To Follow The Goddess

remonstrate with him about letting Clytaemnestra go, I found him at his desk busily writing, and suddenly my voice dried up. I was overcome with such fear that I wanted to run and hide, for somehow I knew from what quarter our danger came. And here he was facing it all alone without any help from me. At such moments I felt that he was born to be King.

Early one morning the ambassador from Mycenae was announced and cried through the courts. I jumped out of bed and dressed by myself, too impatient to wait even for Atossa. I knew this ambassador would not be turned away with the rest.

By the time I reached the throne room, Menelaus had already received him. Perhaps he had been sitting alone all night waiting for him, even watching out the window as he had often done of late. He was reading a missive with a face of stone. My legs turned to water, and I could hardly command them to move forward to his side and sit down. Although he had not looked my direction once, he sensed that I was coming and held out his hand to me before the whole court.

"Tell Agamemnon I shall leave at once as soon as I can dispose of matters here," he told the ambassador, who bowed and took his departure.

The soldiers and the courtiers were all whispering furiously to each other and crept out.

Before I had a chance to say anything, he answered me, "King Catreus of Crete, my mother's father if you will remember, has died. I am to attend the funeral. But another matter has surfaced. It seems that the Cretans were only waiting for Catreus to die as their signal to revolt. They say that Agamemnon has no right to rule, that he has offended the Mother."

"I knew it would come to this. In Crete the Old

Religion still has sway. Agamemnon should have seen it coming. And now he would sacrifice you!"

"It was all foreordained before we were born," he said wearily. "The fortunes of the House of Atreus are not good."

"You must not go," I said.

"I must take my army and leave at once."

With the sun that rose three days later Menelaus was to leave Sparta. I could not sleep that night. He came into my room early before the dawn. "Everything is in readiness," he said. "I have taken my leave of the children. My ships wait at Gytheum to set sail."

My grief was so great I could not speak at first but only fight back my tears. All was numbness now. I could not believe it was happening. Later would come the pain, a pain so great that I would almost rather die than bear it. He was going away to war. He might never come back.

"You know as well as I the danger of my mission," he took a seat on my bedside. "We must be at peace with each other at the last."

I started to protest, but he put his finger to my lips. He paused for a moment of the heaviest silence I have ever felt. Then he took my hands. His head was bowed. When he raised his face, I read naked adoration in his eyes. "They say that a man's feelings for a woman can be only such as he would properly feel for his bed-mate and the mother of his heirs. The nobler passions of love he must reserve for the gods and for fellow men who share in the spark of the divinity of Zeus.

"Once I imagined I loved my brother so. I admired him in all things. He had a grace in his dealings with the world that I lacked and knew always what to say. Now I see he is little better than a beast turned into a monster, and I love only you. But happiness is not the lot of Kings and

Queens."

Perhaps even in the days when we roamed the hills together I should have seen what would happen to us. In those days I was heedless and begged Menelaus to run away with me and live in the mountains. "My father will stop searching after awhile," I stroked his hair as he lay his head in my lap.

He took my hand and kissed the palm. "You know we were born to this, and there is no escape," he said. "To such as us, there is no freedom." He knew even then. Now his words took on a quality of prophecy.

I could no more keep myself out of his arms than I could keep my skin from cleaving to my body. Our tears mingled one with the other even as our bodies did this one last time. And that it was to be the last, a kiss of parting, somehow the gods had made us wise to. Ten long years of sorrows were our destiny until we met again, and then we were two different people, knowing not each the other.

But even now as we kissed, it was not the present we dreamed of. We saw rugged Taygetos rising up from the valley of the Eurotas green with olive and orange groves. Up the mountain we would always climb even if only in spirit with a red anemone here or a hyacinth there, a bright splash of color amidst a rocky landscape, to lighten our way as hand in hand we went.

"It is not fitting to speak of these things," I whispered at last. "Or we shall not be able to bear it." I kissed both his cheeks and then his eyes, as one takes his last farewells of the dead.

After he turned away from me and even his shadow departed through the doorway, I gathered up the children and slipped out onto my balcony, high above the acropolis. The sun was rising for the first time in days, making a mockery of my sorrow. My hair hung loosely about my shoulders just as he had left it in wild disarray. My robe hung on me without even a belt. I looked more like a wood nymph than a Queen. All my life was in my eyes that would reach out and grasp him if they could. I watched him call out to his soldiers, mount his horse, and ride off, and I stared after him until I could see him no more through my tears.

"Not yet!" I said aloud. I could not help myself but ran to another balcony, bereft of all pride, not caring if anyone saw me. Higher and higher I climbed until I was even on the roof. Like a madwoman I stood there. Barely could I make out a form. Before he disappeared over the crest of the last hill I fancied that he turned on his horse, unable to bear it any longer himself, and gazed back at me as if he had known I must be there all along.

For me he should always be there in the last chamber of my mind that I visit each night right before I drift off into sleep. I would never love another.

VII

The Treachery Of Aegisthus

Aegisthus was left in command of all the forces that remained in Sparta. I should have grown suspicious then of his rapid rise through the ranks, but my thoughts were always turned towards Crete and Menelaus.

Aegisthus bowed even lower than usual in his courtier-like fashion and asked me, "Shall I take up a new conscription among the people to fill up the ranks of my troops?"

He could not ask Tyndareus, although Menelaus had appointed him regent. The very day after Menelaus departed, my father took ill and retired to his bed. The winter rains were creeping into his bones.

"I shall write to Menelaus," I said. I did not dare take authority for military matters. That would be rebellion indeed. I wrote to Menelaus again and again, but I never received any answer. Menelaus had never been one to spend much time penning letters as he was always too busy. But I found this silence more than passingly strange.

"Perhaps the King has other matters more important to think about," Aegisthus lifted his eyebrows in disapproval, trying to plant seeds of discontent in my head.

Sometimes I feared that the spirit of my mother from beyond the grave had sent him here. "The next time you speak against the King, I shall have you removed from

The Treachery Of Aegisthus

my presence," I pointed at him, not thinking that all the soldiers were under his command and loyal to him. Since many of them were from Mycenae, they had no reason to revere the Goddess on Earth of Sparta.

No sooner had the dust of Menelaus's warriors settled than a horse troop arrived from Mycenae under orders to break the agreement Menelaus had struck with Agamemnon. They demanded that I yield the Princess Iphigenia up to them. Remonstrate as I would, they would not desist.

Aegisthus began to look the hero, for he pleaded with me not to give up the Princess. He agreed to help me hide her. Even as we plotted, however, Agamemnon's guards took the short way and seized her from her bed. They were carrying her off by the time we answered her screams. Armed resistance would be the only protest we could make, but there were more of them than were left of us, and a battle would strip Sparta of all defenses. Weakly I insisted that they carry to Agamemnon a letter of protest.

One morning I was summoned all unsuspecting to my father's rooms. They were already anointing his body with rose-oil. It was as simple as that. He had been fine, better than he had been in days, at the supper the night before. We chatted of old times. Little did I suspect it would be our last conversation. The silken nets that hemmed me in were being woven tighter and tighter by the invisible spiders that seemed to surround me everywhere.

I questioned his servants as soon as I regained my senses. They told me he died in his sleep, and no one saw him pass away. "The spinners have cut short the pattern of his life," his attendant said.

Aegisthus swept into the room, threw himself to the floor face down, and said, "The King is dead. Long live the Queen." At that instant, as if by pre-arranged signal, all the officers of his guard crowded into the bedchamber and fell on their faces.

My life passed before my eyes as if I were drowning. I remembered my mother and her short-lived rebellion against my father. Not that I was afraid to die if my city needed me, but I would never betray Menelaus so cruelly. If I set him aside and proclaimed the return of the rule of the Mother, I could count on the support of the people and the remainder of the army, but I would deal the death blow to my lord.

"Get out of my sight," I ordered, and they all crawled away.

But soon Aegisthus had persuaded me that he must take up a conscription among the remaining men of Sparta.

I do not know how long I could have gone on being the ruler of Sparta in all but name. It was my destiny never to find out. One night Atossa's scream awakened me. There stood Aegisthus. It was the first moon of the planting season, and the air was still chilly. I clutched my goatskins about me and said, "What presumption is this?"

"Forgive me, Highness, but a runner has arrived from Gytheum. Those who guard our coast have sighted tall ships bearing the Spartan flag close upon our shores."

The Spartan flag! My heart soared. I could almost have hugged Aegisthus with gladness. "What are you waiting for, fool?" I said, "make ready to receive the King!" He left to carry out my orders, and as I dressed danced my last dance about my room. Aegisthus's disloyalties were misconstrued. They were excesses of zeal and loyalty to the old ways. I decided to carry a good report of him to my lord.

Aegisthus and I scurried about the palace in the dead of night awakening everyone. Riders hurried into the town to knock on doors and spread the news. This would be a day of festival, for many of the villagers' sons had ridden with Menelaus into Crete. The difficulties he encountered there must not have been as great as he feared, for he was returned so soon.

By morning we were all in readiness. The townsfolk lined the streets with aprons full of the earliest crocuses of the season to toss over the heads of the army. The servants had donned their red and blue holiday attire instead of the usual white and stood on the acropolis. Hermione at two had just learned to toddle, and Atossa and I watched her as we each held one of the twins. Perhaps that was why I did not carefully study Aegisthus's face as he stood beside me.

Aegisthus said over the noise of the crowd: "Highness, it is only fitting that I take my troops out to greet the King."

I nodded, for I had no eyes. In those last moments I had taken my leave of this world and only dreamed. "Hermione, you will see your father soon!" I said breathlessly.

The sun rose higher in the sky, and soon it was the time of day when a man loses his shadow. We all waited and strained our eyes to catch sight of our returning troops. Shouting could be heard approaching us, and we all perked up our ears. My heart beat faster. I wanted to be the first to see my lord.

But as the shouting grew closer I could make out screams. These townsfolk who had gone out to greet their King came running back as if pursued by demons. Farmers and peasants from the surrounding countryside seemed to have abandoned their farms with their families to take refuge in Sparta. They dashed up to the gates and pounded on them.

"Open the gates!" I shouted hoarsely to the servants, for all the guards were gone. Something had gone terribly wrong. Marching up the valley of the Eurotas I saw the banner of Sparta, the lion and the griffin locked in combat. But beside it rode a flag I never encountered before, that of a giant bull breathing fire. Thus for the first time I saw the Bull of Heaven.

If this made me shiver, the soldiers under the banner did so even more. I had never before seen men so short. Once I heard a bard sing of a race of Pygmies in a land faraway where the sun bakes the earth and turns one's skin black, but these warriors were of the complexion of our Dorians. They were olive-rich with black hair.

I looked more closely and found men who were tall, and as black as if they had marched straight out of the mouth of Hades. Gold rings pierced their noses. They carried spears and looked fearsome.

Those officers riding horses and leading the men were as white as the milk of a goat, just as my people were, and with hair the color of sunshine. Never had I seen such an assortment of peoples from different lands making up an army. None of our cities of Hellas had such exotic allies.

Still I hoped this was a new ally of Menelaus's. Perhaps my Spartan common folk had taken leave of their senses because they had encountered something alien and were so superstitious. The troops, as fearsome as they were, made no attempt to fight or chase the Spartans. They merely marched inexorably forward in a long column with children chasing around the legs of their horses.

My hope died in an instant. There in the place of my lord rode Aegisthus, triumph blazing in his face. He seemed to have swallowed one of Aphrodite's love charms he looked so happy.

The Treachery Of Aegisthus

So many things fell into place. That was why he wanted to ingratiate himself with my lord and myself, why he wanted to build his army, and put himself in a position of trust. The traitor! I had been his fool, but even if I had known that he was planning to hand Sparta over to an alien power there was little I could have done as long as his troops remained loyal. He had intercepted my missives to Menelaus and probably Menelaus's to me, while I had thought it was Agamemnon's doing. The dark suspicion crept into my head that he had hastened Tyndareus on his way to the Underworld, isolating me, making me think I was in charge to conceal his real designs.

The motive alone was lacking. I had never trusted him, but why would he, a man of Hellas, an Achaean if not a Spartan, betray our city into the hands of a foreign power? For foreign they were to judge by their oriental splendor.

It gladdened my heart that Tyndareus was already in his winding sheet so that he could not see this day. The words of my mother, long dead, returned to haunt me: "Menelaus is more important to you than all of Sparta. I see it now. It was foretold. My daughter will be Queen here, and under her Sparta will be no more." She had proved a prophetess. While I longed for my husband, Aegisthus wrought his will. The lesson was bitter in my mouth.

"Close the gates," I ordered the servants who looked at the foreign army as if the soldiers were not human. Not all the fleeing villagers and farmers were yet within the gates, but the soldiers were getting too close for safety. Better for some to perish than for all.

The soldiers of the Bull of Heaven filed out of their ranks and rounded up the fleeing villagers. The women and the children they quickly dragged to one side of the road and put them in chains. These did not resist but only wept. The men they dragged to the other side of the road. I feared what they would do with them and sent Hermione and the twins back inside the palace with Atossa.

Aegisthus never stopped laughing in his crooked fashion as he rode up to the gates. Hatred gleamed in his eyes as he stared at me, "Wretched woman, some god was determined to make me happy. On this day begins my revenge upon the House of Atreus. I am even the very son of that King Thyestes whom Agamemnon, Menelaus, and Tyndareus slew to take Mycenae."

So that was why he had killed my father! Again I cursed Agamemnon. "You are an Achaean, yeah even one of her princes," I wasted my breath. "And even Thyestes, High King of Mycenae, would not hand over one of Achaia's chiefest glories to a barbarian prince. He is no doubt one of your Sea Raiders."

"Tut, tut," interrupted the foreign prince in our language, "I have been called many things in my time, but I fancy 'Sea Raider' is a bit too strong." I took a long look at him. I could not imagine a man dressing like that, except maybe a pharaoh of far-off Egypt. His armor seemed fashioned by some god of solid gold, and in the sunlight it was almost too bright to look upon. His face and features were as fair as Apollo's, his hair done in a mass of golden ringlets. At first I feared he was a god, but then a god never says, "Tut, tut!" in such an urbane fashion.

He was studying me with the fascination of a man beholding some rare wonder even though I was still hidden behind my veil. Then I noticed that the eyes of the whole army were fastened upon me. For once I was glad of my veil, for I was blushing.

The foreign prince leaped from his horse with a grace more at home in a court than on the battlefield. He swept a low bow to me so that the plumes on the crest of his helmet brushed the ground, "Prince Paris of Troy at your service."

The spear of gall was driven even deeper into my side. Aegisthus had waited until Menelaus was gone from Sparta to report to his masters, the Trojans, how they could best defeat Hellas. They would capture unopposed her second most important city and steal her Queen. "Keep the gates fast shut," I ordered my servants, watching the invaders below. "There is only one King of Sparta, and his name is Menelaus".

"How tiresome!" sighed Paris, as he rolled his eyes towards heaven. "Strike your tents," he ordered his army with an easy wave of his arm as if he went through this every day and had expected it. "We wait on our lady's pleasure...But I am obliged to warn you that we can wait only two sunrises for your decision, for our generals grow impatient to get Sparta between their teeth."

As soon as he gave an order, no matter how casually phrased, his whole army instantly with one will obeyed.

Aegisthus whispered into his ear. "No, no, no!" Paris waved him away impatiently. "We don't need anymore of your bloody tricks. Take them away from here and do your dirty business. What do you know about wooing a woman anyway?"

The Spartan men wailed out to me, but I could do nothing as they were dragged away except say, "I would witness their execution."

"Maybe you would like the bloody business," said Paris, contorting his face in disgust, "but I would not." He waved the prisoners away. They held out their hands to me, and I blessed them.

Aegisthus nodded, waved good-bye to me, and

departed, taking his troops with him. As it turned out he knew plenty about wooing when he needed it, for he rode straight to Mycenae and into my sister's heart, practicing his usual strategems on Agamemnon. No one was left to tell the tale of his treachery except his men, and they dared not speak on pain of their lives.

I would not fail in my duty a second time. All that remained of my life was for the common good. Menelaus would forgive me once I was dead.

I wept and prayed on my knees to the Goddess that she enlighten me. After my knees were blistered from pressing them hard on the floor, she finally answered. The room was cold, for the coals in my brazier had burnt out, and I was shivering. "Helen," she said, "I have shown my power. Now use it. And walk with pride."

"He is my wedded lord," I said.

"He has tried to make you the instrument of his will in many deeds of darkness. This son of Atreus has led you from me. You must teach him a lesson he will not forget easily."

"But I love him," I said.

She did not answer.

I hoped never again to endure the torment I felt in coming to a decision. But the Sisters wove and spun all the same, and I was but one of their threads.

Again I thought of Queen Leda, but I had no choice. I saw fear in the eyes of all my servants and the people who had fled inside our walls. I was the only one who could bring them their last comfort before they either died or were carried away in slavery, though I would give Aegisthus the chance to crow that he had defeated Menelaus.

Atossa wept as she helped me don the tiered skirt of the Queens of Old Crete, the one my mother had worn

The Treachery Of Aegisthus

the day the sun disappeared from the sky. "Indeed, the sun has disappeared from Sparta's sky once more," I thought as Atossa helped me paint my nipples gold.

I called everyone together in the throne room. For the first time I dared sit upon Menelaus's throne which no woman had occupied in ages of men. I declared the return of the rule of the Queen, the return of the Goddess to Earth. In the distance I thought I heard my mother's thunder.

As each person filed past my throne I laid hands on him and blessed him. They came to me sorrowing and left smiling as if they had seen Elysium. It was little enough I could do for them. Among the last came Atossa, her face radiant with tears as she was torn between pride for her mistress and the pain I must feel.

It fell to my lot to play general.

All night before the two-day truce was over we were up making preparations, and we could hear the Trojans pulling their siege engines into place and preparing for the attack. I sent the children inside.

I gave orders for those stationed on the wall to keep down so that the Trojans might think we were undefended. In fact, at my signal the women inside the citadel began to wail, lament, and beat their chests. I wanted the Trojans to think this would be an easy victory and walk into our trap.

I myself stood in the watchtower. I could look down upon them through a peep hole. As soon as the hooks were in place, the Trojans began to climb up the ropes laughing to each other. When they were halfway up I raised my hand, knowing all eyes were on me, and suddenly vats of burning oil rained down like fiery lava from heaven upon the heads of unsuspecting Trojans.

From all around the walls screams rent the air. One

would think the world was coming to an end. Blinded and maddened with pain, the soldiers in the lead turned upon their comrades and fought their ways back down the rope ladders, that was those who did not fall to their deaths. Back they fled from the walls in a rout. Those that still had eyes looked back fearfully over their shoulders, screaming, "Amazons! Amazons!" for we were mostly women.

Officers had to jump in front of their own troops and threaten them with the sword to stop their flight. Horses reared and bucked. Some soldiers looked as if nothing could stop them before they had run down the hillside and plunged into the Eurotas to cool their hides. I was proud of my people and satisfied to see the shock on Paris's face. I had made good use of our amphoras of olive oil.

They retreated to plan their strategy in face of this unexpected resistance.

The feast I had ordered in another life to welcome Menelaus I now set aside and rationed. Only those foods that would perish were consumed right away. Those doing the heaviest work were given the most food. I myself took less, Goddess on Earth though I was.

Soon their intentions became too clear. Since they could not drive us out by fire (for they had to take me alive) they began to tunnel under our walls. They started to dig a great enough distance from us so that neither our cauldrons of oil nor our arrows could reach them.

Paris rode up close enough to the watchtower to talk but not close enough to be greeted with the oil. I met him in my robes and veils of black. "This is getting boring," he said. "You know you must yield despite your nasty little cat-like tricks. Why not humor me and open the gates now? It would make everything much easier." Did I read a plea in his face, genuine distaste for the military

The Treachery Of Aegisthus

life? He had said he did not like to witness executions. Perhaps he did not like to see sieges or battles either.

"What kind of fool do you take me for?" I shouted down. "If I open the gates you will slay all the townsmen just as you did with those you captured, enslave all my women, and burn the palace. Do you suppose I would voluntarily consent to have my sons murdered?"

"Come now," he said, "do you suppose I could ever harm anything of yours? You, who are the loveliest woman I have ever beheld and whom I seek for my bride and Queen?"

"For your slave!" I spat.

He fell to the ground on one knee with the practiced ease of a courtier and said in his purr, "You are wrong, so wrong. It is I who would be your slave."

"I trust you not."

"Did I ever tell you that you are loveliest when you are angry?"

"And did I ever tell you that if Menelaus returns home he will sever that smart tongue from your body?"

"Yes, I did imagine that Menelaus of yours was a barbarian. All of the House of Atreus are, you know. Deplorable!" he said. "Personally, my guiding divinities are Apollo and Aphrodite."

As soon as the darkness came, I called my people together in the throne room. I beheld their eyes, trusting me. "We have only one hope left," I said. "It is a slim one, but a risk we must take. If you would prefer to stay here and be slaughtered or dragged off into slavery in a foreign land, I will not stop you. But whoever wishes to fight for his life to the last shall follow me this night. You must bite your tongues and say not a word from this moment forth."

In truth we had no time to waste. Night was longer during the cold season, and we needed ever moment of it. I ordered the cooks to break open all the food stores, excepting only the wine, and to line it up in a neat row. One by one my people passed silently down the line, stuffing their pockets with what they could carry, eating hurried meals on the spot as a protection against the cold.

Nor could I allow them their shoes. We must be as silent as the foxes of the forest creeping across the blanket of leaves on the floor of the world during the season of dying, barely making a rustling sound. We had become creatures who would learn to hug the ground, dart from hole to hole, cave to cave, and despise the light.

Still my heart was moved to pity for these my people. I ordered my women to bring all the contents of the palace laundry, all my wardrobe and my robes, our finest linens and woolens. My maids and I showed them how to cut up the cloth and tie it around their feet.

I could not keep tears from my eyes when I watched the little ones weeping silently. They did not understand what was happening, but they still tried to act brave. My heart was again moved to pity. I led my eunuchs to the palace armory with the village men behind.

My father had not been buried in his suit of armor as was the custom of our warrior kings because of the great need of bronze. Tyndareus's suit of armor was waiting in the Armory to be melted down. I snatched up his sword and put it in my belt. This would be its last battle.

"Arm yourselves," I said. The men took what swords they could carry, and the eunuchs took weapons enough for the palace women and themselves. All that remained now was to distribute poppy dust to drug the babies and the small children.

It was past the middle of the night and time to get

started.

"Disperse and hide yourselves in the caves and high in the mountains. Live off the land. Seek sanctuary in other cities. I who was your Goddess on Earth can protect you no longer," I had told them. Those were my last words to my people.

I stayed behind to be the last to go. Atossa tearfully remained with me. "I owe you my life," she said. "I will do anything for you." Not yet had she forgotten that on the day the sun disappeared from the sky I saved her from the sacrifice.

"That is nonsense," I said, touched. "Let us hear no more of it." But I knew I could rely on her. Her love for me was as great as her loyalty to the children.

Atossa went first carrying Hermione. I strapped the twins to my back. We could carry no torches so I was glad the moon was full to light our paths as we made our ways across the great aqueduct that spanned the Eurotas Valley.

Its sides were as high as a man, but as a precaution I ordered everyone to walk crouched over. We would have no hope if the sluices had been opened, but the engineers were gone with Menelaus's army. No drop of water was in the aqueduct other than rainfall.

During the night I knew the hauntings of terror for abandoning my city so. I had done what I could for my people, but the Goddess on Earth never leaves her citadel. I told myself I had no choice. Atossa read my thoughts and whispered, "Mistress, do not worry. The Goddess will understand."

"No, Atossa," I said, breaking my own law of silence, "if only it were so! But the Goddess does not think as we do. She cares only for her own honor and her shrines. I fear she will yet wreak savage vengeance upon Sparta.

She would have me keep her vigil no matter if my babies starved to death and if I died. The noble course would have been to open all our veins."

"You must save the twins. They are part of Sparta too."

"So I keep telling myself. But I fear I care more out of a weak mother's love than I do for honor. And the light is sweet to me. The Furies will not let me rest."

When we climbed out of the aqueduct in the early light of dawn I knew fear again. Lower down on the slope I saw a Trojan military camp. The soldiers were still asleep, and the fires were burning low. We were that close to disaster, for they had seen our aqueduct and were searching for its source.

But that night, high atop Mt. Ilios, we were treated to a savage sight. Paris had marched into the city ready to receive his bride. He had searched and soon discovered my treachery. I awoke in the middle of the night because I thought it was morning. Light blazed into my eyes. It was no sun but Sparta in flames.

"Look," I woke Atossa, "the Goddess knows no pity."

I could not keep out of my mind all that was dying with Sparta, which I would never see again. In each room of the palace where the servants lived sat tiny likenesses of the Mother, ancient and much cherished. Those personal goddesses that could be carried in a pocket were more real to many of my people than the Mother who can never die. They were burning, and for the benighted, the gods were dying with the night. What a world in which there was no longer any defence against evil, any force for good!

And the great image of the Mother that dwelled for the ages in the palace shrine, which I had defended for so long, was finally and at last melted into bronze.

Atossa and I clung to each other and wailed the night away into morning. But now that my city was no more, I was no longer Goddess on Earth, and the Goddess was no longer here to listen. She had taken flight to find a new home, leaving us homeless wanderers.

Of course the Trojans soon discovered our escape route, for it was the only one possible. They fanned out on Mt. Ilios hunting for us. Our only hope was our familiarity with the mountains and their lack of it. We hid ourselves in caves concealed by moss, hanging ivy, and pine trees and did not build fires at night no matter how frosty.

But they were persistent, and time and numbers were on their side. One by one and group by group we could hear the villagers screaming for help as the soldiers ferreted them out of hiding and slew them or put them in chains. Atossa and I were lucky to hold out as long as we did, five sunrises all told. Atossa was foraging for berries, and I was feeding the twins in our latest cave of refuge. Hermione was playing with some pinecones at the mouth of the cave, when she screamed, "Mother!" and ran for me. I looked up to see a band of soldiers.

Flight was impossible. I sprang to my feet, grabbed my sword, and pointed it at my heart, hoping Atossa would have the sense to stay away now that it was too late for the children and me. "Bring Prince Paris to me," I commanded, "or these words will be my last." I hoped I still sounded like a Queen.

Three of the soldiers stayed to watch me while the fourth went running for his prince. I had the distinction of being the last captive taken.

Paris was facing me in the time it takes for a leaf to flutter to the ground. "So, my lady, you have played me false," he said. "I have played many games of love in my time, but never one so tiresome." He had dark rings around his eyes and looked like the kind of person who could not endure such inconvenience.

But when he got a good look at me his annoyance changed to alarm. I must have appeared like the wild woman of the forest after days of living off the land. My hair was in disarray for I had taken no combs and had no time to care for it anyway. I had slept on it, making my bed on a pile of dead leaves with the sky for a blanket, and it was wet with the morning dew. I wore no shoes, and my feet were thick with callouses and blisters and scuffed with the bruises of rocks and uneven pebbles of the stream bottoms. My robe was torn, and I had ripped it to the knees to make my flight more swift as I was pursued by these curs, nor was my veil in place. My eyes looked like those of a ghost from nights of wakeful watching.

I felt that last of my power still with me. I said, "Son of Priam, you will swear to me a great oath by the River Styx, even the Oath of Death that Zeus himself cannot break. You must swear by that very life that you hold dear that never may you see the light more if you lay hands on my sons or my little daughter. Swear it, or here before your eyes I will do away with myself."

"I grant you gladly all you wish, my lady. I swear by the River Styx never to harm your children in any way as long as you will let me do with you as I will," he said as if he were relieved I asked so little. "Now swear it by that same River Styx."

"I swear it by the River Styx," I gulped. I felt as if I had that day taken a marriage vow with death.

I dropped my father's sword, and for all I know it still lies there on the mountain. Paris stepped forward to take my hand. He was smiling.

VIII

Menelaus Learns His Fate

Aegisthus insinuated himself into Agamemnon's service and convinced Agamemnon that he should be the one to carry the grave news to Menelaus. After all, he had served as Menelaus's Captain of the Palace Guards.

Menelaus's task in Crete was complete and he was embarking on his flagship to return to Sparta when he sighted a ship bearing the insignia of the double gold lions on red sails. It must be news from Agamemnon.

Aegisthus always owned a flair for the dramatic. He had already taken the liberty to robe himself in black and shave his hair in mourning. "I claim the protection of Hermes, the messenger of the Gods, for I am the bearer of bad tidings," Aegisthus knelt before his liege. "You have always been a fair lord to serve, so I beg of you my life."

"Come, Aegisthus," said Menelaus, turning pale, as he later told me, "if what you have to say is in no way your fault, I will not hold it against you."

"Yeah, but never in your life have you heard such news. Imagine the worst thing that you ever feared and multiply it a hundredfold, nay a thousandfold."

"Out with it!" Menelaus was losing patience. "I will receive whatever the Fates have spun for me, for no man has any choice."

"Hear then what Agamemnon, High King of Mycenae, says to his brother: 'You who were once King of Sparta have no kingdom. You who were once husband of the fair Helen have no wife. You who were once blessed with three children have no heirs, and you who were once the wealthiest king of Hellas next to myself have not one gold coin left to command.'"

My husband raised Aegisthus to his feet, "If you lie I shall have your tongue cut out."

Aegisthus assured him it was no exaggeration. In fact, it was worse, far worse. This time Menelaus did invite him inside the house he was using as his administrative headquarters at the port of Amnisos.

Aegisthus told my husband his version of what happened. "We sighted ships bearing the Spartan flag," he said, and that was as far as his truth went. "We marched out to greet you, thinking you had returned sooner than we dared hope. To our horror we saw a massive fleet of Trojan ships. We tried to beat them back, but they overwhelmed us and forced us to retreat back to the acropolis," he lied. Later I learned that he engaged bands of brigands to attack him on his march to Mycenae to lose enough men to make his story plausible.

"The Queen immediately proclaimed herself sole ruler of Sparta and usurped your throne just as Queen Leda had before her," Aegisthus knew what to say. The rest about me eloping with Paris after I married him at the altar of the Goddess was all epilogue. "And what could I do, lord? I could not take up arms against the Queen?" Aegisthus said innocently.

Many besides Agamemnon criticized Menelaus for his indulgences towards me and said that I had bewitched him. He became the butt of jokes about husbands who allow their wives to lead them by the noses like oxen with rings. Odysseus might guess at it, but only Menelaus knew for a certainty that I loved him and had done so since childhood. "Go," said Menelaus, bowing his head in his hands.

Menelaus became more tight-lipped than ever. His admirals were afraid to go near him. They feared he might lash back at them for his great tragedy. But if he had woes, he kept them to himself. Their wariness changed to admiration. Everyone wanted to share his burden.

"I am glad old Tyndareus is in his grave before he lived to see his daughter come to this," Agamemnon greeted him when he arrived at the palace in Mycenae. And thus Menelaus received another piece of bad news. Aegisthus had not bothered to inform him that his stepfather was dead.

"I wish to see Clytaemnestra," Menelaus said, not responding to his brother's caresses and hugs.

"I thought you had all the problems a man could stand and more without adding that bitch to your roster."

"Let me see her, or have you something to hide, my brother dear?"

Menelaus had expected to find a mere ghost of a woman, bruised and scarred from repeated beatings. And he expected her to be glad to see him. At their last meeting she had called down blessings upon him. But instead he found an impeccably dressed woman very much in possession of herself and cold. Her eyes glittered dangerously.

"Do you think Helen capable of eloping with Paris and burning Sparta?" he asked his sister-in-law.

"Why not?" Clytaemnestra spat at him. "Who would willingly choose one of the sons of that accursed Atreus for husband? Not even you, my lord brother, can keep your promises. You let Agamemnon take Iphigenia after all."

In that cruel way Menelaus learned that Agamemnon had played false to that vow too. But neither son of Atreus suspected that Aegisthus was already beginning to work his charms upon my sister. From him she drew her strength. Whatever he believed she accepted, and he hated Menelaus.

Menelaus strode up to Agamemnon, High King of Mycenae though he was, and pinned him against the wall with his strong hands. Agamemnon was so taken aback he let his mouth gape open. "If you arranged for Sparta to be burned and Helen abducted along with my heirs just so you would be able to get up an expedition against Troy, you are much mistaken."

"Are you crazed? Do you think I would strike at you?" Agamemnon said. This time he was not blustering.

"You have long yearned after Troy's riches."

"Troy yearns after ours as well. Look to your wife, brother. It is she who has played you false."

"I will not condemn her until I hear her treachery from her own lips," Menelaus insisted.

Menelaus had never been an admirer of the Ithacan. To me he had called him "dishonest" and a "pirate king". But in a situation that called for diplomacy instead of force of arms he might need one famed for his oily tongue and quick wits rather than his brawn. Odysseus was one of the few kings of Hellas either not allied to Agamemnon or not under his sway. Ithaca was too far away from the main centers of power.

Menelaus and his army traveled by sea, exchanging the duties and privileges of guest-friendship with each of the kings at the ports of call. He sent runners ahead to announce his arrival so no one in these troubled times would be taken by surprise and think him a Sea Raider. They were only too glad to greet Menelaus, for he was popular among his peers. They knew they could trust him at his word. His misfortunes had flown ahead of him, and they were only too eager to make war against the Trojans.

On his way to Ithaca he forced himself to stop at Gytheum and march to Sparta, retracing the path that his people had taken into slavery only moons before. All along the way he saw farms burned, the countryside deserted. Only a stray goat here and there remained. And even now we are more a goat herding people than the farmers we used to be, just like the Ithacans. Our once fertile land is too barren for anything else.

What the Earth-shaker had not done to Sparta, accursed of the Mother, Paris's generals had completed. Not a house stood, and Sparta was inhabited only by ashes and the wraiths of the unburied dead howling for vengeance.

Menelaus immediately assigned his men to burial details. "These Trojans are barbarians," his men heard him say, "to pay no respect to the dead."

His eyes traveled slowly up the slope of the acropolis to where the palace stood. Even that was only a skeleton. A few walls remained; the rest had collapsed in on itself under its own weight of stone after the timbers were consumed.

"Stay behind," he told his generals. He must ascend the acropolis himself to this place which only the winds could inhabit now. They must not see his face.

The stone echoed beneath his feet a hollow sound. Even in the throne room there was no symbol of his authority left, for the throne was made of wood which the vandals had stripped of ivory inlay and gold foil. On the floor scattered about he found my combs and pins from the upper story. He picked up one and stared at it as if it alone could tell a tale. He seated himself on what used to be the hearth and gave vent to his emotions. There was no man about to call him a woman.

Atossa had been living on the acropolis in what was left of the palace awaiting his return. She heard him moaning and came in to him. She knelt down on the floor in front of him and waited until he looked up finally and saw her.

My lord was in no mood to stand on ceremony. "In the name of the gods, Atossa, what are you doing here?" he pulled her to her feet.

She looked at him sorrowfully, big tears running down her cheeks.

"Do not keep me in suspense like this!" he shook her.

Only then, when she had no other choice, did she open her mouth and point to the wound where her tongue used to be. She would not be able to tell him the truth of my story after all, and of course she did not know how to write.

"Atossa!" he was filled with pity for her. "Did the Trojans do this?" he said.

She shook her head vehemently "no". Atossa pointed towards the hills and opened her eyes wide in fear.

"The bandits?" he pressed.

She shook her head "yes".

"But why?"

She blushed and looked down.

"I will take care of them!" he sucked in his breath. "But just shake your head. Did the Queen elope with this Prince Paris willingly?"

She shook her head "no" so vehemently that

Menelaus told me he thought her neck would snap.

"And yet everyone else condemns her for lightly deserting me, betraying her children into the hands of my enemies, and burning her city and her Goddess shrine behind her...Yet I know I can trust you. You are loyal to us both."

Atossa still looked very frustrated as if there were something she still wanted to say but could not. She tried to gesticulate with her hands meaninglessly until Menelaus had to say, "Perhaps later...." There was no way she could warn him about Aegisthus, and he would not think to ask.

"Follow me. I shall take care of you," he said. She bowed her head, blushed, and followed him gladly several steps behind him. She wanted nothing more than to be with him.

Menelaus was in the mood for vengeance, so he took his soldiers into the hills and cleared out the bandits to the last man. Then he rode about the countryside of Laconia impressing peasants into his army.

The sea was a smooth sheet of blue as they sailed into the harbor of Ithaca with no waves but those created by the keels of their ships. No fishermen were at the dock casting out their nets, and not even a stray orange or gray cat lolled about waiting for his dole of fish. A few boats lapped up and down on the placid surface, brushing against the rocks beneath. The seagulls told no tales.

Ithaca was no Laconia. It was a small island. Most of its few inhabitants made their living herding goats in the hills or fishing, and they pretty much minded their own business. But it was highly unusual for even the privacy-loving Ithacans not to gather at the dock when a fleet of ships came in. They would want to trade and hear the news.

Immediately Menelaus wondered if plague or sickness raged on the island, but he saw no red flags of warning to ships. He sent a delegation to the palace to inquire what was going on and if they needed assistance. The delegation went armed as if to ward off the invisible ghosts of the island or perhaps pirates, though there was no sign of a recent raid. Up the goat trails they climbed into the hills.

They returned quickly enough. When Menelaus asked, "What news?" they seemed puzzled.

"Highness, we could get no straight answer from the palace women. They could do nothing but beat their chests and wail."

The second soldier added, "Yes, and the gates to the palace were not even guarded. We did not see a man about."

Only the death of a King could throw a kingdom into such confusion. Straightway he prepared to offer Queen Penelope his condolences and what protection he could to little Prince Telemachus, for after all Penelope was Helen's first cousin.

Penelope suffered from none of my boldness, and it was all Menelaus could do to persuade her to receive him. He was so accustomed to dealing with me that it took him aback at first when he encountered a Queen who behaved like a modest woman should. At last through intermediaries he persuaded her to leave her rooms and talk to him. She walked with such shuffling steps that it took ages for her to arrive, and then she moved like one whose ankles were bound together. But she was so thickly veiled and surrounded by her women that he could not make out her form or features, only that she was rather short and carrying her baby son Telemachus in her arms.

When my husband began, "I would like to tell you how sorry I am for your bereavement...." Penelope broke into such sobbing, that was picked up and echoed by her women, that Menelaus could not make himself heard. He had time to reflect how odd it was that no one wore mourning.

"How did he die?" my husband finally had a chance to say.

Penelope shook her head and finally managed to say a few words between her sobs. "Sir," she stumbled, hardly able to conquer her shyness at addressing a man, "my husband...is not dead...His wits are gone...."

Nothing could have shocked Menelaus more. Odysseus would be the last man he could imagine going mad. The servants took him out onto the acropolis and pointed down into the valley where the people were gathering in great crowds. Menelaus and his escort rode down to take a look.

There was King Odysseus of Ithaca indeed. At first he was hardly recognizable. He was clothed in a peasant's garb with a felt cap instead of a King's fine tunic. His face was blackened with soot and his feet bare. His beard and his hair had not been trimmed or combed, and swarms of gnats and flies buzzed about him. He did not slap at them or try to drive them away as any sane man would.

He had yoked an ass and an ox together, and sweat dripped down his brow as he tried to plow his fields. Odysseus was not making good progress, for the mule would constantly stop, stall, and refuse to go forward. The ass was a poor draft animal and could not carry its share of the burden of the plow. Any simpleton would know that.

What was worse than a King plowing his own

fields, doing the work of the despised Dorians, and even worse than using a donkey in place of an oxen team — Odysseus threw salt over his shoulder instead of cow manure. Salt would destroy the soil. Enough salt would destroy it for generations. If an enemy hated another city enough it might plow it under with salt after burning it to the ground. Not even a madman would thus destroy his children's inheritance.

The peasants and fishermen were gathered in groups whispering among themselves in their own language and crying. Others were fleeing in terror to the hills, for a madman brought bad luck and a mad King meant disaster. No one dared try to stop him or tell him what he was doing. They feared that some god was behind this.

Black thunderclouds gathered overhead, blotting out the clear sunny day. The wind picked up in one of those sudden storms of the hot season. Odysseus's cap blew off, but on he plowed. He seemed not to notice even when the thunder crashed, the lightning streaked across the sky, and the rain pelted down upon him drenching his clothes and making him slog through mud.

"Odysseus!" Menelaus called, cupping his hands to be heard. "Do you know me?"

Odysseus looked up and grinned as if to no one in particular. He stared straight through Menelaus and beyond.

"Have you known some terrible grief?" Menelaus asked, wondering what could be greater than his own. But madness and misfortune are not always bedfellows.

"Yes father, yes father, I shall be in for the evening meal soon," Odysseus said in a child's small voice.

Menelaus knew that Odysseus was older than he but still much too young to have the aging sickness loosening his wits. He was still only thirty summers.

"Bring Queen Penelope here to me, no matter if she resists," Menelaus gave the order. Still Odysseus plowed his fields, and still the rain plastered his dark hair to his face. Yet he owned more gray hairs than several cycles of the seasons ago.

Penelope would not willingly leave her house, but the soldiers brought her anyway. "Speak to him," Menelaus said to her, "and see if he knows you." With much urging Menelaus had to nearly push her forward.

"Husband...." she whispered, afraid. "Husband...." she said a little more loudly. She sidled towards him hesitantly as if each step might be her last. She was now standing with the wailing Telemachus in her arms at the edge of the field, right in the path of Odysseus's plow. She had gotten too close. Menelaus, seeing the danger, stepped forward to snatch her to safety when at the last possible moment Odysseus himself swerved aside to avoid her and stopped, leaning his forehead against the plow in exhaustion.

Menelaus clenched his fists. He did not relish being taken for a fool. "I see I have come to the wrong place to ask for help," said Menelaus. "I had not heard you were turned coward."

"Don't puff your plumes too far, son of Atreus," Odysseus said in his normal voice. "My parentage may not be as illustrious as yours, but I lack nothing of courage. You cannot win this war, and I want no part in it. I would not see the world come to an end over one silly woman."

"Yet you were the author of that oath we all took to defend Helen's husband against all comers," Menelaus reminded him.

"I will be getting myself into no end of trouble" Odysseus said, wiping the sweat from his brow. "Yes, I know I am honor-bound. Come inside and be my guest.

Maybe I will yet be able to dissuade you."

Then Odysseus took notice of Penelope kneeling on the ground with her hands raised to heaven giving thanks that his wits had been restored. "Wife, get inside with Telemachus, or he will catch his death of cold," he said angrily, and she obeyed as if used to doing nothing else. Later Menelaus confessed that the contrast between Penelope and me was amazing.

Odysseus ruled over one of the smallest kingdoms in Hellas. His palace on the nearby hill was less than half the size of our palace that burned in Sparta. Nor was it defended by a wall. His lack of riches and obscure location tempted few comers.

No guard stood at the propylon gate, for Odysseus had not the money to hire one. He had to depend entirely on the goodwill of his citizens and the other landowners on the island in times of war. With his small military force he maintained his position as King more by force of personality and his wit than by blind authority. He could not merely snap his fingers and expect to fill Menelaus's quota for troops.

It was but a short distance from the gateway into the throne room. Menelaus saw what a difference Penelope's dowry made to a King like Odysseus. Here and there new sconces appeared on the walls to hold candles, and it seemed that old stones that had crumbled and fallen out of the walls had been replaced.

Odysseus received Menelaus with all the state due his rank as one of the two chief Kings of the Achaeans. Odysseus would omit nothing. A maidservant brought a pitcher of water and washed Menelaus's hands. Odysseus might boast more tin and bronze ware than gold, but his servants displayed the finest he owned.

The women brought tables for the two Kings and

served them with a plain, simple fare but a hearty one. They partook of goat's milk cheese, milk curds mixed with honey, fish caught off the coast of Ithaca, and vegetables grown in the palace garden, and completed their meal with wine of a local vintage.

Only then did Odysseus resume the topic of war, for a guest's rights were sacred to Zeus. "If the Kings and princes of Hellas remember their oaths and send their ships to your aid, we may yet take Troy, but our homelands will also be for the taking," Odysseus argued.

"I know, and my purpose is first to avoid war," Menelaus said. "I propose that you and I, two Kings alone, journey to Troy on a diplomatic mission. We will meet with Priam and demand the return of Helen and the children with all the riches of my state treasury. If they comply, we will do nothing. If they refuse, we shall outline to them the consequences of their actions."

"But why would they give up what they have gone to so much trouble to take?" Odysseus said. "Helen and Hermione give them the right to rule Sparta. Priam will lose face. He cannot give in to you so easily, or he will be mocked in all the courts of Asia."

"Not so if we leave the way open to him to blame the raid on Paris. Everyone knows how Paris would rather play the lyre and chase women than fight. Perhaps Paris, in his lust and foolishness, put Troy at a greater risk than Priam is willing to take. Troy by herself is far mightier than any one of our cities, including glorious Mycenae, and is the greatest since Knossos fell. But against the combined Achaean host she and her allies are well-matched."

Odysseus frowned in concentration as he fingered his goblet, "Tell me, why do you call on me when many Kings of Hellas stand greater in the esteem of the world?"

"I admit I have not liked you and in the past would not have trusted you. You have the reputation of a pirate."

"Some of us inherit a well-stocked state treasury," said Odysseus, "and some of us must go in search of one where we can find it." He looked at Menelaus pointedly. "But, proceed. Your greatest virtue is your honesty. If you flattered me I would not trust you."

"You are one of the few Kings of Hellas not allied to my brother or under his sway."

"Go on."

"You helped me once with your ready tongue and wit."

"Continue."

Menelaus was puzzled. Odysseus stared at him so intensely that he seemed to look through him, weighing him on the bronze scales that judge the soul after death. "There is no more," my husband said. He stared back, for he would never flinch under another man's gaze.

"But you have not yet told me your real reason for going," Odysseus insisted. "I have an intuition that King Priam could restore your treasury, your heirs, return your title and even your enslaved subjects, could even rebuild your palace, and still you would invoke the oath of the suitors. It would not matter to you that Hermione would be Queen and you could afford to buy yourself another wife."

Odysseus was a man who would not settle for less than complete honesty. "Odysseus, it is said that you can see into the minds and the souls of other men with a wisdom far exceeding your years. Very well, then. As silly as it seems I love my wife, and I cannot believe that she would willingly betray me for Paris."

"Despite what I have heard, I know Paris could not command the respect of her little finger," Odysseus sounded very sure of himself. But suddenly a veil was drawn across his eyes so that it seemed he could neither look out nor could anyone look in. He even appeared to have forgotten Menelaus's presence as he remembered something painful. Then his mind snapped back into focus. He grabbed Menelaus's hand and said, "You have a bargain."

Menelaus was much relieved.

"But," said Odysseus with a twinkle in his eye, "you must promise me that if the mission is not a success, we will take time out to raid the coast of Asia Minor before returning home. And if you should be successful, you will share your treasury with me."

"I had not expected this, but I cannot do without you. You are a hard man who drives a tough bargain."

"I must be," Odysseus laughed, "that is, if I want to remain King of Ithaca. Everyone will be asking me what they can get out of this mission."

Odysseus entertained Menelaus for the better part of a moon as they made final preparations to set sail. On the last night before retiring they were drinking wine with each other. Odysseus said, "You are a fool, you know."

"What is this?" Menelaus said. He was not used to being addressed so.

"For loving a woman like Helen. And yet you are the only man in Hellas who has the courage to."

IX

Troy And Inanna

With weary eyes I first beheld Troy. Even then I was dazzled. Early one morning I opened my eyes and was nearly blinded. There stood the city on the hill rising sharply above the plain and the harbor. Sparta was surrounded by hills. One came upon this suddenly. It looked something like one imagined Mt. Olympus must, the home of the gods.

The city was built in terraces of white stone, all planted with trees, vines, and flowers in a spiral design. At the base of the hill were the humbler dwellings of the citizens, rising up from level to level to the houses of the rich, to buildings of state, and finally to the palace of Priam and the temples of the gods at the summit. And the little black dots milling about everywhere must be people, hundreds if not thousands!

Paris's flagship signaled the shore, and all the black dots poured out of the city, ran across the plain, and crowded into the harbor. They kept coming and coming like a colony of ants until I imagined the city could contain no more. Paris was standing at the oarlocks beside me, for he would not allow me a moment of peace or reflection. I said, "They seem anxious to greet you."

"No, you, my Helen, you. The reputation of your beauty has arrived before you."

I blushed, and yet I did not know why. That was merely another of his inane compliments which meant nothing, for in the whole time of the voyage he had never claimed what was now his to take. Instead he had courted me and had seemed to enjoy the music, food, and wine more than any sight of me. I was the daughter of a soldier King and the wife of another. Even my mother had come to her death wielding a sword in a rebellion. I too had fought off Paris rather than submit, for the Achaeans were a warrior race. But this Prince seemed to hate his very armor. He left everything to his generals when he could and spent the rest of the time preening himself. He thought of little but his own comfort or the pleasure of his senses. Even this morning he took me aback by asking if I liked his new scent which he had imported from Egypt. In a woman I would have counted such a question mere folly and vanity. I was a Spartan.

I remembered my modesty and checked to see that my veil was fastened. He caught my hand and stopped me, "You will not be needing that here."

I was shocked. "Don't the Trojan women wear veils?" I asked.

"Mere women do," he answered, "but not goddesses."

I was angry and wondered what game this was. Soon I was to learn to my everlasting shame and sorrow. Whatever little innocence I had left was to be gone forever.

Asians love a show. Their child-like natures incline naturally to spectacles of all kinds. As soon as we put down anchor I had a chance to study them.

At the front of the crowd that came out to meet us were curtained litters and carrying chairs. Although the rulers of Troy were Achaeans they had long ago adopted Asian conventions of ornament, nor had they lost the opportunity their litters presented for engraving and silks.

The nobles could hardly be seen for their clothing. Not only were the materials fine linens and silks, as with our Achaean lords of Hellas, but they were bordered with designs of mythical beasts: lions with tails of dragons, griffins with wings, and snakes with heads of dogs. It was hard to imagine where they found such brilliant dyes of red, purple, blue, and green. Nor were their faces or hair visible for the jewelry and cosmetics. And here I am speaking of the men, for the women lay behind curtains. I could feel their eyes studying me.

Down fell the gangplanks, and the ships carrying my people, my Spartans, unloaded their human cargo. The Spartan women wailed and clutched each other for comfort. They had to parade through the crowd and veiled themselves in shame. They were chained together and progressed barefoot, driven forward by soldiers with whips. As soon as they passed beyond the litters a loud clamor of pots and pans beaten together rose to the skies, and jeering yells were heard. Cowbells rang, and my people were pummeled with sticks. The guards tried to keep the crowd back from this valuable merchandise and hacked away at the mob with their swords. Jeers turned to screams.

My people turned and looked up to me for comfort. I was still their Goddess on Earth though I had no power in this alien land. Tears came to my eyes. I could imagine what their future would hold among a people so heartless and savage. But I had to do something. Although my heart was not in it, I held up my arms in a gesture of appeal to the heavens and with hope on my face.

Suddenly, in the time it takes to snuff out a candle

or a life, there was silence. The flies of the ship buzzed near me. Everyone had turned and was staring in the direction of the ships. Paris took my hand, and we stepped to the head of the gangplank. When two of the sailors came forward and blared forth on their horns, I realized that everyone was gaping at me.

I balked, feeling naked under their gaze, but Paris's grip had become iron, and he moved me forward as surely as if he were one of the whip masters. At the foot of the gangplank two sedan chairs and eight palace eunuchs awaited us. Paris led me to one, he took the other, and up we soared over their heads.

Murmurs shot through the crowd. I saw women peeking out from behind their curtains. I seemed to be a great curiosity. Never had I realized that, stripped of the accoutrements of my office, I could be so fascinating. I glanced towards Paris. He was basking in their admiration, drinking it in, and smiled like a cat who had just finished a huge meal.

I looked ahead, and for a moment I was blinded. The great gates of Troy seemed to be two balls of sun spitting forth sparks of light. I shut my eyes, stinging like a nest of wasps, and saw nothing but red. When I could open them again we were passing through the gates. Looking at an angle I realized they were fashioned of solid bronze. In the afternoon sun setting in the west they were for a space of time too bright to look upon. Such was my introduction to the power and might of Troy.

Behind me they closed suddenly like the jaws of the sharks in the great Sea and never were to open again for ten long cycles of the seasons. But now I was too stunned to have such forebodings.

Sparta boasted so few citizens by comparison that her humble dwellings could be lined up side by side along a scattering of streets. Hardly could I have imagined it, but here the people lived one on top of the other like bees in a honeycomb. Three or four stories into the air I saw people peering outdoors at us. Many more were crowded onto the flat roofs where it would seem they had gardens planted, although right now they appeared rather brown and dry.

The population looked polyglot just as the army had. Men and women came in all sizes and colors. The natives were short and dark with large eyes, and they lived on the bottom of the heap. They were by far the most numerous in this metropolis. Again, all eyes followed me as I passed.

Just as we turned onto the road that wound up the hill, I looked over my shoulder down into the marketplace in the center of the city. There were my people, the women of Sparta, stripped not only of their veils but of all their clothing. The slave masters had chained them together on the auction block. Many of the litters were crowded around the market as the nobles shopped for women for their households. Such was the fate of slaves. I showed my anger to Paris, but he merely blew me a kiss and shouted that I was beautiful when angry.

The Trojan army lined the sides of the road. The people from the lower town were filing up the hill in a mass buoying us along. From their awed expressions I guessed that this was not their usual privilege. Then I began to notice that the buildings we were passing by were decorated.

The more elaborate houses of the rich were hung from window to window with garlands of summer flowers, and their rooftops were blanketed with them. At first sight charming, but when I looked closely they seemed as dry and stunted in their growth as the gardens in the lower town. Entire households stood there cheering me, picking up poppies, carnations, candytufts, and marigolds and tossing them down on me. These were the usual decorative flowers. But immediately I was struck by the prominence of the flowers of the sun.

In Hellas we have a legend about the flower of the sun. A beautiful young maiden, the daughter of a King by the name of Clytie, fell in love with Apollo. She spent her days gazing ever upward at the yellow orb. The god punished her for her hubris in presuming to think herself worthy of him. He changed her into a flower, condemned to perpetually turn her face upwards. But not only that, instead of giving her a graceful face and a lithe form such as other flowers, he made her ungainly, tall, and gawky, an awkward plant with no beauty in a bold yellow color with a brown face.

"Also," I thought, "she endures drought better than other flowers."

It was hardly the bloom one would imagine being chosen as anyone's favorite. Yet here it was painted on the stone facades of houses, painted large so that it could even be seen by the birds of the air. Women shielded behind veils began to throw flowers of the sun and seeds down upon our procession as we wound up the hill. All around me veiled women and men were carrying them and chanting something in their language which I did not understand. It sounded like "In-nanna!" So first I heard that name.

Finally we reached the palace on top of the hill. If not as large as Knossos it would have swallowed our palace at Sparta. Its design was more sprawling and open. Strange to say, it was painted in bright colors on the outside in motifs of giant bulls breathing fire, the same symbol I had seen on the Trojan standards. The background was sky blue, the bull black, his horns gold, and the fire red.

Paris helped me down from the litter. Everyone was gathered in a crowd barely kept back by the guards to watch us go in. They were staring at me as if trying to memorize my every movement. We passed through the great stone pillars. Entrance way led to vestibule led to inner court and still on and on through a maze of rooms. The floors were tiled in designs of dragons and strange monsters with forked tongues breathing fire or half-human, half-monster creations. The walls were painted in frescoes of monsters of the sea or bright geometric patterns.

In the throne room high on a dais sat a figure barely distinguishable as a man so obscured was his form by his robes of state. They were sky blue trimmed in gold foil, emeralds, rubies, and bright lapis lazuli stones. All over they were embroidered with the same insignia of the bull breathing fire. On his head he wore a bull's head fashioned in gold surmounted by horns as a crown. This must be Priam.

Around him stood a crowd of blue-clad figures veiled in gold, one a little forward of the others. They were too richly dressed for serving women.

"Who are they?" I whispered to Paris.

"My father's wives, and Queen Hecuba in front."

"All of them?" I gasped.

"One hundred all told," he smiled.

I was horrified at the barbaric customs of the East. Was I to become one of the one hundred wives as well?

I did not have time to think. Paris was addressing his father, "Shepherd of the Great Sea, Bull of Heaven, Priam, King of Troy, I bring you Inanna, Queen of Heaven."

At the name "Inanna" everyone in the room from

the one hundred wives, to the guards, to Paris, with the sole exception of Priam, fell to their knees. Only I remained standing, and turning towards me they all touched their foreheads to the ground.

"But I am Helen, Queen of Sparta," I said, unable to fathom why Paris suddenly named me "Inanna". I had never heard of anyone named "Inanna" before. It was too primitive and foreign to suit me. Then I recalled the crowd had been shouting it.

Priam rose to his feet. Suddenly from out of the crowd darted a young man as big and brawny as Achilles and equally as tall, but with a bushy black beard. His dress was almost as elaborate as Priam's. He lent Priam his arm, and they both knelt before me. "Inanna, Queen of Heaven," Priam said in an old man's voice. But the young man stared from Paris to me and back again as if he could not believe what he saw. Envy was written all over his face.

It seemed I must be Inanna whether I would or no.

Paris led me away before I had time to wonder what was happening. We retraced our way through the palace and out into the light of day. The crowds were even thicker. The guards beat a path for us so we could cross the acropolis to another building that looked like a shrine. Still they shouted, "In-nanna!"

As we passed through the pillars a young woman about my age with a head of startling red hair hanging loose and uncombed around her shoulders, wild green eyes, and long red fingernails appeared before us. I could only marvel at her appearance and at her skin as white as the powder of talc, which was fully revealed to us. All I could think was how did she resemble me that she and I were the only two women in the city who wore no veils.

"Welcome, Queen of Heaven," she saluted me. "Welcome to the Shrine of Inanna." She took my hand from Paris. I was to go with her.

"So, Inanna is your Goddess?" I asked as I followed this red-haired beauty into the shrine.

She pointed towards the ceiling and spoke, "See, the Bull of Heaven." I stepped back afraid. "The Bull of Heaven belches forth fire and breathes smoke. His red eyes blaze down on the earth and scorch us in the season of heat and drought." The Bull was fearsome of aspect and painted as huge as the ceiling was wide. He hung over the worshippers as a black cloud hangs over the day.

The priestess pointed at the floor beneath our feet. "He singes the earth and leaves us with famine and no water," she said. In tiny pieces of colored tile was the depiction of a field of wheat at the moment the breath of the Bull strikes it, setting it aflame. In the far corner was the wasteland it became afterward, turned brown and straw-colored with not a drop of green.

She pointed to the wall on our left. "The people die," she said. "The God Tammuz feels sorry for us and dies with us." I saw a picture of the most beautiful youth imaginable with bright blond hair and eyes the color of the skies falling to the earth as the fire struck him. In the next picture he descended beneath the mountain, buried in his tomb. Around him the mourners wailed and beat their chests.

"Inanna takes pity on us," the priestess said and pointed to the wall on our right. "She sends Im-dugud. He brings rain in the cold season." Depicted was a huge lion-headed eagle with wings the span of the entire wall. Dark clouds of rain and lightning swirled around him, and water flooded the earth.

"But still the earth is dead. Nothing grows, and no one can bring Tammuz back to life. Inanna marries him, and he is born again. Our life is restored to us," she said, pointing to the shrine ahead of us. Painted on the wall was a goddess holding two flowing vases as her breasts. Next to her stood the God Tammuz restored. All around them the earth had again sprung into life. All creatures were staring transfixed at the beautiful, golden-haired goddess.

"But what does she have to do with me?" I asked.

"This time the sacrifice was not pleasing. There was no rain. We must repeat it. The time for the sacrifice is propitious. You are Inanna and will bring us rain."

I was beginning to feel very uneasy in my stomach as I recalled the parched-looking flowers that had greeted me. "I have no such powers," I tried to explain. "I was the Goddess on Earth in Sparta. But all I could do even there was bring comfort and succor to my people."

"Yours was a dying religion," she stared at me. "Here you will bring rain." She reached out and touched my hair, pressing it between her fingers. I felt a sudden shock of recognition. My hair was flaxen just like their goddess's.

She beckoned, and I had no choice but to follow her through a door into the back rooms of the shrine. Even if I could escape her there were guards outside.

Priestesses were at work everywhere just as my women in Sparta used to occupy themselves with the affairs of the Goddess. Some were washing her sacrificial vessels. Some were preparing her offering and her meals, some the sacred wines for her priestesses to drink. But everywhere they stopped and stared at me, and some even clasped their hands over their mouths and pointed. One priestess even touched her hand to her hair, which was black, and then pointed at mine. I wanted to hide myself.

Finally the red-haired priestess ushered me into a room where in the shadows stood a man in a long, white chiton bordered in gold and blue bull-motifs. He was turned in profile with only one side of his face towards me. I gasped. He looked the very image of Paris without the blond ringlets, for his head was shaved and oiled in the manner of eunuchs. Somehow I felt he was aware of my presence almost immediately.

He turned and walked towards us. I held my hands over my mouth. The other side of his face was terribly scarred and burned so that he was horrific to look upon. By contrast it seemed as if the beautiful moon had a dark and pitted side, gutted by monsters. Yet he walked with a dignity and presence alien to Paris.

So self-possessed did he seem, at first I did not notice his second affliction. He limped, dragging one foot turned inward so that he had to step on the side of it, clumping the sandal of his one good foot on the floor. A club foot. Spartans regarded club feet as marks of the demons, setting a child apart. He would have been exposed at birth or thrown into a mountain gorge to rid the family of the curse.

"My brother, Prince Deiphobus," the priestess said. "He was dedicated to Inanna when he was a youth."

I found it incredibly strange that a royal prince should become a eunuch. But perhaps that explained why he was still alive. When he nodded his head to me in greeting his eyes quickly but instantly traveled up and down the length of my body, in moments taking in everything, then coming to rest on my face. Even more strangely he smiled as if in recognition, as if he had been looking for me all his life and had finally found me. I shuddered. I could not look at him.

"But you said he was your brother?" I asked. "Then you must be...."

"The Princess Cassandra," she said. "Chief Priestess of Inanna."

Before I could say anything more, Cassandra left me with Deiphobus. I did not want to be alone with him and tried to creep away to the other side of the room.

"You need not look at me," he said in a voice that sent thrills of horror through me. It was the same soft, silken purr that I had often heard in my mind since girlhood when I thought of the evil gods of the universe.

"What else do you want to know about me?" he asked. "Yes," he said, "I was Paris's twin at birth. But he was beautiful, I deformed. When Priam saw I had a club foot he threw me into the fire. That explains my face. My mother saved me and promised me to Inanna. But more of that later. Now you must do exactly as I say. You have a severe trial ahead of you."

"What is all this talk of my being Inanna and bringing rain?"

"No more and no less than that you are Inanna, the loveliest woman alive," he smiled at me queerly, and his voice carried nothing of Paris's courtly flattery in it. He was stating a fact. "Now, drink this wine. It will soothe you." He talked in riddles. At least Paris never did that.

"No, I refuse."

"Drink it," he said more sternly, thrusting it at my face.

I stepped backward.

"Very well, you shall learn the hard way. It would make you senseless so that you would remember it all only as a terrible dream. Now it shall be a waking nightmare. But you shall learn that you must always listen to me."

He pulled me after him to a sunken tub of tile filled with water where the decoration of cavorting nautili, squids, octopi, and snails mocked my horror. "You must bathe," he said. Before I knew what he was about, he was deftly unfastening my clothes.

I freed myself. "If I must bathe, I shall bathe myself!"

"I am the servant of Inanna, but if she shall persist in fighting me, I shall call for assistance."

One of him was certainly better than ten. I shut my eyes and pretended I did not feel his fingers brushing against my skin. Hot anger shot through me. He was deliberately lingering over my breasts longer than he needed in order to remove my clothes. I shrank from him as he traced the outlines of my body from my breasts down to my ankles.

Keeping my eyes shut was doing me no good. I stared at him, expressing my disdain. "Eunuch," I spat, "do what you will, but hurry up with it. I cannot long endure you." It was insufferable to me, having him touch me where only Menelaus had preceded him.

Deiphobus's eyes glittered with anger. He took hold of my hand and helped me into the tub. He washed me in the perfumed water, dried me, and anointed me with oil. I awaited my new clothing, which would no doubt be the costume of this Inanna. Instead he led me to a large, curtained litter covered with flowers of the sun. He gestured for me to climb inside.

"This joke is a poor one," I said, trying to cover myself with my hands. "Your revenge is both petty and stupid. What will you say if I tell Paris what you are doing?"

"He would be very angry at you. He would think you were trying to seduce me with your ample charms and that I spurned you as I must do. Alas, I am a eunuch," he laughed, "as far as my poor benighted brother knows or anyone else for that matter."

Then I became more afraid than I had ever been before. What kind of demon was this? Fear coursed through me until I shook and could hardly stand.

He took advantage of my discomposure, which I was later to learn was his specialty. He took my arm and forced me into the litter. He laid me down and bound my ankles and wrists with ropes plaited with flowers so they could not be seen. Around my neck he placed a garland of yellow flowers. That was the only garment I was to wear.

Suddenly I remembered tales of how victims used to be sacrificed in times of drought and famine. Would they slit my throat and leave me to bleed out my life on some altar, then immolate my body on a pyre? Was I brought all the way to Troy just for this? I remembered that Paris had not touched me. Did he intend to marry Hermione instead? "Deiphobus," I said, "in the name of mercy, do you intend to kill me?"

"Hardly," he laughed in a most cynical fashion. "Paris means to marry you after the ceremony. By bringing you to Troy he has risen more in the favor of our father than he ever has before. Poor Hector is much put out by it. Oh, he was the big, burly one you saw in the Throne Room helping old Priam about. He is afraid Priam might name Paris heir instead."

"Then what are you going to do?" I said.

He disappeared and returned wearing a mask. It was the head of a sphinx painted in red and blue with a flattened nose and bright rosettes on its cheeks. It stared out at the world from under judgmental brows. "Everywhere I go except inside this temple I hide my face. But you, Inanna, wear nothing. If I were as beautiful as you, there would be no need for shame. No one can look at you and do anything but marvel."

I could no longer hold back my tears. "Don't speak in riddles," I wept.

He shocked me by suddenly slapping my cheek

with the back of his hand. "From this moment forth as soon as the others arrive, if you so much as make one whimper, you will spoil the sacrifice. This is supposed to be a joyous occasion, and we celebrate it only once in seven cycles of the seasons. Remember, you turned down the drink of forgetfulness. I shall be with you the whole time. If you make one sound, I shall have you gagged."

I choked on my sobs.

Priestesses bore the litter out of the temple with Deiphobus keeping pace with the sound of the drums that struck up as soon as we started. All the rest is a blur of the most horrific misery I ever endured. Nothing in ten cycles of the seasons until the very end could equal it. They lay me down in the square between the palace and the shrine. I saw Cassandra with her flaming red hair and the priestesses forming a ring around me and the people in mobs beyond.

"Inanna! Inanna! Inanna!" they chanted until it had the rhythm of a heartbeat.

A young man of the nobility, as I guessed because of his fair skin and golden hair, stepped forth from the ring of priestesses. He wore the kingly raiment of gold and blue. On his head sat Priam's crown of the bull with horns. But his eyes looked faraway. He had accepted the drink of forgetfulness that I had spurned.

Around and around my litter he began to circle, stepping in time with the chanting. The dust rose with his tread, while all else was still. Closer and closer he came. I shut my eyes and thought of the sharks circling our ships on the way to Troy, imagining how cool the sea was. Here the sun had no mercy, and all was as dry as dust. I coughed and choked on it, and still he approached closer.

He stopped in front of the entrance to my litter and suddenly all was silence except for the thudding in my chest. Was he a priest? Would he kill me? I tried to struggle away, but I could not move. And I could feel Deiphobus's eyes scorching through me as pitilessly as the sun. He touched my cheek in warning.

But the young man, as if still in a trance, lightly tapped his own shoulder. At once the priestesses stepped forward, converging on me. Two stepped beyond the others and disrobed him with reverence. He stood before me as naked as I, and as pale. The sweat stood out on his skin. He parted the curtains and gazed upon me, big with desire. Perhaps they had given him an aphrodisiac. At once I understood, or perhaps had understood all along and had fought off the admission. A distant memory of a muggy summer night alone in the shrine of the Goddess in the mountains of Sparta flashed through my mind. As frightening as that had been, I longed for it with the fierceness of hunger. Menelaus would not come through that curtain to save me this time.

I turned my head away and swore I would not open my eyes until it was over. Deiphobus's fingers dug into my shoulder where my head was turned. Nor did he let go of me the whole time. It would be easier if I let my body go limp, and I willed it. This young man wanted this no more than I did. He was so nervous it took him a long time to work his fate upon me. I could feel nothing I was so numb, and could think only of reaching the end of time where the trial would be no more.

Barely had he withdrawn, when I heard him suck in his breath sharply as if in fear. Alerted, my eyes opened before I had time to think. Now both Deiphobus's hands were fastened upon my shoulders, holding me. Paris stepped forward out of nowhere. He was dressed as if for battle in his bronze helmet and cuirass. He raised his hand and plunged his sword into this youth who fell dead upon me, spilling out his blood. A bitter bile rose in my throat and I retched, drowning out my scream.

Cassandra and her priestesses removed the body with great ceremony, laying it reverently on a bier of flowers of the sun. Others poured ewers of clear, perfumed water over me, and as they did so the crowd erupted into cheers.

I began to shake uncontrollably. Deiphobus laved my forehead with a cool cloth and explained to me, "They have shown Inanna what they want. The earth and the sky must dance together the dance of copulation, break forth into bud, and flourish. The sky must let down its floodgates of life-giving rain. They have sacrificed a King to Inanna and fertilized the earth with his blood.

"In the old days of Knossos, Priam himself would be sacrificed. At first the ceremony would take place every year, and every year the King would die and a new one be chosen. Then it was once in seven cycles of the seasons. Soon the King began to choose a surrogate so he could live out his reign."

I prayed to Our Lady of Sparta. Perhaps out of pity she might listen to me wherever she now was. I thanked her for having more mercy than this Inanna who demanded such cruel sacrifices. Our Lady had been more kind. But this was the custom of the Trojans.

I wondered if even my mother would go this far.

The priestesses carried my litter back into the palace. Deiphobus gave me to understand that the marriage ceremony would take place immediately and that I was not to be allowed to rest. Again he bathed me, but this time he dressed me. I was married to Paris the same night by the light of the torches. Deiphobus stood in the shadows, watching all the while.

X

The Will Of Deiphobus

While Paris was building our house, we continued to live in the palace of Priam. Priam, as Paris said, was so pleased with me that he gave us the apartments of state next to his own. Prince Hector and his wife Andromache were forced to move down the hall. Paris was now acknowledged to be the heir apparent, and nothing could contain his jubilation — unless perhaps it was I.

Finally even he grew tired of courting me, and consummated our marriage. It was quite distasteful to him, for I would do nothing to cooperate and lay passively in bed. I considered myself a captive of war, nothing more, and still called myself Queen of Sparta.

"My lady, I am afraid you have no taste," he said. "You are now well on your way to becoming Queen of Troy. You see how old and feeble Priam is. Why can't you appreciate it instead of lamenting about the past? Certainly Sparta cannot compare with our city."

"Maybe not," I said, "but as a husband, ruler, and man you do not compare with Menelaus."

That would anger him, for above all things, Paris prided himself on his lovemaking ability. He could not understand how I should fail to succumb to his charms. To soothe his vanity he soon took to leaving me alone as often as he could. His previous mistresses were only too willing to take my place and console him. Perhaps he thought I would come to my senses, but I could feel only vast relief to be rid of him and be alone with my children.

All too soon I discovered it was my destiny never to be alone. When Paris was not with me, Deiphobus was. The Trojans did not find this strange. All of Priam's wives, including Queen Hecuba, had their own eunuchs who kept watch over them as personal bodyguards and jailers. They were called "harem masters". Since I was soon regarded as the chief woman in the land, my eunuch held the highest rank.

One morning I looked up after Paris left, and Deiphobus was the shadow darkening my doorway. He startled me, for he was wearing his sphinx mask. Hermione screamed and ran crying to me. I picked her up into my lap and stroked her hair. She had been through too much for a child of only two cycles of the seasons. Lately I had been answering many questions about where "daddy" was. And from this time she began to dream of a man in a sphinx mask. The twins stared from where they were playing on the floor, and then they crawled over and clutched my robe.

"The face that can put even the birds to flight," Deiphobus said. "They shall get used to it in time. All things come in time." He approached the children slowly. He stood there silently until they had the courage to touch him. He took Hermione's hand, led her away, and summoned the maidservants to carry the twins out.

He seated himself beside me on the bench. When I tried to move, he caught my hand fast and would not release me.

"Out with it," I said. "What do you want of me?"
"Nothing and everything."
"Riddles again!"

The Will Of Deiphobus

"I want you to be nothing but what you are, but I need all of you."

"I have no choice in the matter?"

"How very wise you are!" he said. "I did not overestimate your worth when I went to all that trouble to send for you."

He still held my hand fast in his grasp. When I again sprang up, he yanked me down. "But it was Paris who — "

"And who do you think put it into Paris's head?" he said. "Do you imagine that Paris knows how to go about things? Ever since we were little he has relied totally on me for everything except how to play at dalliance."

"Paris is too vain to listen to anyone," I said, hoping that what I was hearing could not be true.

"And I play to that vanity, as you will see."

"But why?"

"Priam is an old man teetering on the brink of the grave. Hector is like that hero of yours, Achilles, all brawn and daring and no forethought. Paris is, simply put, a fop with grandiose ambitions. Troy and her empire need a ruler. I plan to rule through Paris, and you will be my Queen."

"But I am Queen of Sparta," I wept.

"You are Inanna," he said, lifting my hand to his lips and kissing it through his mask. There was no sense of gallantry in his movements as there was in Paris's, only a strong sense of possession — that I was his as much as some poor bird caught in a trap.

Indeed I was Inanna whether I liked it or not. Since the ceremony, it had actually rained. Now no one would believe that I was not their Goddess. Everyone called me "Inanna" down to the humblest chambermaid.

"I cannot be your Queen," I said, putting scorn into

my voice to conceal my fear. "You are a eunuch."

He laughed, "Come." He led me by the hand, which he had never relinquished, but was careful not to hold me so hard that he marked my skin. He took me to his quarters.

"Besides my rooms in the temple I live here."

The court was open to the sky. It was filled with music, not of the flute or cithara, but of singing birds. The winged creatures flew about freely or sat on perches or in golden cages. They were the most colorful and exotic creatures I had ever seen, instead of the small songbirds that perched on my windowsills in Sparta.

He introduced me to a black bird with an orange bill that came from the Land of the Sunrise far to the east over the Mountains. Others strutted on the ground and spread their tail-feathers like brightly-colored fans. Yellow and green birds sporting long tail-feathers and peach rings around their necks, perched on tree branches. Two small green birds with orange heads sat in a golden cage. Deiphobus called these "lovebirds". He patted their heads with his finger, and they rubbed against it.

But the perch of gold decorated with blue lapis lazuli stones in the center of the room was most elaborate. The parrot who occupied it was by far the plainest — all gray with a little white underneath and a red patch of tail feathers. But the large yellow eyes that fixed on me looked wise, and perhaps it was the oldest of all. Deiphobus put out his elbow, and the bird stepped onto it. "Helen," he called the parrot, "today you meet your namesake. Meet Helen the Queen."

"Helen," the bird addressed me.

I jumped backward in shock. Was this bird magical? This man a demon?

He saw the panic in my face and again laughed.

"This bird is from the farthest reaches of Ethiopia, the Land of the Setting Sun. There birds talk, or at least the most talented do. Of course I had to cultivate it. And I had to clip the feathers in her wings when she was young, or she would have flown away."

"You practice black magic!" I said. "And you named her Helen so that you could curse me through her."

"Hardly," he said, in his most purring, sycophantic tones, "when I have waited so long for you. I named the bird Helen because it is a thing of beauty and the smartest of all my pets."

He still held me fast by the hand as he led me to an adjoining chamber. Then he pulled me down upon something soft, of the texture of silk and yielding. I could not see, for it was completely dark here. Little did I think in that instant what this bed was to mean to me, the couch of Persephone in Hades in the black pit of Tartarus.

He began to stroke my cheek and say in a low, warning voice but one already husky with desire, "Now we shall see just how smart you really are. I will not hurt you, but I will advise you that I have Paris's ear as well as the charge of your children."

I sat immobilized, my eyes shut, biting my lip, thinking hard on my children as he ran his fingers through my hair, combing it. I tried not to think of the loathsome monster next to me and gagged on my sobs as his fingers touched me lightly, now on my cheek, my neck, my breast, and my thighs. Wonderingly they lingered now here and now there, exploring me as if I were a novel being from a foreign land, unimaginable until this moment. "Perfect," he said, "perfect. You own not a flaw anywhere."

I braced my body for a quick violation like the one I had received at the ceremony. That would be over before the bile could rise from my stomach. It was unendurable to lie still while spiders skittered across my skin. I began to squirm and draw back wherever his fingers lighted.

He stopped. He got up but was soon back. He held my head and said, "Here, drink this. It will calm your fear, and this time you will listen to me."

Now his fingers felt heavier. My limbs were weighed down and could not move. My thoughts were racing ahead and screaming as he undressed me and pushed me back against the pillows. I was strangely awkward and numb, stunned, like those victims of the spiders frozen with enough venom to keep them still but not yet to kill them.

I seemed to be floating over myself. I kept waiting for the pain to strike. I seemed to be searching around for it, expecting it at every turn, either that or a blackened, burned face belonging to a denizen of the Underworld. But these might have been dreams, detached, for he never hurt me, just as he promised.

I must have fallen asleep, for when I opened my eyes I was back in the room filled with birds and music, reclining on a couch and even garbed in new clothes. I would have imagined I dreamed it all, except that I could still detect a faint scent of him.

Shame broke out all over me like a cold sweat when I saw Deiphobus coming towards me carrying a tray of fruit and cheese. I felt corrupted and vile and wanted to put my skin away and not touch myself ever again. "I would bathe," I said.

"I have bathed you," he said as he served me with grapes and the ripe red flesh of pomegranates slit open to display them to better satisfaction.

Suddenly I could endure his ugly mask no more. I grabbed for it and pulled it away from his face. I had caught him off-guard, and for a moment he looked unsure of himself. But he regained his composure almost instantly. I stared at the blackened face that I vaguely remembered. He stared back at me, breathing hard, daring me to flinch at the sight of him. But I did not. Curiously, I felt relieved. "I would know my enemy," I said. "Do not wear that mask in my presence again."

"Very well, if that's the way you would have it," he said, flinging his mask across the room. He sat down beside me with studied nonchalance and helped himself to a pomegranate.

XI

An Heir For The Throne Of Troy

And so it went. Every day Paris left me, and every day Deiphobus was my gaoler. If I had duties to attend to as Inanna, he would accompany me as my chief attendant. But I dreaded even more those days when I had no duties. He would take me to his chambers and make excruciatingly prolonged love to me, caressing me and touching me softly as if I were his pet. At first I defied Deiphobus and complained to Paris that his brother was abusing me. And I dared to do this in Deiphobus's presence, wondering how he could be brazen enough to deny it. I made my eyes two red coals.

"Poor Defy," Paris objected, patting Deiphobus on the head condescendingly where he was sitting beside him. Deiphobus drew himself up almost imperceptibly. "How could you complain of him?" he asked as if the subject in reference were a pet dog. "He never harms anyone, let alone my wife!"

"You know I seek only to serve you, my lord," Deiphobus bowed his head behind his mask and spoke in the smooth voice of a courtier. Yet I thought I could detect a note of irony.

In the presence of his family Deiphobus acted the slave as if he had no right to claim that he was Paris's twin. King Priam could not even endure the sight of him, and when the court banqueted together in the megaron, a screen of gold and mother-of-pearl always separated the Bull of Heaven from the sight of his despised offspring. When Queen Hecuba had to acknowledge the presence of her son, she forced a smile that hid her true feelings. Hector, that "godlike man" as the court called him, who was blessed with powerful shoulders, muscular arms and legs, big feet, a broad chest, and in short resembled Hercules, seemed to think Deiphobus an offence to the male sex. He blushed to acknowledge as brother this lame creature who was forced to drag his right leg along to the too familiar "clink" of his sandal on the plastered floor. And Cassandra, well she never joined family gatherings, preferring to remain aloof in her temple dedicated to Inanna. But when I had opportunity to gauge her reactions, she seemed to think of Deiphobus as a fellow rebel in her cause against the corruption of the royal family. Yet she was so grim I do not think she liked anybody.

These banquets were far more sumptuous than anything at Sparta, and bards nightly entertained us with their lays of gods and heroes. Yet I was never more stunned than when Paris turned to Deiphobus and asked him to sing.

"It is not for one with such meager talents as I to send you all to the land of Lethe and Sleep," he protested. "Surely all would enjoy your golden tongue more, my Prince. Your voice is like honey."

Paris drank in these words as if they were sweet nectar and he the honey bee that buzzed about them. "Go on, Defy," Paris urged. "We don't expect you to be a bard."

Deiphobus bowed his head, and the eyes in the mask lowered themselves. Bards were wont to walk among their audience and sing to each listener. I was wondering how Deiphobus would manage that without making a fool of himself, when they brought a special couch for him.

He announced his theme "Pysche and Love," which I scoffed at. In Sparta we would sing only the sterner martial lays, the tragic epics, and not concern ourselves with such frivolous fancies. But I could well believe this would please Paris.

From the moment Deiphobus strummed his cithara until he concluded an indeterminate amount of time later, I found myself in a state of shock. His voice discarded its sycophantic purr and took on a tenor's mellow softness with a richness of tone and timber that could have rivaled Orpheus himself. The servants in the megaron put down their trays to stop and listen. Even the royal family quit eating and shifting restlessly about. I could well believe that Deiphobus's canaries and parrots stopped singing at the sound of their master's voice. Perchance the Fates themselves ceased spinning, and Time herself stopped.

I was familiar with the tale but never before had I found it so poignant. Princess Psyche was so famed for her beauty that the Goddess Aphrodite grew jealous and plotted her downfall. She made her own son Love fall into a passion for the princess. Aphrodite caused Psyche to leave her home and come to Love's house. Love could reveal himself to her only in the darkness and at night, and then all Psyche could know was his soft voice and tender touch. She could never see his face or know his name. He was invisible, for so Aphrodite in her cruelty decreed.

The pathos in Deiphobus's voice as he sang of Love's plight brought tears to my eyes. He expressed the bewilderment of Love who knew Psyche's heart and could by magic make anything she wished come to her — except him. If she desired a particular food, it would appear before her even as she was thinking of it. If she longed for new clothes, invisible fingers would spin them. But if she grew lonely for her home, he could do nothing and could not even reach out to console her until the sun had disappeared, and small consolation his ghostly fingers were. She was afraid that he might be some brigand or even a demon or vampire because he could not show his face.

Love knew the night of reckoning would come. Psyche, despite her vow, one night lighted a candle and shown it full upon Love's countenance when he was sleeping beside her. She was aghast at his beauty. In that instant that she learned his identity and her own folly, he vanished, gazing sadly at her. Aphrodite had her revenge.

As his song ended I realized that when he spun tales the audience forgot who Deiphobus was. He too became a thing of beauty just like his song. The royal family forgot that he was lame and scarred for life, that he was a thing apart, a thing of ridicule. His tragic mask took on a certain dignity and became a part of the song itself. For once he could gain approbation and acceptance.

One advantage of the sphinx mask for Deiphobus was that no one could be sure whom he was looking at. But I felt his eyes on me all during the performance. So strong grew the conviction that I stopped looking at him and tried to hide my face, which was not so easy now that I no longer owned a veil. "What if someone else sees what he is doing, what he is saying!" I feared.

"Paris," I summoned enough self-possession to say, "may I please be excused?"

"You are such a bore!" he sighed. "Suit yourself." And he waved me away, for he could not long endure my coldness.

"I refuse to play Psyche to his Love," I said to

myself as I drew up to my full height and swept out of the room. Only when I was again alone in my chamber did my stunned feeling at this unexpected side to Deiphobus's character leave me. I grew angry. No doubt he was trying to make me feel sorry for him to better manipulate me to his own ends. No one could trust him. He was incapable of sincerity or love.

Every day I was witness to Deiphobus controlling Paris through Paris's vanity. Deiphobus would approach his brother with a necklace of amber beads. "Look what the bazaar keeper had for me today," he would proclaim to Paris. "I told him what a connoisseur you were of foreign works of art, so he saves them for me. This is from the land of Ethiopia."

So Paris would again be beholden to his brother for some expensive trinket that he could give to a mistress. The most costly ones he presented to me. Not that he liked me, but I was his wife and thus a reflection on him. He enjoyed seeing me well-dressed without realizing that Deiphobus was in charge of my appearance too. Deiphobus knew exactly what would become me and what jewels I should wear. No doubt that was merely another way of intimidating me, showing me what power he held in case I should try to defy him.

Or he would say to Paris when he brought me back to greet him for dinner, "Hector was chumming up to Priam again today while you were in town attending to your affairs." Then Deiphobus would shake his head. "That brother of ours is a disgrace. He is so idle that he cannot think of anything to occupy himself while there are no wars. He does not have your taste or the manners of a gentleman. If only Priam would make war against the

Cimmerians and send Hector away!" he would sigh imploringly to Paris, and of course plant the seed of the idea that Paris should suggest to his father that he make war against the Cimmerians and send Hector away.

The rivalry between Hector and Paris burned hot. Ever since my appearance, all Paris had to do was bring me to see Priam to persuade his father to grant almost anything. Priam was one of those old lechers who loved a pretty woman better than meat or wine, for indeed he had one hundred wives. If I were not already married to Paris, I imagined Priam would not be above adding me to his collection.

The farce continued unchanged for the entire first cycle of the seasons I was at Troy. Deiphobus used me — body, mind, and soul — to advance his own kingly ambitions without anyone so much as suspecting. He had gained much prestige at the temple for being Inanna's personal attendant and chief bodyguard. People began to bow to him too as some of my supposed divinity was shed on him. Even Cassandra asked his advice.

Paris trusted him implicitly, for Deiphobus was making him King of Troy. Priam finally announced it publicly and held an investiture ceremony. That Deiphobus was sleeping with Paris's future Queen as the price did not matter, nor that Deiphobus was making himself the power behind the throne, deciding when to make war and conclude peace and how to tax the people as Priam grew more and more feeble and leaned more heavily upon Paris. Paris did not care to know what was really going on as long as he could revel in the show of pomp and ceremony.

In the season of flowers I missed my moon madness, grew queasy in the stomach, and began to experience all the signs of conception. I grew furious with Deiphobus.

I could not endure the thought of the loathsome creature that was in my womb, whom I was sure was just like my oppressor. It would never see the light. I would rid myself of it, even if I risked my life in the process. To carry it to term would mean certain death. I would be executed for adultery. If a midwife butchered me, at least my maids could carry me back to the palace to die, and I could bleed out my life in peace. Paris would think it an accident, and no one could blame my children. Perhaps they would take pity on them and send them back to Sparta.

Since arriving in Troy never had I taken any independent action. I was at a loss to know what to do, and Deiphobus had intimidated me to the point I thought he watched my every move. Now I was desperate. I persuaded one of the palace maids, who was one of my old Spartans, to find me a practitioner of the art.

The maid sneaked at night into my room in the new wing that Paris had built onto the palace where my husband and I occupied separate bedchambers. The maid and I crept quietly out, feeling our way along the walls without even a lantern to guide our steps. We feared to wake Deiphobus when we passed his chamber in the Old Palace.

Suddenly something was blocking our path. We tripped and found ourselves sitting on the floor. Deiphobus's door quickly opened. He was carrying a lantern, and I noticed that even at this hour he had not forgotten his sphinx mask.

"Get back to your quarters!" Deiphobus hissed to the maid, who fled into the night.

He whispered to me, "And where, I pray, do you think you are going? The gates of Troy don't open by magic, and even if you did slip through there are sentries. If you evaded them, would you take to the marshes? Come to your senses! I wondered if you would ever act rashly, so

I keep this rope tied here."

I could see by the light of the lantern a rope tied across the hallway, fastened from wall to wall. I did indeed feel trapped. Instead of answering him in kind as was my wont, perhaps because of my condition, I burst into tears. Suddenly, I did not care what he did with me or said. Nor did I care who heard.

When I would not stop he picked me up and carried me inside his room. He threw aside his mask, took me to his bed, and laid me down. "Stop!" he ordered. But there was a tremulousness in his voice I had never heard before.

I rolled away from him and kept on sobbing. Nothing he could say would silence me. "Are you possessed of some demon or god? What madness has come over you?" he tried to shake me.

I had not eaten that day and coupled with the excitement and my condition I felt giddy. I was sick into my hands.

"Helen...are you ill? Why didn't you tell me and I would send for a physician!" he said, beginning to sound confused and worried. He ran for a basin and sponged me with cool water.

"If I am sick it is all due to you," I spat. "You lied when you said you could not make me conceive."

Instead of laughing as I had expected or making some other callous remark his face went blank. He looked stunned as if a god had drawn all the life out of him. He sat down upon the bed and hardly drew breath as he stared at me in stupefaction. Then he left the room. I heard him clumping around the aviary, awakening his parrots. I imagined I heard him stifle a sob or groan, but it was hard to tell over the squawking. "How far along are you?" he whispered hoarsely when he finally returned.

"I have missed one moon madness, but what has

that got to do with your guilt?"

"Are you sure?" he said, not listening, looking off into space. He was totally absorbed in his own ruminations.

"You lied to me, didn't you?" I pressed the point.

"Paris...I must talk to Paris," he said as if to himself, his eyes glazing over.

"You wretch! You are going to betray me then!" I was so enraged I slapped him across the face, and that felt good.

He grabbed my wrists, but continued to look off into space and mumble to himself. "I shall tell Paris that Hector...yes, Hector's wife is going to have an heir. He will want to emulate him. Yes, that should work. Vain poppycock."

"What are you plotting? What next?" I spat. "If I could I would do away with both you and your child."

Finally my words seemed to penetrate the veil he had drawn over himself. "Do away with!" he lunged at me and pinned my hands against the bed. "So that's what you were about? You were sneaking out into the night to do away with my son. You would kill him just because you hate me. Well, change your mind, my Queen. We must both protect him with every bit of strength and cunning we have left, and I am beginning to see you have plenty of that."

"So you did this to me on purpose?"

"On purpose?" he laughed bitterly. "No, I would never have dreamed of a boon such as this. This is a gift from the gods indeed," he looked wistful. "At last they smile upon me. Neither of my brothers has even one son nor so much as a daughter, and they have walked in the light all their lives. Small use they have made of it. My son shall become Paris's son, and when Paris becomes King he shall rule after him."

"And I'm sure your brother will be happy to comply with your dynastic schemes."

"He shall if I have to make him drunk myself and drag him to your bed...And you, my Queen, shall do your best to be compliant," he warned me.

And so it was. Paris was reconciled to me through this ruse. Deiphobus made him envious of Hector, and to ensure the succession Paris came to my bed. I had to pretend to like it for the sake of my children's lives and my own, for Paris was ever put off by coldness.

So matters stood when one morning without notice early in the season of flowers Deiphobus appeared at my door as usual, and Paris escorted me to the throne room. I should have suspected that something was afoot, for the courtiers were gathered in groups, whispering. Everyone seemed to be jostling each other to peek into the throne room. But I was too miserable to do other than keep my eyes fixed straight ahead.

The Bull of Heaven sat on his throne, aloof in regal splendor, his bull's head fixed on his shoulders. Beside him stood his wives, faceless ghosts in blue. I was reminded of the time I came here as a stranger to be received into my new life. Now two more foreigners stood before the Throne of Heaven.

Their attire struck a discordant note. Everyone in the Court of Heaven was perfumed and bejeweled until they looked like images of gods and goddesses. Even I who was once a Spartan Queen walked shamelessly without my veil. My nipples were painted gold and shone through a diaphanous silk draped over one shoulder, leaving the other breast bare. These two men looked plain by comparison dressed in tunics and sandals tied with leather leggings like mainlanders.

"Helen!" said a voice from my past. Menelaus stepped forward like one in a dream and started towards me before the guards could stop him. But he stopped before the guards could even lay hands on him. He stared in shock at my breasts which had already begun to swell and then down at my womb.

Paris urged me forward to take my place beside the royal ladies, but my knees locked. If I went forward I would stumble. I felt my blood freeze and turn me into a statue as it drained from my face. A cry of despair welled up from within me, and as I turned to flee I caught sight of the furrows wrinkling Odysseus's brow as he stared at me more as if I were a puzzle than an abomination.

I did not care who saw me as I fled so fast I lost my sandals. My shoulder brooch slipped, and my dress fell to my waist. My hair came undone, and I was brushing strands back as I wiped my eyes when I saw him. There before my bedchamber door stood Deiphobus wearing his sphinx mask. He had known what would happen. In fact, he was holding the door open for me. As I passed him, I realized he had planned this meeting carefully.

XII

The Achaeans

"Your husband is as much a naive fool as you used to be," Deiphobus laughed scornfully, closing the door behind us. "But I suppose idiocy runs in the mainland blood. Menelaus tells Priam that if we Trojans return you, Menelaus's children, and all the Spartan booty we took, all will be forgotten and forgiven. But if we don't, the Achaean host will sail against Troy."

"My husband does not speak idle threats," I spat at him as I tried to cover my breasts with my hands. I would not give Deiphobus the satisfaction of seeing me cry, so I forced myself to stifle my sobs.

"The Achaeans would just as soon tear themselves apart like a pack of curs as sail against us," Deiphobus said. "And even if they did, who not possessed of a demon would challenge the might of the Trojan empire?"

"Of course you told him no," I said, stiffening as he approached me.

"No answer has been given as of yet. Paris and Priam are considering the matter in council, which is a fancy way of saying they are waiting for me. I am waiting for you to give me your answer," his eyes glittered dangerously.

He threw off his mask, grabbed the elbows which I had raised against him, and pulled me to him. I closed my eyes to better endure what I must as he kissed me full on the lips and forced my mouth open with his tongue. He explored my mouth possessively and held me so tightly against him I had to squirm for breath. I could feel his heart beating against my breasts, and I could tell as surely as if he had said so that he was afraid, perhaps for the first time — afraid of losing me.

"This will surely drive him mad," I thought. "If Paris would even look at me with interest, Deiphobus would probably kill him. And he must see he can't compare with my Menelaus." I tried to push him away. "What are you up to now, wretch?" I said, trying to distract him from the inevitable.

"What would you give for the life of his companion Odysseus?" said Deiphobus. He kissed my ears.

"For proud Odysseus — nothing," I answered with confidence. "He needs not my help. In that man you have met your match for cunning, Deiphobus. I would pit him against twenty Deiphobuses." I let his hands do as they would, running up and down my sides and cupping my breasts.

His hands fell. He liked not my reply and grimaced as if I forced him to swallow vinegar. In snippets here and there, that was my only satisfaction in life — to foil Deiphobus. "Speak, woman," he said. Now I had done it. Deiphobus was furious. I could even see his hands shaking. He ever did hate me to compare him to other men. "Tell me what you would give for your husband's life?" he pushed me down on my bed and climbed on top of me.

"For my husband — everything," I said, and whimpered against my will. "His noble nature is too generous. He errs in thinking others are like himself."

"Which is a foggy way of saying I am the better man," Deiphobus said as he loosened his own robes.

"Which is a way of saying you are no man at all but a creature," I struggled against him.

I knew my punishment and prayed only that it would soon be over. Usually he was more careful about where and when he took me even if he had bolted the door. But this afternoon he was in quite a passion, and I thought he would never be satisfied.

Afterwards as we lay exhausted and he drew lines in the sweat on my belly, sneered and said, "Know then, woman. Menelaus's life is in your hands. After we refuse his generous terms," he snickered at the word "generous," "I will arrange a last meeting between you two at which Paris and I will be present. To make matters more poignant, your children will be there. Yes...." he pondered with a grin of satisfaction. "And you will convince him in no uncertain terms that you eloped with Paris out of love or lust I care not which, and that you wish Menelaus to leave you here."

I had listened to his plan with growing horror. "He will never believe it!" I nearly shouted as I pushed his hand away and sat up. This was too cruel even for Deiphobus. But it was all my fault; I had put him in a fury of jealousy.

"It is your business to make him do so," he got up and dressed himself. "And, remember, I shall be there to gauge your behavior and to see if you try to send him any secret messages with your eyes or lips, and I know them well."

Now there was nothing left for me to do but fall on my knees, grovel, and plead. Nor would that do any good in his present mood. It would just give Deiphobus satisfaction, so I mastered myself.

Deiphobus was already rummaging in my wardrobe. He got out a red skirt with a diaphanous red silk robe and ruby brooch pin. It was even more useless to plead about my costume, for I was Inanna, the goddess of love and fertility.

Deiphobus gave me no time to prepare, to catch me the more off guard, and speedily arranged the meeting. I had not even the time to tell Hermione she was to see her father. At least the twins would be spared the pain of recognition, for they had been too young when they were abducted.

Hermione was now three cycles of the seasons, and Deiphobus kept her dressed like a little lady, properly robed and veiled. When she saw her father she screamed and ran to him, only her little feet poking out from beneath her skirts. He caught her up in his arms, and there were tears in his eyes as he hugged her and kissed her cheeks. I looked away and bit my lip. Fortunately I had cried so much in my room before this meeting and had applied so much powder that I had not a tear left, or so I told myself. I concentrated instead on how much I hated Deiphobus, and that kept the ice in my bearing.

Paris held my hand, and Deiphobus flanked me on the other side as we advanced to meet my love. Odysseus was not with him, but I had not time to wonder why. I knew only that if I looked into Menelaus's eyes all would be lost, so I stared at his chin or looked beyond him. Strangely, I thought of Taygetos and Parnon where we had first known our love, and how far above my present hell that was.

Paris let go of my hand and stepped back. Menelaus put the twins down and stared at me. I could see his muscles stiffening all over in rigid disapproval of my attire and my condition even more sternly than he had done in the throne room, for he was closer. I opened my mouth to explain, but I could feel Deiphobus's eyes searing through my flesh, hating Menelaus even more than his twin brother Paris, for Paris was no rival.

"Helen, what is this?" Menelaus said.

"Greetings, husband," I said as distantly as possible, thinking again only of Deiphobus. "Or rather I should say, my former husband."

"I do not understand," he pressed his lips together until they turned white. He looked like a man from whom all hope had been drained.

"You must make your peace with fate," I said. "It is hard for all of us." Still I struggled to keep my voice toneless. "You left me to go to Crete, and with that departure you lost all right to me and your family, son of Atreus. We have found another home that appreciates us more. And call me not Helen. My name is that of the Goddess Inanna."

"So, it is true, what they all say!" I could feel the pain in his voice. "You proclaimed yourself Goddess on Earth to rebel...Just like your mother."

I cut in. "You married me knowing who my mother was. I hope I am worthy of her," I said like one already dead. "The Trojans know how to appreciate a Goddess," I concentrated on the one aspect of the situation I knew he was predisposed to believe. If I told him I was in love with the fop Paris, he would know I was lying.

Menelaus paused for a long while, staring at me, and I thought I should faint under his scrutiny. I wanted to reach out to him, to touch him softly, but the chasm between us was forever. "Cursed be your name!" he said finally with all the force of Atreus in his voice. "I hereby put you from me," he said, "calling you wife no longer. Paris is welcome to such a creature. But it is indeed my cruel fate that I must fight to recover my heirs and your person, for in you is invested the kingship of Sparta. Only then will I deal out justice to you."

It is fortunate that he was a man of swift action. If

To Follow The Goddess

he had not turned on his heels and stomped out of the megaron he would have seen me fall. Only Deiphobus reaching out in time kept me from striking the pavement. For with his curse, my knees gave out and I shook so violently it was as if I had the ague.

I sobbed all the way back to my room, but still peace was not to be my lot for long. Soon Deiphobus was back grumbling about the airs my husband gave himself and how dare he come here like this. The more I wept the more agitated he became, pacing back and forth as if he would wear a groove in the floor. His clumping drove me mad.

Suddenly he smiled as if an amusing thought had struck him in his misery. "This crafty Odysseus of yours seems like a lout to me," he said. "When I met him in the portico he was drinking with the common soldiers and was quite drunk indeed. Your Menelaus," he spat, "was even shocked as I showed him out. Odysseus played at draughts and seemed to be gambling away what little money he had left. Menelaus accosted him and asked him what he was doing, and at first Odysseus seemed not to recognize his friend. Odysseus, bless his soul, was joking about you and calling you a common whore."

Immediately, deep within the blackness that had become my soul, one ray of light sprang into being. I knew hope for the first time in over one cycle of the seasons. Odysseus had saved me once. Not that he could rescue me now, but that he was up to something no one else but me suspected, I would bet the lives of my children on. Odysseus had aroused all my faculties in an instant. I stopped grieving, for my mind absorbed all my energy. I began to playact. "I have said Odysseus was proud and I had imagined clever, but I never said I liked him," I pretended I was offended. Somehow, magically,

Odysseus was here, whispering the words to say for I knew not what purpose — as yet.

"He then complained of you, saying that you stole his horses. I must say he sounded like some drunken fishwife in the marketplace. Menelaus was so disgusted he left him," Deiphobus grinned. He was so far gone in his hatred of Menelaus he could not see what I was about.

"Horses?" I said, genuinely surprised. I indeed did not know what Odysseus was getting at. But I searched and searched and searched the dustiest recesses of my mind for clues. Horses...Then I remembered that the last time we met he was consoling me for the loss of my favorite horse who had just been sacrificed. Yes, horse was the clue just to let me know I should trust him.

"I am no horse thief," I said. "Not even you, scoundrel, could accuse me of that." I was as huffy as I knew how to be.

"Yes, your pride still needs taken down a few notches. I had not decided, but I think I shall grant his wish to present his silly complaint to you personally," Deiphobus took my chin into his hand and forced me to look into his eyes. Deiphobus was intent upon hurting me as much as I had hurt him with my incessant weeping over Menelaus.

Odysseus wanted to see me! My heart pounded in my chest. My head was whirling, and I was in a cold sweat with anticipation. But I had to conceal it. "See him?" I shouted. "Never! I wish not to be insulted by such an unmannerly lout. As if I have not yet had enough grief today. Why must you annoy me so?"

"It pleases me," Deiphobus took my arm and led me to the throne room. I complained all the way there to conceal my eagerness.

Odysseus was in rare form. He was joking with the

guards trying to get them to laugh and taking such liberties as poking them in the ribs. As soon as Odysseus saw me his eyes fixed upon mine, and a spark of sympathy leaped between us. I could tell he was as sober as I. In an instant I knew his mind and he mine. I felt I should be open and receptive to the smallest clue he should give me. It was as if we two had rehearsed this play before in another life.

He guffawed in a drunken tone and held out his arms. He was all comic theater and exaggeration. "My dearest cousin!" he cried and advanced upon me, smacking me loudly upon both cheeks and pounding my arm.

I sniffed and held myself aloof as if he reeked of the fish from the very market where he got his manners.

"We used to like each other," he grinned and pinched my cheek. "Remember?"

"No," I stepped backwards. "If my cousin Penelope had not had the misfortune to marry a pirate and a ne'er-do-well I believe you would not even be given a bone in my kitchen when you came a-beggin'."

"Now is that a nice way to greet your cousin?" he persisted. "I mean, fair is fair. I tagged along with Menelaus just so that we could be fair about this little matter."

Deiphobus was grinning and chortling with glee behind his mask at what he supposed to be my discomposure, I could feel it. But no matter how I looked I felt light and fleet of foot, laughing in my soul. "I have no dealings with the likes of you," I said. "It is truly said that one cannot choose his relations."

He crossed his brows and pretended to frown in great concentration. He even pulled at his beard like a man in thought. "You know my cousin Menelaus and you were keeping some of my studs in your royal stables for breeding purposes when Paris came along and burned the entire city. A nasty deed. The stables were outside the city, but when I got there to recover my horses I found only my chief stud, the one I called King Horse."

"Fool, we had none of your horses," I shouted in impatience. "They were our horses."

"Now, my dearie, King Horse languishes without his mate. He is sad of countenance. His favorite mare is missing. Now I know that mare had the reputation of a flirt," he raised his eyebrows, "as much as mares can be flirts, if you know what I mean," he whispered to me.

I stepped back from him and drew myself up regally. "Sir!" I said, knowing in a flash of inspiration that Odysseus meant Menelaus to be the King Horse and me to be the flirtatious mare. I sifted all the meaning I could from his parable.

Deiphobus was now laughing aloud. Odysseus could charm even Hades himself.

"Well, my meaning is this," he slurred his speech and hiccuped. He winked at me, leaned closer, and whispered, "Did the pretty mare go into heat when she saw one of Paris's steeds? Did she follow him to Troy? Or what happened to her?"

My mouth felt dry, and I wondered if Deiphobus would notice I moistened my lips before I dared answer. "Fool," I said, "my lord Paris took what was his by right. He is now King of Sparta and can claim everything that belonged to me by patrimony."

Odysseus nodded to me in a barely perceptible manner, and I glanced at Deiphobus. "Horse thief!" Odysseus shouted and spat in my face.

"Deiphobus, I have had enough!" I demanded, as I crossed the room to his side in another flash of inspiration. "Why will you always be abusing me like this? Why must I listen to this lout? You are in charge here!" I dared to say, daring no more or Deiphobus would pick up on it. I would be ashamed to admit as much to Menelaus, but somehow I could confide anything to Odysseus.

Deiphobus's jealousy was great, and as I have said he was infinitely amused at what he supposed to be my discomfiture. He clapped his hands and called for his servants to drag away Odysseus who played his bit of theater to the end. "Wait a minute!" he called, stumbling over his feet as the guards surrounded him, "I demand satisfaction!" We had communicated something very important. He was asking me if I had gone voluntarily with Paris or if he had abducted me, and I had answered that I was abducted against my will.

Much later I learned from Odysseus what followed. When he and Menelaus were alone on the ship and had set sail from Troy, Menelaus was upbraiding him for his obscene behavior, "If I had known you were going to make a fool of both of us, I would not have asked you to come."

"You brought me to help discover what happened to Helen," Odysseus said coolly, "and I have. My methods are not yours, and that is why I succeeded."

"I will listen to nothing more about Helen," Menelaus waved him away.

Odysseus grabbed him by the shoulders and shook him, daring so much for me. "Paris abducted her! What disturbs me more is that I think she is trying to tell me that all this has something to do with this fellow Deiphobus, the eunuch."

"She would never lie to me," Menelaus said, taken aback by these oblique methods of communication in which he had no part.

"What if her life or her children's were at stake?"

"She is changed."

"Helen can lie when she must just as I can," Odysseus tried to explain. "You cannot see that because of your more noble leanings."

Odysseus had taken a chance, and now Menelaus was angry. "She was my wife, not yours, Odysseus. Remember that," he frowned and stalked off. He refused to discuss the matter further beyond vowing, "She will die."

XIII

Sacrifice At Aulis

Menelaus found the palace at Mycenae crowded with idle mercenaries standing and sitting about in the porticoes, hallways, and waiting rooms, drinking wine and playing at draughts. The palace had become a military barracks. Menelaus was shocked at the sight of all these former enemies claiming hospitality and making free with the serving women. "Brother, this is unfit," he protested.

"How else do you think we will clear free passage for our ships going to Troy? We need them," Agamemnon was proud of his foresight.

"Can you trust them?"

"As long as I have this," Agamemnon flipped a gold coin into the air and let it fall with a ringing sound on the stuccoed pavement. He possessed more gold than anyone else now that he exacted tribute from Pisa, Perati, and Lerna as well as the cities he inherited from Atreus.

"But if we come upon hard times and Fortune deserts us these troops will decamp to Priam," Menelaus protested. "I would prefer soldiers who fought out of loyalty instead of for money."

Providential as his words proved, they went unheeded.

Agamemnon was too preoccupied to listen to wisdom. When Agamemnon was near, Iphigenia huddled in corners, wrapping her veils tightly about her. If he called her to him, she would pretend not to hear. If he took her hand, she would jump. Menelaus wondered what had transpired in his absence.

Once he was bold enough to question her. "Pray, uncle, do not ask me that," was all she would say. "I am accursed of the gods." Menelaus took his brother to task.

"I will brook no interference," Agamemnon said with a wave of dismissal.

"Is it not enough that you murdered her infant brother?"

Agamemnon said in his most winning way, for he had spent a lifetime whittling away at his brother's over fine sense of honor and justice, "She is just a woman."

Menelaus went next to Clytaemnestra and asked what was going on. "What indeed?" she said. "I prayed to the gods that my husband would learn to leave me alone if I hated him enough. They answered my prayers in the cruelest way of all." She took the medallion from her neck and handed it back to Menelaus. "Take it. You are no protector of mine." She walked back into the shadows from which she had come.

The criticism stung my husband, but Odysseus said, "You can indeed do nothing unless you would take up arms against your brother. That would split the Achaeans, and now the word is unity."

Menelaus had never forgiven Odysseus for his actions in Troy, but he had to admit the man was wise if interfering. He and Odysseus left to remind the Kings of Hellas to honor the pledge of the suitors. In this pursuit they were gone another cycle of the seasons.

But that was not the end of the matter. When the Achaean host was assembled at Aulis, Agamemnon doubled his folly. One thousand ships sat in the bay. And one thousand ships could not leave that harbor. The winds died for moons at a time. When a breeze sprang up and the captains tried to follow it, the thunder and the lightning quickly passed, and the winds and waters were glass-like again. The men had to lower sails.

Soon the common foot soldiers, the Dorians among them, whispered to each other that the Mother was angry. If I had been there I could have silenced them, but men know not these arts. The only women with the group were those who made their living following armies.

The soldiers reminded themselves how dangerous the sea was. The earth was a flat disc surrounded by Oceanus, the sea that lived before men. One could get lost and sail off the edge.

No matter if Menelaus assured them that they would never be out of sight of land. He reminded them that the Great Sea was dotted with islands which were ports of call, and then they would sail up the coast of Asia Minor raiding as they went. Not even the promise of booty seemed to influence them the more and more convinced they became that the Goddess was against them.

They whispered that the Goddess was making known her displeasure by not letting Agamemnon's expedition succeed. She would not have him known as "the King of Kings" since his hubris was too overweening. After all, he was the one who had dragged Clytaemnestra away from the altar of the Goddess.

As these rumors grew louder, men stole away at night. Odysseus took matters into his own hands and bribed the lesser seers and prophets to predict good fortune. But Calchas, chief prophet, would not toady even to Agamemnon's gold.

Agamemnon could not long endure these reflections upon his manhood and right to the kingship. He would think of a way to prove to everyone who had challenged it that he was indeed the King of Kings. The chief of the doubters were his Queen and his stepdaughter. They would be the first to pay.

He sent for Iphigenia to join him at Aulis. So that Clytaemnestra would let her go and not suspect a ruse, he announced that he was going to marry her to Achilles. Agamemnon was now at the summit of his power and took no one into his confidence. The boldness of this stroke of genius would be his own — or so he imagined.

Iphigenia came gladly. She believed he was tired of her and willing to hand over her guardianship to someone else. She was only too eager to escape him into the arms of a husband. She arrived in record time, complete with trousseau.

Even her mother accompanied her, happy that fortune had smiled at last upon her darling. Aegisthus's warnings for once could not keep her in Mycenae.

Agamemnon strode forward to greet them in the presence of the whole army, assembled for the occasion. He took his stepdaughter by one hand, his wife by the other, and announced, "The Great Goddess has kept our ships at anchor for these many and wearisome moons. Last night the Mother appeared to me. As your leader I must sacrifice up to her the thing that is dearest to me. That way she will know if I am worthy of victory. So I have pledged to her the life of my stepdaughter Iphigenia."

Iphigenia fainted into Agamemnon's arms, and Clytaemnestra was dragged away. The soldiers were silent, gazing at him in awe. They felt his power perhaps for the first time, those who were not his own men, drank deeply of the draught, and were amazed by it. Few men had the resolution or strength of will to sacrifice their own daughter, and to them that spoke of devoutness. Their leader, son of Atreus or not, would be found worthy of victory by the Great Goddess.

Only later were they to learn that Agamemnon lacked divine inspiration for his deed and had committed the blasphemy of pretending that he did. Only then was it recognized for what it was — another and almost final step towards the ruin of the House of Atreus.

At once Achilles stepped forward in front of the army, "I thought I was to become your son-in-law!" His face glowered forth his challenge. "I will not let you play me false, Agamemnon." His hand was on his sword hilt.

Menelaus stood beside him, seconding the mightiest of the Achaeans. "I will not support you in this, brother." He and Achilles then took their armies apart.

In private Menelaus sought audience with Agamemnon and shouted at him, losing his temper at last, "You are no longer my brother if you do this deed of darkness. Will you let your lust for that poor Princess and your desire for revenge on her and her mother addle your wits?"

Menelaus accosted Odysseus and demanded to know why he had not formed a third to their challenge. "Fear not," he placed a reassuring hand on Menelaus's shoulder, but his smile was a grim one for once. "My heart is with you, but once again my means are different."

Odysseus's mind concocted schemes as some men's minds concoct excuses. He told me later that sometimes they would spring upon him full-blown with all the details worked out, and sometimes he would act first without knowing what he was going to say next. But his tongue never deserted him whatever the circumstances.

This extremity would require all his ingenuity. He was at a disadvantage with Agamemnon. He had chosen to spend a cycle of the seasons recruiting with Menelaus, after already spending another cycle sailing to Troy and back in his company. As far as the High King was concerned, he was Menelaus's vassal. Nor could he deal with the "King of Kings" as one conqueror to another.

Agamemnon was not in the best of humors. Many of the allied Kings were against him even though he had more than regained his popularity with the men. Odysseus knew Agamemnon would not receive him, so he sneaked into his tent.

Agamemnon was lounging on his cot, his legs spread apart, dangling an empty goblet between his knees. He twirled it this way, now that. He dropped the goblet and looked up in surprise. Odysseus knelt before him, his head bowed in reverence before this King of Kings.

"What do you want?" Agamemnon rose to his feet unsteadily.

"I always admire wisdom when I see it," Odysseus smiled at him.

Soon Odysseus had convinced Agamemnon that his bold stroke of policy that afternoon had changed Odysseus's estimate of him. He freely confessed that before today he had thought him something less than King of Kings.

Agamemnon was completely taken in. He knew that Odysseus was reputed to be the wisest of mortals. If Odysseus proclaimed it a bold stroke of policy, indeed it must be one. This pirate fellow, who had seemed such a lout, was proving to be quite genial. He slapped him on the back and invited him to seal their new alliance with a goblet of wine.

Now Odysseus could hold wine better than any other man, for the Goddess had taught him the advantage of it when he was very young. Often while his companion would be gulping and toasting, he would be watching him closely and sipping when his fellow was not looking, or even pouring it back into the krater if the man was in his cups. Of course Odysseus had no trouble pretending he was possessed by the spirit of Dionysus.

When Agamemnon was thoroughly drunk, Odysseus dared to put his plan into action. He spoke more boldly than he would have dreamed if this had been a sober King of Kings. After all, he was a mere nobody from Ithaca. "Too bad we could not have spoken soul to soul sooner," Odysseus sighed like an old man who has seen his lifelong ambitions come to naught. "I always wished to betroth my son Telemachus to your daughter Electra. You do own comely daughters. If I were not married already, I would ask for Iphigenia."

"I can tell you about that wench!" Agamemnon snorted indecently and clapped Odysseus's thigh with his hand. "She would warm no man's bed." Then he showed he was really far gone in drink by reciting a few indecent anecdotes. This went against the laws of the gods, and yet Odysseus not only had to restrain his temper but had to laugh.

Odysseus gave every indication that he was as lascivious as he seemed. He concocted tales about his adventures with serving women in the days when his father Laertes ruled Ithaca. He pretended to sympathize with Agamemnon's plight. He too could simply not resist women no matter what the barriers to their seduction. The two toasted the ladies among a number of other unmentionable attractions of theirs.

"You whet my appetite," Odysseus forced himself to say. He even threw in a smack of the lips and winked like a satyr. "Yes, I would give anything to taste your stepdaughter once."

By that time Agamemnon could do little but laugh

and jest. He could barely raise his cup to his lips. He was positively ribald. "Taste her you shall then," he said. "She need not die until morning."

Odysseus had been waiting on his very words. In case Agamemnon did not say them, he had plans to trick this chieftain into signing a paper granting him Iphigenia as a slave.

Agamemnon's guards brought Iphigenia to Odysseus in his tent. As soon as they were alone Odysseus untied her. "Sir, I beg you," Iphigenia immediately fell to her knees, "please do not lay hands on me. Let me retire to the Underworld in peace." She was a wasted thing, all white and trembling.

"Would you not rather escape and live?" Odysseus whispered.

Iphigenia was confused. "Sir, there is no haven for an accursed one like me when the man who calls himself my father is my worst enemy."

"Listen closely," Odysseus said. "This very night there lies a young girl about your age dying in this very camp. The illness is one with which the gods afflict the practitioners of her art. This devotee of Aphrodite is past knowing what happens to her and longs only for a swift end and a decent burial. A royal princess like you would be given a spectacular tomb."

"You would have her exchange places with me?"

"It could be done. The madam who owns her services owes me a favor. She has agreed to take you into her tent as a cooking drudge. It is not much of a life for a princess, but at least it will preserve your honor. When we set sail from Aulis, she has promised to send you on to Ithaca where my lady wife Penelope will take care of you as is fitting. She has always wanted a daughter and now has little prospect of one, for I fear I shall be away many cycles of the seasons and may never return."

"You are a bold man to cheat the Goddess of her sacrifice."

Odysseus took hold of her and shook her. "Do you believe for a moment that Agamemnon was divinely inspired? He is the one who profanes the Goddess with his words. His is a political move."

Iphigenia hung her head. "But won't they know the difference — between her and me I mean?"

"No. You would lie on a mat of straw carried by four soldiers. Your face would be covered, the rest of you draped in a sheet covered with flowers and vines. Your hair would be wreathed about and is the same silver color anyway. Only your white neck would be exposed to the glare of day."

Iphigenia cringed and raised her hand to her throat. Tears filled her eyes. "May my lady mother never know that I live?"

Odysseus squeezed her hand, "She could not command her tongue. But I shall let your Uncle Menelaus know the truth. Someday it may yet be in his power to do you justice."

And so it came to pass. Standing upon the rocky cliff above the sea, Agamemnon slit the throat of a whore. To prevent rebellion Odysseus told Menelaus what had happened. The chief second in command was again stupefied by the means Odysseus would take. "I believe you would stop at nothing," Menelaus said. "You are both a dangerous man, the most dangerous in the army, and the one we cannot do without."

"The words are yours," Odysseus grinned. "I am, as you well know, too humble a person to claim the distinction for myself." His words were light, but there was added another crease to his already much furrowed brow.

Sacrifice At Aulis

Odysseus invented a story to tell Achilles and thus placate his wounded honor. Odysseus and Menelaus both convinced him that Iphigenia was spared by the Goddess in this fashion: Clytaemnestra was overcome with grief, and at the last moment before burial had removed the winding sheet that covered her daughter's corpse. In the place of a young maiden she found a hind. Athena had at the last moment taken pity on Iphigenia and transported her to a far distant land to preside as the chief priestess of her temple and had substituted a deer as the sacrifice more pleasing to her. Thus did Odysseus, favored of Athena, keep the peace and prevent the outbreak of hostilities before the Achaeans even encountered the Trojans.

But the Goddess would not forget how King Agamemnon prostituted her name to his designs. She handed over the pattern of his destiny to the Three Sisters who are always spinning and weaving, weaving and spinning. One Sister took out her shears and poised, ready to cut off the thread of his life.

XIV

The Power Of Inanna

By the time the Achaean host at last beached their ships in Troy's harbor, nine cycles of the seasons had gone by since my capture — and I had borne four sons to Deiphobus. Paris named the eldest Deiphobus in honor of his brother and never knew how that left his sibling grinning.

But though Deiphobus could still triumph over my body, he could no longer triumph over my soul. Odysseus had restored my self-confidence that I need use only my wits to defeat him. I was Inanna, Deiphobus merely my priest and eunuch. As far as the people were concerned, I was divine while he was merely mortal.

Perhaps I would never have seen my role myself, but the people called me to it. For seven cycles of the seasons the Achaean army lived raiding the coast of Asia Minor and fighting their way ever closer. Panic spread, for no one had taken the threats of Menelaus and Odysseus seriously. The ninth summer brought the Breath of Dryness, more severe than the drought the season Paris brought me to Troy. One morning I awoke to the sound of far-off but distinctly heard chanting. I went to my window and looked out. I saw Paris at the bedchamber window next to mine.

"Mere rabble!" he sniffed. He pushed a lock of his

golden curls behind his ear. "If they keep it up, I will send the guards into the city." Paris spoke with authority, for Priam no longer had his wits about him and was merely the King in name. Troy waited only for his death to proclaim Paris King by right as well as in truth, but Priam lingered stubbornly on.

Far below I could barely make out the sight of a mob gathered at the start of the road leading up to the acropolis. Only the hirelings and the slaves of the merchants and wealthier citizens kept them back. I shut my eyes to hear them better. They chanted, "In-anna, In-anna, In-anna...." Their great need washed over me like a wave. Their pull was like that of the tides returning to the sea.

So preoccupied had I been with Deiphobus I had ignored their call. My soul had too often been one pulsating misery. Now their need was like a balm, lifting me far above my mortal state. I could forget....

I do not know how long I stood there mesmerized by the sound, staring down at them until my vision blurred. The touch of an all too familiar hand on my shoulder brought me back to myself. I felt the chill followed quickly by the flush of shame. I had never gotten over darting my eyes about quickly to make certain no one could see us.

"Don't go," Deiphobus said, for over many moons and cycles of the seasons he had begun to know me. "It is too dangerous." He never wore his mask when we were alone, and I saw fear in his eyes.

This was a surprise. I had seen anger, rage, jealousy, cunning, irony, and lust in that face, sometimes even a glimmer of what I would rather not name, but never fear. I assumed that he had nothing left to make him tremble, for from his birth the Fates had done their worst to him. "How now, Deiphobus, what is this?" I said, trying to cover up my confusion. "Have all your sins risen up against you and stared you in the face?"

"Mock me if you will," he said, "but I can assure you the people will not please you in their present mood. I forbid you to go." He tried to put that iron in his voice with which he had so often intimidated me in the past, but somehow it had begun to sound more like tin. His pace was too rapid. He was too anxious.

I was about to lash back at him, feeling my advantage, but that was no way to accomplish my purpose. I said nothing. I would outwit him instead.

He thought I would obey him. He took my chin in his hands and kissed my cheeks as if I were a good little girl. I could feel the accustomed self-assurance in his hands. Already his tension had begun to ebb as I stood very still and closed my eyes.

I pretended to return to bed, for it was very early. After I could no longer hear his "clop, clop, clop" on the floor, I leaped to my feet and hurriedly summoned one of my Spartan maids. "Tell Cassandra to come at once and very quietly with my priestesses," I said.

Cassandra stayed awake at night, gazing at the stars and the moon, long after everyone else had retired to bed. She rose before dawn to greet the sun. This was her life and all of it, rejoicing in the creation of Inanna. She believed in every ritual and knew every article of the creed. In short, she was a religious zealot and fanatic, and just the person I needed at the moment.

Cassandra was at my door before I thought it humanly possible, but she would say the Goddess had guided her footsteps. Her eyes were luminous as she gazed at me adoringly. "I knew you would send for me. I awoke this morning, dreaming it," she said. Her red hair still hung loosely about her shoulders in wild array.

"Yes, I knew you would," I tried to humor her,

although she was not normally much to my taste and hardly the woman I would have chosen for a friend or confidante. She possessed about as much human feeling as a far-off planet which, if beautiful to look at, was impossible to touch.

Ordinary mortals could not keep pace with her, and her fellow priestesses arrived only awhile after she did.

"We must go at once to the lower town," I said. "My people call me."

"They yearn for Inanna," Cassandra said as if she had said, "I love you."

Deiphobus was upon me again. He must have heard the chatter of women's voices or the footsteps. Or perhaps some sixth sense had told him I should not be trusted. Since the others were present he was wearing his mask, but I could always tell when he was glaring at me. I shivered, remembering the mastery of those hands and fingers.

Cassandra said to her brother, "We must hasten to the people."

He could not contradict her or she would spread the word among the commoners that he was a heretic. "Very well," he said. "But I shall summon the palace guard." I could feel his lips curling themselves into a bitter grin. He would have said "nonsense" if he had dared. In his heart he believed in no gods or goddesses except one, and I did not know her then. By the time I discovered her, she had proved herself but a mortal.

Cassandra did not like having the guards accompany us. But it was her policy never to meddle in military matters. That was the province of her brothers.

Deiphobus ordered the litters. As he helped me up into mine, I felt his hands heavy with the weight of disapproval. They lingered longer than usual before letting go.

The roar of the crowd was deafening long before we reached the base of the hill. Despite the curtains of the litter, the people knew me. Deiphobus signaled to his guards to form a ring about our litters as we edged our way into the mob. The people were reaching out to touch me, jumping up and down clapping their hands and stamping their feet. They threw flowers, grains, and it seemed anything else they could possibly associate with me. They were pushing on the wall of guards surrounding us as if seeking to storm the barricade.

Deiphobus raised his hand, and the guards drew their swords. Now that I look back on it, that was the last distinct action I can remember from that day. The rest was a blur like rushing through a nightmare. The people were so desperate to get to me, calling, "In-anna, In-anna, In-anna," that the first wave gave up their lives hurrying upon the swords of the guards, perhaps not even seeing the gleaming bronze in their mania to reach me.

After that, not even the guards were safe. The crowd kept coming and coming. Those behind rushed across the bodies of their fallen friends as if they were merely the bridge to reach me. The guards too could do nothing in a ring one deep. They were trampled with the rest. The mob pushed aside those carrying my litter and took charge of it themselves. I was their captive goddess.

I thrust aside the curtains and tried to catch their attention, shouting, "Tell me what you want!" There was no safe way I could climb on top of the litter to command their attention. I remembered Menelaus lifting me up onto his shoulders to stop the Spartan riots. But to descend to the ground here would be suicide even for Inanna.

"What do they want of me?" I asked Cassandra

The Power Of Inanna

who rode beside me.

"They are taking you to the People's Shrine," she said. "I can feel it," she stared off into space.

I was afraid to ask what that was. I was still haunted by memories of the day I arrived in Troy. Deiphobus had been there, holding me and explaining everything that happened. I looked behind me, searching for him in the mob that surrounded us. Though I hated him, he was still a kind of security. But I could not find him. I supposed he had saved himself first. How could I blame him when he had warned me not to go?

In the center of the city where the lords and ladies rarely ventured stood a circular building of unhewn gray stone — frightening in its very plainness. It looked like something that had survived from the Age of the Gods Before Man. Smoke billowed from a terracotta pipe in the roof.

They set me down on the Throne of Inanna elevated on a dais a few handspans above the rest of the room. It reminded me of the days when I used to receive the women of Sparta in the portico before the Throne Room. Although both men and women waited outside, in here only the women had entered — the women and the children.

Cassandra stood beside me, surveyed the scene, and smiled. Why shouldn't she? This was simple enough. I laughed at my fears. Deiphobus must be a cowardly dotard to dislike this.

As I shuffled my skirts and prepared myself to settle their disputes, with one motion they fell to their knees and held their children out in their hands in front of them as if offering them to me. This was odd. I was accustomed to seeing small children who had not yet reached the age of wisdom running about making light of my ceremonies. Instead, the only sound was the wailing of infants. To this day I cannot hear my grandchildren wail for the most innocent reason, be it ever so softly, without starting in fear and trembling. Only then do I remember that I am in Sparta once again. We are all safe, at least as safe as any can be in these latter days when we have only charred walls and the ruins of our palace to protect us, where we live like mice in holes and crevices.

Then the women rose to their feet. "You may begin," I said to them in their own dialect which Deiphobus had taught me. Instead of coming forward by rank, they lined up at the hearth. "How odd," I mused, "I have never seen a hearth like that one. Why does it have a bridge crossing over it? Would they walk through fire?"

The keening began. The women tore their hair and ripped their robes. They pounded their chests with their fists and raked their nails over their faces like my women the day Menelaus ordered the shrines to be desecrated. I was horrified that they would ruin the only clothes they owned, for these were the poorest of the poor.

Their faces were emaciated, and I felt guilt that I had allowed matters to progress so far without doing anything to aid them. I could see the bones of the wrists of women who had not yet known twenty summers. The babies whimpered from hunger. Their mothers had no milk.

The women huddled together in a mass and moved forward with one will in a procession up the ramp. They cried out "In-anna!" as if in great pain. I have never heard a more piteous sound, like the wind howling. The first stopped at the top and turned to her neighbor for support. They embraced each other. The mother kissed her baby, closed her eyes as her lips moved in a prayer, and incredibly down the baby fell straight into the flames. It wailed for a moment.

I could not speak. I tried to move, but I was as immobile as an Egyptian statue. Woman after woman consigned her baby to the flames. It seemed like a nightmare, not quite real, until I smelled burning flesh. That brought me to my feet. Cassandra clutched my arm. "You mustn't," she said. "The sacrifice is sacred."

I smacked her across the face hard enough to send her flying backward. "Swine!" I cursed her. She stared at me uncomprehendingly. I ran down the steps and pushed through the crowd of women going up to the altar. When they recognized me they fell back, terror in their eyes. "Stop!" I yelled as loudly as I could in their language. "You do not please Inanna. Stop it!"

"How could you do this to your own children?" I accosted a group of bereaved mothers kneeling in a circle on the beaten earth floor pouring handfuls of dust over their heads. "How?" I insisted, but they were beyond even hearing. They just stared past me at the flames.

It seemed the women could not understand. What I was saying was beyond their experience. Inanna lived in a separate plane and knew no mercy.

"No! No!" I hollered in a fury. I shoved my way to the front of the line. I snatched the next sacrificial victim from its mother's arms and shouted at her, "Murderess!"

The mother stared at me as if she had seen her fate. Her thread had been cut. She crept around me, made a sign with her hands, and leaped to her death in the inferno below. She cried longer than any baby had.

Holding the baby under one arm, I tried to block their path to the flames when soldiers in gleaming bronze poured into the shrine. The women scattered screaming, but they were cornered and cut down on the spot. Many mothers crept over to the flames to toss their babies in as a last act to propitiate an angry Inanna.

Now I was shouting, "Stop!" to the soldiers who did not see or hear me.

At first I thought Deiphobus had gone mad too. He headed straight for me as fast as his club foot would permit and caught me up in his arms. "Stop them!" I yelled. "Don't you see, this doesn't solve anything to add murder to murder!" But no one could hear me today, and Deiphobus was no exception. He held me until I stopped struggling.

He whispered harshly, "Fool, didn't you know? But then I guess I never told you, and Cassandra would not. Sometimes when these women are in a frenzy, they take whomever is their embodiment of Inanna for the moment and throw her into the flames. They want her to retrieve the souls of the dead, to bring them back to life. Then they wait for her next incarnation to arrive, and with her will come the rain and the new life...Don't you see? I thought they would kill you."

Suddenly I had no strength at all. I had been through too much and was more weary than I knew. I said nothing, but just let him carry me out clinging to him.

XV

To Provide For My People

I was determined to persuade the Trojan people to give up their barbarian practices and obey me. I had to gain the same influence over them that I once possessed over my Spartans. But first I had to show them that I had power and could provide for their needs.

Drought was still on the land in the hot season. The commoners suffered from a lack of both water and grain. At the same time the palace and the houses of the rich were fed water by aqueduct. The temple granaries were bursting with wheat, barley, and corn; the pantries and storerooms of the palace with pithoi of olive oil; and the wine magazine with imported vintages. I smelled the wine fermenting as I passed by. Its acrid odor burned my nostrils.

I was determined that Deiphobus persuade Paris that the temple and the palace stores be distributed among the needy. I disdained to flatter Paris, and that was the only way to move him. He thoroughly despised the lower classes. When I took issue with him he said, "So what if they die? They breed like rats."

"You are about to be attacked by the Achaeans," I tried to appeal to his self-interest. "You must feed the people as if they were your soldiers. You may need their help." But Paris did not have his brother's intelligence.

I could see why the Trojans thought their gods

were merciless. Their overlords were.

Occasionally I would take the trouble to appeal to Priam himself. But he could only look through me and smile. He would pat my hand and call me, "Cassie." No doubt he remembered Cassandra as a little girl.

Cassandra I would not call upon. I abhorred her presence.

So I was again left with no one to help me but Deiphobus. As much as I tried to avoid him, it seemed I could not.

I sought him out and found him sitting in the shade of the afternoon in the patio of Paris's wing of the palace. Our sons and the twins were frolicking and wrestling on the floor as the slave women ran about catching their balls and scolding them. The very youngest sat with his wet nurse and watched the action. I marveled at how none of our sons showed any signs of Deiphobus's deformity. They were all perfect, and I knew that was one of the great boons of Deiphobus's life.

Hermione was seated beside Deiphobus on the bench. Deiphobus was bent over a pile of papyri. It was funny how little I noticed it anymore, having become so accustomed to it, but Deiphobus rarely wore his mask when not in public. At first he had shed it in my presence only, and now whenever the children were about and he was "at home." They were able to accept his scarred face more easily than the mask. Now no one suffered from nightmares, least of all Hermione.

She held his cithara. "Deiphobus, listen to this!" she said proudly. She strummed a few notes. He looked up and smiled approvingly. That stopped me. I had never seen him smile before except in sarcasm or in a mood of irony. This was a real smile from the heart. I saw him in a flash as he could have been. He would have had Paris's perfect face but with a far greater depth of feeling and perhaps compassion. He could have been a great man if it were not for the bitterness that had deformed his soul. But then perhaps tragedy had given him song.

"Deiphobus," she said, her golden curls bouncing about her shoulders as she jumped up and down in her seat, "sing me that song about the one-eyed giant!"

"Polyphemus?" he asked gently, a cloud darkening his face.

"Yes!"

Deiphobus took the cithara and tuned it with a few expert manipulations of the hands, tightening the strings here and loosening them there. Then he began to sing of a faraway land and a lonely cave by the sea where lived a one-eyed Cyclops named Polyphemus. It was his misfortune to see one day while he was tending his sheep the lovely sea nymph Galatea. She walked in the sun while he walked by night, so he loved her. But when she saw his face, she was appalled and pelted him with apples. When he tried to pursue her, she flew like the spring breeze and left the sound of her laughter tinkling in his ears. He was as clumsy and slow as she was graceful and swift. There was nothing left to Polyphemus but to sit alone on his rock and let the waves lap over his feet as he sang of her.

Hermione looked thoughtful. "Why didn't Galatea love Polyphemus? She was mean."

"Not so," said Deiphobus. "Polyphemus made himself as ridiculous as he was ugly by reaching for something that was forever beyond him." There was a bitter knowledge in his voice that brought the blush to my cheeks.

"But why couldn't Polyphemus do something to change her mind?" Hermione persisted, for she did not like the ending.

"Perhaps he did not know how. A creature who has lived apart all his life, an object and a thing of ridicule, grows bitter and pities himself. He shrinks into the shadows like a creature of the night and cannot hold a spear to fight like a man by the light of day. No woman can love him."

I felt the gall rising in my throat.

"He should do something noble," Hermione said, putting her hand on his arm. "Then she would love him."

"Yes, he said, "noble...."

"Hermione," I said in a tone of dismissal, "you should be attending to your duties in the temple."

Deiphobus nodded to the maids, and they cleared the patio of children and slaves. Hermione lingered behind pouting, "Must I go too? I'm not a child anymore." She was already eleven cycles of the seasons. She looked to Deiphobus and not to me. This was a girl who had yearned for her father and had now found him in a man who was as unlike Menelaus as the chaff was to the wheat grains. I could not help but feel he was a dangerous man and a bad influence.

Deiphobus said, "If you help your Aunt Cassandra collect the offerings, I shall teach you a new song tonight." That worked far better than my approach, and she was off right away.

"Leave her alone," I found myself growling through my teeth, barely able to wait until everyone was gone to show my spleen.

"My, my, we are getting testy, aren't we?" he said with just as much restraint as I had shown lack of it. I ignored the fact that his voice was quieter than usual.

I was used to a certain sequence of events. I thought, "Now he will take my hand, and the talking will be over." It was with a certain resignation and relief that

To Provide For My People

I knew the outcome of the struggle.

But he did not touch me. I looked at him, and my surprise must have shown. He was smiling at me, but sadly.

I was blushing and completely out of sorts. So I said, "I need corn and wheat from the temple granaries to give to the people. I would like to divert water from the palace aqueduct to quench their thirst."

"The very grain we trade for gold talents to pay the mercenaries. Agamemnon has used all the gold of Mycenae to steal them away from us. Many sail with him. But then I forgot, you are not a Trojan," the bitterness was creeping back into his voice.

That fortified me. I had learned to live on bitterness. "Enough of a Trojan to want to assume my responsibilities," I said. "They look to me as Inanna, and I must provide for them."

"That casts a different light on matters," he said. "I can't lend you grain. Our defense needs it all. But I have a better idea. Maybe we should send the palace guard out on a foraging expedition. Of course we would accompany them."

I could not believe what my ears said I heard. Was he compromising, or did he have an ulterior motive? In nine cycles of the seasons I had not left the city. Its walls had been my prison. Only in dreams did I relive my days of freedom roaming the Parnon and Taygetos Ranges with Menelaus, and now Deiphobus proposed setting me free if but for a day.

Deiphobus was true to his word. Within a few sunrises he had organized an expedition. Half the palace guard were to be spared from their usual duty of guarding the King's family. They were to carry their bronze-tipped spears into the hills. The temple women who prepared the food, the sacred meals, also got ready their sacks to gather wild herbs and berries.

The land surrounding Troy was mostly a plain watered by the Scamander and the Simois, which emptied into the Great Sea. But like all rivers they had their origins in hills and mountains. The mountains were not as high as the ones I was used to in Sparta, but at least they were hills high enough to look out upon the waters. We followed the Simois upstream to a height called Callicolone.

The air away from the heat and stench of the city was bracing. Of course it would not be seemly for Inanna to travel any other way than by litter accompanied by a contingent of her priestesses.

I was Inanna. They should obey me. I ordered the guards to set down my litter, and I walked free the last part of the journey. I went faster, thinking that Deiphobus would soon catch up to me. He had exchanged his priest's costume for a coarse hooded cloak with peasant's walking sandals. It would be a second life not to always have Deiphobus dogging my footsteps.

I felt young again, a girl Hermione's age. My feet flew on ahead of me. Perhaps I was not yet so old that I had forgotten how to run.

As Inanna I kept my own tent. Deiphobus as a prince and chief eunuch kept his as a matter of state. The priestesses kept to a third, the guards a fourth. We set to work immediately. I kneeled on the ground, gathered medicinal herbs, and put them into my own sack. It mattered not that Deiphobus objected to Inanna working with her hands and shocking everyone. I was Inanna and would do as I chose

Deiphobus spent most of his time organizing the

soldiers into hunting parties and giving the priestesses orders. I sniffed and thought what a busybody he was. But after everyone else had gone about his business, I saw what I would never have believed if someone else had told me. He too was kneeling on the ground looking through the bushes studiously.

  He was only pretending to know what to do. I wanted to burst out laughing, but instead I returned to my own work. Out of the corner of my eye I watched him cast looks at my hands from time to time to see what I was doing.

  He was out of his element. His hands were sleek and smooth like those of a palace eunuch, instead of roughened and calloused with outdoor use and fighting. Certainly no one would mistake him for a soldier like his brother Hector who was several shades darker.

  I would not let him spoil my day no matter what he was up to. Whenever I found a sunny patch of clearing on the hillside, I searched for bushes with small gray leaves and sniffed for thyme. I looked for the white flowers, thin stalks, and green leaves of oregano. It was easy to confuse with basil, but even after all these years of neglect my mother's herbal lore was returning.

  That evening my priestesses returned to their tent with their herbs and berries, the soldiers with their catch of wild goat, squirrel, and rabbit. But I decided I would not go back. I found myself a comfortable rock. It was the hour of sunset, and I looked out to sea and dreamed that I was no one and had nobody to answer to but myself. Soon I could see nothing but the lanterns on the ships of the Trojan navy anchored in harbor, the few that had not sailed, and the stars. It had been ages since I had thought of it, but in an inspiration I picked out the twin stars, the Dioscuri, that I had long ago told my father were my brothers Castor and Pollux. I felt very safe with them watching over me. A bright sheen of silver crossed the tops of the waves like a magic carpet to take me to them.

I did not even realize that I was crying until I felt fingers touching my cheeks. I jerked my head to the side and stared at the ghostly apparition of a hooded figure. Only then did I recognize Deiphobus, so far away from him had I been in thought. Let him drag me back to camp if he must. I leaned back against my rock.

But he did not stir. He leaned back against the same rock. Finally he said like the lament of the dead, "You still want to return to the land of your birth, don't you?"

There was no longer any Sparta to return home to. Deiphobus had seen to that. Nor did Menelaus want me back. I had even begun to identify myself with the Trojan Goddess Inanna instead of the Spartan one who had left me. In unguarded moments I felt I had to protect my new people from their enemies, the Achaeans from Hellas, my old people.

Yet I had been born the Spartan royal heiress, and Spartan blood flowed in me. The blood of my slain father called upon me for vengeance, all the blood of my massacred people. Right sailed with Menelaus, Odysseus, and the Achaeans.

I did not know how to answer Deiphobus. I only hated him for asking the question. He said not another word the rest of the night as we both sat there leaning against the rock and looking out to sea — sleeplessly.

XVI

The Goddess Returns

We stopped in Troy to drop off our new supplies of food and medicine before heading out to sea on a fishing expedition. Hermione asked Deiphobus again if she could come. He tried to placate her with a gold bracelet of paired argonauts, but that did not work. He had denied her the first time; this time he could not resist her pleas. I thought it might be dangerous, but I had no say in the matter.

I resolved to teach her something. As I knelt by the shore to pick caper flowers, I called Hermione to my side. I pointed out the pinkish-white blooms on the bushes and warned her not to prick her fingers. It was a game to her, and she soon had picked a whole sack full. Pickled or boiled, they could help keep the Trojans from starving.

"Deiphobus," she called, "come here!" He had been busy choosing crews from among the fishermen to man the warships along with the officers of the navy. He seemed reluctant and looked awkward as he stood there until she took him by the hand and led him over to me. Hermione threw the contents of her sack over him, carpeting the rocks around Deiphobus's feet with petals. A morning's work — ruined.

"Hermione!" I shouted in my sternest voice.

She stared at me in shock as if she did not understand why I was spoiling her fun. Then she stuck her lower lip out and stalked off.

I was about to go after her when Deiphobus stopped me. Why he was not wearing his mask I could not imagine. Ever since our trip to the hills he had shed that part of his costume in public as well as in private. Those who dared cast surreptitious glances at him, but for the most part his scarred face did not excite half the gossip that his sphinx mask did. There was little terror in the known.

But my greatest shock was not to come until the very last day we spent fishing.

Every evening at sunset the ships would return to shore and unload their catch of squid, octopus, red mullet, and tunny fish. Those fishermen who had stayed on shore for the day drew in their nets and finished their crabbing. Even the small sharks caught in the nets were killed and cut up for meat. Fishermen's boys beat the octopuses on the rocks to soften the meat before carrying them into the city.

And every night after dark I would go from house to house in the lower town to supervise the distribution of the food. Most of the dwellings were poor mud brick and only one room with a floor of beaten earth. Here whole families lived and died in crowded squalor. They buried their babies with little ceremony under the floor. Here too they threw their refuse and garbage when they did not toss it onto the streets.

They had little enough room for even their mats, let alone storage, so they dug holes in the floor and buried giant pithoi filled with dried meat, fruit and fish. Some houses held so many of these pithoi that they formed a kind of paving to the floor. One could step from lid to lid.

Paris raised a fuss about his Queen going from door to door like a common trollop. It was one of those rare occasions when he bothered himself with anything I did because it reflected on his regal dignity. But Deiphobus came to my aid. He persuaded Paris to relent but insisted upon taking the guard. He would not let me enter any dwelling because of the stench. Yet I could see the inhabitants stare out at Inanna from their doorways, do reverence, and even try to rush out and touch me. The guards blocked their way with crossed spears.

On the morning of the last day we set sail, I stood on the prow of our ship and poured a libation of wine into the sea from a giant bull's head rhyton. I prayed to the Earth-shaker, Lord of the Sea, to grant us a good catch.

It was early, and there was no wind. I took my place on the quarter deck with Deiphobus and Hermione, who could hardly be restrained from running about the ship in excitement. She clung to the figurine of Inanna on the prow, for the ship was named "The Goddess", and swung from it irreverently. I saw in her the ghost of my dead self even as I chastised her. I was becoming like my mother.

Deiphobus gave the order, and the fishermen took their places at the oars and began rowing us out to sea. Only then was the mainsail raised to pick up the breeze. It was brisker than usual for the morning. No one thought anything of it at the time, though in the hot season the wind does not usually pick up until midday.

The catch was so plentiful that we stayed out longer than we normally did. Sometime past the high sun the wind suddenly and without warning turned into a squall. Deiphobus gave the order to head back, but it was too late. I had heard tales about this wild meltemi wind that blows from the north during the dry season. On land it brings much needed coolness, but on the sea it brings sudden death.

In minutes the sea had gone from a clear blue to

white froth as the wind churned and tormented it. The rigging groaned. The sails filled to overflowing as if they would burst. We were suddenly doing battle with a head wind, and it was winning. We had to hold onto our bench to keep from being swept overboard.

The meltemi increased, and the ship spun about and leaned far over to one side. Deiphobus dragged the hysterical Hermione and me to the other side of the ship as fast as I had ever seen him move. All the rowers had long since fastened their oars, locked them in place, and were likewise running to the side of the ship that had reared high in the air like a giant whale surfacing from the depths. We clung to the railing, and some of the fishermen leaned way out. The captain of the guards yelled to pull the brails in. The mainsail bellied to catch the breeze, and we righted again.

Deiphobus threw Hermione and me to the deck and spread his body over ours as the spray flew over us. We plunged, rocked, and jumped high into the air. The horse we were riding had gone mad. I prayed to the Goddess to save us.

At such times one can think only of the moment. The past and the future are erased, for every moment may be our last. I was holding onto Hermione's hair. That was all I could reach. I was crying out to her, but I do not know if she could hear me, for I did not hear the death agonies of the many men who were swept overboard that afternoon. I was holding on as hard as I could, but suddenly the ship lurched, and sea water was washing between my empty fingers.

I screamed and tried to scramble after her. Deiphobus pinned me down. I managed to turn over and face him as I struggled with the opponent I could barely see for the spray. The desperate have a strength they hardly know. It must have been nearly impossible for him to contend with me and hold us both on the ship.

His lips pressed down on mine. The wind, the waves, and the constant jerking about seemed to be him and not the sea, and while I could not best the elements I could fight him as I had done for nine cycles of the seasons. My hands and legs were pinioned so I used the only weapon I had left — my own lips. I thrust and jabbed at him, but he would not release me.

The sun was going down by the time the wind and the waves were calm enough for us to sit up again. I felt my grief more keenly with the returning stillness.

I looked at the frightened faces of the crew and felt a dawning strength. I had suffered but so had they. It was my duty to help them.

I rose, and as if Deiphobus sensed my thought he helped me and guided my footsteps to the figurehead on the prow, the deity of the ship. It was the head of Inanna with her hair streaming over her shoulders and breasts. Through my tears I raised my hands, and everyone knelt in the thickening darkness to give thanks for their deliverance. "Praise be to Inanna," I managed to say as tears streamed down my face. "She is merciful. She is good, and we are her people." To myself I said, "Her will be done." Every soldier and sailor was crying with me.

The air was sharply cooler of a sudden. I felt a light breeze, gentler than what was just past, and my skin prickled. The Goddess said to me in the voice she had always used in Sparta, "I have been wroth with thee, Helen, but now I am well-pleased. You no longer rebel against my will but serve me. Your courage and worthiness show in that you have remembered me at a time like this. You are truly my daughter."

Tears sprang to my eyes. I imagined that she had

deserted me. But she was here, the same, here in Troy as everywhere. Inanna was only one of her names. I had found my path again.

Deiphobus was no longer supporting me. I stood alone. He knelt like the rest with his head bowed in reverence. He felt my gaze as surely as if I had touched him, and he looked up, drawn to me as the flower of the sun is to the sky. I felt the Goddess in me and her power. She called to him in the same language.

His eyes were wet, as hard to imagine as that was. No longer could he conceal from me what was in his heart as his whole countenance blazed forth pride in what I had done. No longer could I disbelieve him. I knew he did love me to his great sorrow.

That certain knowledge stunned me as if I had received a heavy blow. His eyes continued to stare into mine unflinchingly, defying me to spurn him. He was afraid of nothing, perhaps because he had nothing left to fear — not even death.

Then I heard a voice from the shades. "Here I am!" shouted Hermione scrambling toward me from the quarter deck. Some sailor whose hand was stronger than mine had grabbed her as she was falling overboard. The Goddess had seen to that.

"Hermione!" I covered her with kisses, but she pulled away and ran to Deiphobus who seemed equally glad to see her. Again I found myself meeting his gaze.

It was night, and the water was quiet. We could not sail back in the darkness. We bunked down on the planks. I snuggled with Hermione to keep her warm and fell instantly to sleep with the gentle rocking of the ship. Later I felt someone lie down behind me and lay his arm over both of us.

XVII

We Meet The Achaean Host

In the middle of the night we were awakened by a flashing light several stones' throw from the ship. Sailors on a passing vessel were yelling something that sounded like a warning, but we were too far away to hear them. We could not imagine what was left to happen to us and returned to sleep, shrugging it off.

At dawn we sighted a ship fast approaching. We set sail towards it, for the storm had blown us far off-shore and had taken many of the oars as well as the crew. We needed fresh supplies and sailors. Deiphobus had only to give the word and any Trojan or Sea Chief in his employ would aid us.

We were nearly within hailing distance. The sails of the relief ship billowed. That was — not the Bull of Heaven — but the double golden lions of Mycenae! At the prow gaping at us like a cat fixing on its prey stood the red-bearded Agamemnon with his long hair flying about his shoulders in the wind. I think he recognized me at once to judge by the way his lips parted to reveal his teeth. Beside him stood his captain of the fleet gloating over the prize that had just floated their direction.

We had been blown so far off-course that we had run into the flagship of the Achaean Armada heading for Troy! By rumor and report they sailed one thousand strong. They must have beaten the Trojans and their allies badly to surprise us like this. No sooner had I been rendered speechless by the first sight than a second ship, following the first closely, pulled up alongside it. It sported the lion and the griffin of Sparta. There stood the one whose memory had haunted me, my beloved.

I felt almost the same as I had cycles of the seasons ago when I looked for the Spartan flag and encountered the Trojan one. I put my hands up to cover the wet silk that was plastered to my breasts.

"Why don't you jump overboard?" Deiphobus whispered low. His hooded presence was like a condemnation. "I'm sure your obliging Menelaus would be happy to fish you out." I wished he would go away, but he hovered as near to me as he could get without touching.

"Maybe you could arrange a truce? Hand me over and save yourself!" I whispered back.

"Man the oars!" he shouted to the remaining crew. "Head for shore. If we die, we go down fighting." Now everyone knew which direction shore was. It was the direction the Achaean fleet was sailing.

Deiphobus had never been trained for the army as his brothers had. But still he took a seat at the oars and helped the crew pull. It was menial work that his brother Paris would rather die than perform. I was too numb to feel shocked.

Of course the Achaeans pursued us. But they granted us a head start. All the oarsmen leaped up to catch a glimpse of me, the guilty one they had heard so much about. There was much ado to make them resume their places. Menelaus went from oar to oar shouting at them.

As we pulled away I could not help myself but stare at Menelaus. That took great courage, and I had to pray to Inanna first to give me strength. He glared at me

We Meet The Achaean Host

like great Zeus himself sitting in judgment about to cast down one of his thunderbolts. His brows seemed to darken the rest of his face. He was older, his face lined, more beaten about by the elements. I imagined that his hair was graying too, but I was not close enough to see.

Fortune had not done her worst. Before we were too far away, a woman stepped up on the quarter deck beside Menelaus and put her hand on his arm. Was that Atossa, a grown woman instead of a girl? I imagined that even she, who had always been so gentle and kind, stared at me in judgment.

"Who is that?" asked Hermione, her eyes big.

"Your father," I said.

"No he's not!" she screamed and burst into tears. She huddled beside Deiphobus at the oars.

I bowed my head and crossed my arms over my heart. I could stand anything as long as the Goddess stood with me. Let her will be done. She had brought me to Troy for her purpose.

Still another surprise. As we pulled for the shore, a fleet of Trojan ships sailed out to meet us. They had retreated from yesterday's fight and regrouped for another attempt, bringing with them whatever ships had been left in the harbor for Troy's defense. Soon we would be caught in the middle of a battle.

Agamemnon had always hated me. Now he intended to get his revenge. He would kill me and claim credit. His men sent a huge stone catapulting through the air. It slammed down in the middle of our deck and put a hole in our hull. A storm of rocks rained down upon us. We had no weapons except swords, for we were equipped for fishing, not war.

We were fast taking on water. I had learned to swim by stealth cycles of the seasons ago in the mountains

To Follow The Goddess

near Sparta. Menelaus taught me. But Hermione had never learned, brought up as a Trojan princess. There was nothing we could do. We were sinking and could not risk staying aboard any longer, for the whirlpool would pull us under. I saw some floating planking and decided to jump.

First I yanked off her sandals and her robe, for this was no time for modesty. I hardly had time to pull the jewelry out of my own hair. "Do exactly as I say and trust me!" I shouted. With my arm around her waist I made her jump with me although she screamed that she would not. We held on to a board and kicked.

Then I saw Deiphobus. He too was holding onto a small piece of planking, too proud to call for help. He dared me to let him drown. Of course all the Trojan men could swim just as the mainlanders could, but Deiphobus as a eunuch had been brought up confined to the house like a woman from his youth on. Yet again he showed no fear. He would have made a good warrior if given the chance.

All I had to do was ignore him, and he might well drown. But in the night the Furies would pursue me with guilt. He had saved me in the storm as well as in the People's Temple. I owed him something, and he was the father of four of my sons. "Hold onto my waist!" I said. He held on in silence.

Since we had been missed in Troy the night before, Paris had ordered the warships to be on the lookout. When the Trojan navy saw the Achaean Armada bearing down on us, they knew who we were.

The signal went from Trojan ship to Trojan ship to lower sails. The rowers took over. The Trojan flagship was flying straight for us. Two ships aimed for Agamemnon's flagship, and two others went in pursuit of Menelaus. Their strategy was all too obvious even to the untrained eye. They planned to cut Menelaus and

We Meet The Achaean Host

Agamemnon off from the rest of their navy and make them pay with their lives for the privilege of killing me.

Menelaus and Agamemnon quickly perceived their peril. Menelaus's vessel turned away to port to face its adversaries. Agamemnon's lingered, reluctant to leave its prey, like a frustrated bloodhound called back by its master against its will. He let loose a shower of arrows, though he was still too far away for good aim. No one had to warn us to duck. The Goddess kept us from harm. When we again surfaced, Agamemnon too had tacked.

The crew of the Trojan flagship soon dragged us on deck. Paris looked out of place wearing his palace regalia aboard ship. He had been so shaken out of his usual aplomb that he had come along. His relief immediately changed to annoyance. He greeted us by scolding, "I told you not to leave the palace on a silly fishing expedition. You are a Queen, not a fishwife."

Paris gave the order to return to shore. He had no intention of waiting for the outcome. Yet amid the sounds of men shouting and keels splashing through the water I heard trumpets. Agamemnon and Menelaus were giving the signal to lower sails and begin rowing in earnest. All they could do now was barely avoid the Trojan ships that tried to ram them and shave off their oars like a scythe cutting grass. As the Trojan ships slipped past and barely missed, the sailors on the Achaean ships threw a shower of javelins. The Trojans retaliated with fire arrows. One stuck to the mast of Menelaus's ship but was quickly doused.

Soon the whole sea was filled with enemy ships trying to cripple each other. They attempted to make the opposition armless and legless by depriving them of oars, and then went in for the kill. They tacked just so and tried to pierce the defenseless ship below the water line and sink it. The sea was dotted with wreckage, the dead, and survivors.

Our flagship was making progress with its sails but not fast enough. A small Achaean ship that had been closely following Agamemnon and Menelaus slipped through in the confusion and now pursued us with its sails down and its oars under full power. Since it was smaller, it was swifter. Two Trojan ships that had been circling to the port tack had just spotted it and were attempting to cut it off. Incredibly it ignored its own danger and continued to pursue us, heading straight into the bulk of the Trojan navy all alone. No one else could be so mad. I looked at its flag, and there flew the wild boar of Ithaca. Odysseus!

My mind raced. I had to figure out what he was up to. I could be certain only that it would be what everyone else least expected, and that was why it would succeed. Only one motive other than suicide could prompt him. He must be after me. But once taken, how would he escape with me? I did not have time to think. He was gaining on us fast.

Paris had retreated to the far side of the ship as if that would save him, walking backwards all the way. His sailors were running to him for orders, abandoning the oars. He was a fool to have assumed command himself. "Man your oars!" Deiphobus shouted, but it was to no avail. Men ran screaming about, jumping overboard. The rowers were convinced this man Odysseus was possessed by a god to give him such courage. We were all in disorder as Odysseus's ship pulled up alongside.

Odysseus's men poured onto our ship, swords in hand. Paris surrendered at once, and within minutes Odysseus had captured the heir to the throne, the power behind the throne, the Queen, and the Princess Hermione.

The Ithacans threw our rowers overboard and

We Meet The Achaean Host

replaced them at the oars. Without hesitating a moment, they rowed with all their might towards the Achaean ships.

It was not every day that a war was won in the time it takes for a man to snap his fingers.

Odysseus without any organized opposition was sailing his way back to the Achaean lines in perfect disguise as a Trojan ship flying the Bull of Heaven. For all the Trojans knew he was one of them attacking the Achaean fleet. As soon as he had reached safety, he would raise the Ithacan boar.

But fate would not so decree it. The wind whipped about my face, and I heard the Goddess speak: "You must not break faith with me again, Helen. I have work for thee. If you take the easy way and go back now, you will reap bitterness to the end of your days that will make what has already passed look like the Elysian Fields."

I was the only captive not under fetters. All Odysseus's companions and crew assumed I must be greatly relieved to be liberated. They had tied Deiphobus and Paris to the mast. Paris kept gesticulating, no doubt trying to promise his kingdom for his safety. Hermione was clinging to Deiphobus and weeping, her hair blowing wildly about her. He was too proud to say a word. Nor would he look at me.

I went forward to where Odysseus was standing on the quarter deck giving orders. I took him by the hands and said, "Odysseus, listen to me."

"You can shower me with your thanks later, Helen. I'm busy now," he said.

I tugged at him, and he turned around to face me. He looked the same as always with the addition of more gray hairs. When he saw my face he said, "I won't let Menelaus kill you. I'll take you back to Ithaca with me if I must until his temper cools...And we won't leave without the twins."

"Time has changed things," I said, as the Goddess made the words fall from my mouth. "The last time you saw me I would gladly have returned with you even if Menelaus would kill me, just so that I could again see my native land before I die. But you must try to understand, you who were always the only one who could. I have six sons now. Four of them are Trojan. I must not desert my people. They have no one else to look after them."

Even Odysseus stared at me in shock, he who had never failed to understand me before.

"Come to me in Troy," the idea sprang into my head. "I know you will find a way. We must save my new people as well as defeat these Trojan lords who are too proud...Even if you do not understand now, please, I beg you, save it for a quiet moment," I read the puzzlement in his face. "But put Paris, Deiphobus, Hermione, and me off the ship while there is still time." We were nearly into the Achaean lines. "Please sail up to that other Trojan ship. They will never question it. They will assume our ship was sunk and you rescued us. You cannot keep us aboard because you are proceeding to the attack. Menelaus need never know what you attempted."

As if in a trance himself, Odysseus motioned to his crew, and they obeyed. The Goddess was working on him.

"I must be mad," Odysseus said, "to bind myself to a war that could be ended in an afternoon. But in this mood of yours, Menelaus would surely kill you, and all the Achaeans would second him. How could I defend you?"

There was so little time to carry out the commands of the Goddess. I beckoned Odysseus to follow me to a station behind the mainsail where Deiphobus, Paris, and Hermione could not see us. I followed her inspirations without thought. I took his hands. "You are the man the

Goddess would have chosen as King of Sparta and my husband. I never told you and never thought to tell you, especially like this. But the hand of destiny is on you, and you are the only one who can help me."

In an instant, the vision was before me. I could see Odysseus as King of Sparta and myself at his side as his Queen. This war would never have come, just as the Goddess promised. We would have grown old together, and our children would have inherited courage and daring from both of us. But most of all, there would have been little need for speech. We could read each other's thoughts. I saw the regret and the longing for what could have been in his eyes too. He leaned closer, tempted by the path we had not chosen.

Once I was returned to the Trojan ship we headed straight for shore. Paris was much impressed with my unlooked-for loyalty. "I see you have finally come to appreciate our superior degree of civilization," he said as he smoothed the creases out of his robe.

I had expected that incident to erase the last of Deiphobus's doubts about me. Instead it seemed to increase them. "I thought you and that loutish cousin of yours hated each other. What did you say to him to get him to agree to release us?" he whispered to me at the first opportunity.

"That loutish cousin of mine was also one of my suitors. He still remembers those days. I took him behind the mast and kissed him. He was stupid enough to think it meant something," I lied.

"He must be very stupid indeed," Deiphobus said scornfully.

Odysseus's sudden appearance had raised my spirits and made me feel I could endure. The Goddess had sent him to do her will. Together we could do anything. I knew in the end Odysseus would come to me.

XVIII

The Battle Of Champions

The great bronze gates of Troy were thrown open. From morning until sunset of that day the countryfolk streamed into the city in panic. They had heard from returning sailors how the great meltemi, that had nearly drowned Inanna and her daughter, had sunk half the Trojan fleet while they waited out at sea to do battle with the Achaean Armada. The very center of the storm struck them. Few had made it to shore and safety. They feared that the gods had turned against them, and Im-dugud was breathing his fire on the Trojan earth.

I watched from the walls as families with all their worldly possessions piled in haste upon a cart whipped their horses into a frenzy to pass another family. Fathers unsheathed their knives to protect their cowering wives and children. Horses reared and trampled those on foot who pushed, shoved, and tried to run ahead, knocking down those in front of them.

Trojans were shedding each other's blood before Troy, and as yet there were no Achaeans in sight. I had bound myself to protect these, my people. I vowed they would never be carried off to Hellas in chains. Now I had to protect them against themselves.

"You will not go down there," Deiphobus said.

"I don't need to," I said. "Give the order to shut the

gates," I told the captain of the palace guard, and he obeyed me with a quick step. Any doubts about my loyalty vanished from every mind but Deiphobus's once the word spread how I had saved the royal family from Odysseus. I had also learned a lesson in command. I must act with confidence and decisiveness, and others would follow — perhaps even Deiphobus.

The guards had to fight off the crowd to shut the gates. People tried to drive the donkeys against the walls and whipped the animals for balking. Carts splintered into pieces. Men stabbed at the walls as if the stones were alive and could bleed. Some even began to scale them. They were the ones who first caught sight of me.

I stood with my arms outstretched holding in each hand a spear that I had grabbed from the astonished guards. Gradually the scalers fell back and became quiet. Their brethren followed when they too looked up. "Disgraceful people," I said, "you have offended Inanna." I hurled one of the spears down as I had seen the men do it, and it stuck in the ground. The crowd groaned and fell back.

"You fight one with the other like a pack of curs!" I shouted. "You are not worthy to come into this, my city. But I shall give you one more chance. Enter without a sound and in orderly procession. Any who disobeys me I shall put outside these walls and leave him for the Achaeans. Achilles will drive you before him like a pack of geese, and Odysseus, Menelaus, and Agamemnon will mercilessly slaughter you for sport."

I must have looked like the Goddess, for they obeyed me.

Hector had taken command of the army and led

The Battle Of Champions

them out onto the plain in front of the city. They were digging a trench that stretched as far as the eye could see in either direction. Slaves were setting up tents and digging cooking pits. Deiphobus was soon busy directing the transfer of the contents of the temple granaries to the army supply tents. No longer did he have any mercenary sailors to buy, for the Sea Peoples had decided almost to a man that the Achaeans were winning and sold their allegiance to them.

Hector had sent couriers to the Hittite King asking him to honor his alliance and send his troops. All the chieftains in Asia had been alerted, and many were already there in force before Troy. They were bound to the Bull of Heaven, and they would rise or fall with Troy's fortunes. No Achaean mainlander would rule over them. No one would bow to Agamemnon as King of Kings.

Paris wandered around on the walls. No one had believed that the Achaeans would ever get this far, least of all Paris. He imagined he could be Bull of Heaven, get all the glory, and do none of the fighting.

By the next morning the remnant of the Trojan fleet again sailed back into harbor and abandoned their ships on the beach. They had held off the Achaean fleet as long as they could in their crippled state. On the horizon sailed the Armada.

Hector's men lined the beach, Hector first of all, brandishing their spears. Soldiers stood poised with their bows ready to shoot fire arrows. Hector gave the signal, and his men with tears in their eyes set fire to their own ships. The wrecks were of no use now. But no one wanted them to fall into the hands of the Achaeans.

I sent the children back to their rooms high on the citadel. I did not want them to witness battle. Everyone was in momentary expectation of one. But instead of braving Troy's onslaught of javelins and arrows, the Achaean fleet sailed only so far that they were just out of range and put down anchor.

The flagship threw a large raft overboard. It righted itself with a splash on the still surface of the water. Closer it came. One man was rowing and one standing upright. Before him he held a staff of the god Hermes.

Deiphobus grabbed my arm and said under his breath, "What does this mean?"

"I know not," I said in all astonishment.

This made no sense. The Achaeans had decimated the Trojan force, and now they sued for peace? Immediately I thought of Odysseus who was the father of everything that made no sense and was not what it seemed. But this was not what I had asked him, unless he were more tricky than I could imagine.

Hector gave the order for his men to lower their spears. Clearly the raft was not armed, and it was beneath Hector's dignity to make war on such unequal numbers.

The raft sailed into harbor. Hector's men closed in around it, and those behind stood two high to get a better view. For awhile I heard only the babble of voices, all gossiping and speculating. I craned my neck and would climb up on the ramparts myself if it were not unseemly.

The soldiers broke ranks to make way. My heart began to pound. A single champion in full battle dress stepped forward and strode with giant steps toward the Skaian Gates where we were standing in the watchtower. Was this Achilles? Certainly he stood too tall for Odysseus. This man of bronze, gleaming in the sun like the war god himself, stopped beneath us and looked up. With one motion he pulled off his leathern helmet studded with boars' teeth, an ancient device of the Kings of Sparta.

Menelaus! He stared past me at Paris who had

cowered backwards and clutched my arm. "Paris!" he shouted up at the paling ruler of Troy, "you have lost your navy, and our losses have not been light. I have no quarrel with Troy. I challenge you, if you dare to meet me in a single combat, to decide the issue. If I fall, I am no longer worthy to be called King of Sparta. You may keep Helen, my heirs, and all my wealth. But if the gods will your death, you must swear to return what is mine to me. May the gods decide the right between us."

Deiphobus whispered to me, "Is that man in earnest?"

"I can vouch for that," I said without hesitation. "He never gives voice to his thoughts unless his heart is in it."

Deiphobus pushed by me and headed straight for Paris. Paris stood speechless, transfixed by Menelaus's stare as no doubt he soon feared to be by his spear. "You must accept," Deiphobus whispered. "You will lose face with the army if you don't."

"But that man looks like a butcher," Paris whispered. "I shall suggest Hector as my champion."

"The people look to you as King of Troy."

"I am an artist and a King, not a butcher!"

"I shall arrange everything," Deiphobus said. "We shall turn his offer to our own advantage. You see, he's trying to fool us. If we gave up Helen, the Achaeans would try to lay us waste anyway. They have not come so far for nothing. So we shall resort to a bit of trickery of our own. You shall march out to meet his challenge. Then, when you give the signal, I shall order the gates to be opened, and the palace guard shall rush out to slaughter Menelaus. We shall have one of their champions for nothing!"

I could not listen to Deiphobus plotting Menelaus's death without objecting. He had been my lord, and I owed him better than this. I was about to warn Menelaus when Deiphobus checked me with a glance out of the corner of his eye.

Suddenly I knew he was lying to Paris. He would not have spelled out the plan in front of me if he had been in earnest. He would have said, "Accept, and I'll arrange things," and left it vague until they were alone, or said even less.

I guessed at what he intended. It struck me with horror. Not even Agamemnon, cruel as he was, would dream of doing that to his brother. It was more on the level of Aegisthus, that long forgotten creature. "I like not these challenges," I said. "Send Menelaus back and fight army against army."

"No one asked your opinion," Paris said testily. "Vixen, you would want me to lose face with the army so Hector should triumph over me."

His fate was a true one, and he had sealed it. He was beyond my reach. But he was in his glory. He stepped forward to the ramparts and called down in a princely voice, "We accept your challenge." Never had he believed himself so noble.

By the time Paris stepped out to meet Menelaus I think he had convinced himself he was another Achilles. He summoned Hector to stand by the walls and invited Menelaus to bring as many Achaeans as he wished to shore to witness the combat. Perhaps he even imagined he would have no need of Deiphobus's palace guards.

Priam did not know what was transpiring, but Paris had him brought to his room to watch him don his armor. It was the finest metal anyone had ever admired, for it had seen little use. I knew he had not appeared in uniform since the siege of Sparta nine years before, and then he had been fighting unarmed civilians. He fancied that I should assist him in putting it on, for that seemed more dramatic — the warrior's wife helping to strap him into his armor as he strode off to battle.

His cuirass was of silver wrought with scenes of battles of long ago. His ankle-clasps were gold, and he fancied they would catch the light. His helmet nodded with a horse's plume. Nor could he resist tying a panther's skin over his shoulder and around his waist with the verve of an actor.

Hector was the very soul of honor even as Menelaus was. As far as he could see, the dispute would be settled one way or the other today. So he saw no reason why he should not let the Achaeans come to shore and put down anchor. As many who cared to had disembarked and stood behind Menelaus to cheer him on. Even Agamemnon had not been able to sulk for long and had come ashore, taking a conspicuous place where everyone could see him.

To the fanfare of trumpets the bronze gates of Troy opened. Paris drove out in his chariot of cypress wood inlaid with ivory, drawn by two horses with plumes on their heads, raising the dust with his wheels.

As soon as Menelaus caught sight of him, he put down the visor on his helmet and unsheathed his sword. He was the man to be angry at such pretensions. He strode forward like a great bear stalking his prey, ferocious and growling, drawing back his sword arm over his shoulder to thrust home the fatal blow.

Paris jumped down from his chariot in haste, probably angry that Menelaus had shortened his grand entrance. Paris barely had time to put up his shield to deflect the blow. It hit him with such force that he staggered backward. He did not have time to grab his own sword.

The desperation of fear must have struck him then, the realization that this was a fight to the death. He fumbled with his sword until he unsheathed it. Boldly, Paris lunged forward to attack Menelaus. But such force did he put into the lunge that his sword point stuck into Menelaus's shield, and Paris could not draw it out. Now he had only a spear and shield, and a spear was an unwieldy weapon against a sword at close quarters.

Paris panicked and turned to signal Deiphobus. Deiphobus pretended to be ignorant of his meaning and averted his gaze. Of course no one else knew what they had agreed upon. I pitied him and hated Deiphobus. Deiphobus should be the one out there fighting Menelaus now, but it was to Deiphobus's credit that I knew he would go if he could. He was no coward.

Menelaus threw down his sword. He would not take unfair advantage of his opponent. Menelaus grabbed his own spear and began to circle around Paris. Paris took his eyes off Deiphobus long enough to perceive his danger. Disbelievingly, he took out his own spear. I could see his arm shake. Menelaus feinted at him, but instead of feinting or striking back, Paris leaped back, as if that would protect him. There was a roar of laughter from the Achaean camp. Hector was beginning to look ashamed and the Trojans uncomfortable. They were shifting and restless. Some dared to trade lewd jests.

Again Paris signaled wildly to Deiphobus, waving his spear. Deiphobus stared unseeingly past him, his face hardened, probably thinking, "Now no more do I have to toady to you, fool." Menelaus called something to Paris which none of us could hear, and Paris faced him again. How like Menelaus to give his opponent every possible chance! Tears came to my eyes when I thought on it. If the situation could somehow be reversed, Paris would not spare one thought for any other human being but himself. I remembered his cowardly slaughter of my Spartan men.

Menelaus circled around and around Paris, now one way, now the other. Paris summoned up all his fading courage and made stabs at him, thrusts which the practiced Menelaus easily deflected. I could imagine the sweat running down Paris's brow. I could feel his perplexity, for someone had always been there to help him. Perhaps he had accepted the truth and wished only that his fate could close his eyes forever.

When Paris could stand the tension no longer, he took his spear and hurled it at Menelaus, who sidestepped it. Now Paris owned no weapons at all. He began to speak, what I could imagine. He would be trying to plead with Menelaus for his life. I am certain he promised Menelaus that he could have me back as well as half the riches of Troy thrown into the bargain. Perhaps he even offered Troy itself.

But Menelaus said nothing. In a great dudgeon, severely offended by the coward's lack of honor, he threw down his spear and shield, took off his helmet, and tossed it into the dust. He strode towards him to grapple with him hand to hand. Paris did not understand that certain offenses could be righted only by blood.

Paris stared at Menelaus as if he were a lion or a panther. The coward turned and fled, speeding towards the gates. My lord took off after him, grasped him by the fancy plumes of his helmet and hurled him to the ground, knocking the wind from him. Only when Paris recovered did Menelaus throw himself upon his enemy.

Paris struggled and squirmed like a woman being raped, slapping Menelaus about the face and scratching him. His slim body was no match for Menelaus's brawny one. Paris summoned the strength of the panic-stricken to throw Menelaus back and roll on top of him. He kicked my lord in the face and ran towards the gates. Again the Achaean camp erupted into laughter.

Menelaus's patience was at last exhausted. He raced back to retrieve his spear. "Stop, coward, you who had pluck enough to steal my Queen! Stop and defend yourself like a man, or you soon will be a dead one." Paris ran faster. Menelaus hurled the spear. It found its mark and impaled him, going straight through his body from back to front. As he fell, his eyes looked amazed as if he still at the last could not believe that this was happening to him, he the favored one of fortune. But in the end, he toppled into the dust.

Menelaus pulled out his spear. He stepped back and viewed his handiwork. Any other warrior would have stripped Paris of his armor as a trophy of war to hang up in his hall. Instead, Menelaus knelt down and picked up Paris's body in his arms. He carried it over to Hector and laid it down at his feet.

Hector nodded gravely and said, "It was well done. He deserved not even so much from you."

Menelaus approached the watchtower. "Now I demand the woman called 'Helen,' he shouted up. "Yes, even she, my daughter, and my sons as well as all my wealth. I have won them fairly. No man can dispute that."

"The woman called 'Helen'," was still in my ears when Deiphobus shouted down to him, "Want in vain, King, you cannot command us here."

"But you have ratified a solemn oath," Menelaus said.

"A bargain struck by our former King, who was a fool," Deiphobus said. "If you think I would give back to you what was once yours and you could not even appreciate, you are as slow of wit as you are strong of brawn."

This I had anticipated. I knew Deiphobus would never surrender me to be butchered. But what followed took me as much by surprise as it took Menelaus, and all the Trojans and Achaeans.

"Helen is mine," said Menelaus.

"She was yours," said Deiphobus, his hate gleaming from his eyes. "Now she is mine, and I intend to marry her as the rightful successor to my brother."

I clutched the ramparts. I should have foreseen this. Of course this was the perfect time to step in and claim what had been his all along. There would be no change for me, except that my shame would be made public. Menelaus looked at me in amazement. I could not meet his gaze and turned away, but not without seeing the gaping look on Hector's face. Murmurs ran through both armies and through all of Troy, louder and louder.

Menelaus at last said when he found his tongue, "But you are the eunuch Deiphobus. Surely you jest with the gods." The Achaean camp echoed with laughter.

Nothing was more calculated to get Deiphobus's ire up. "I am even Deiphobus, son of Priam, Bull of Heaven, but no eunuch. I have already sired four sons on Helen, whom I now publicly acknowledge as my heirs."

I staggered backwards and turned to flee. Not even in a nightmare did I imagine these deeds of darkness would be revealed so. But I felt a chill, and the Goddess said to me, "Take courage, Helen, I am with thee." I turned and came back to Deiphobus's side. It did not matter what Deiphobus said or did. I still had my own task before me. In the end I would triumph, and he would fall.

"So know your enemy, Menelaus, King of the dust," Deiphobus was saying. "Plot your wars against me.

But fight me with other than spears and shields or you will surely lose."

"One thing I do know," said Menelaus, recovering himself. "No man can long remain King if he has no honor." With that he turned and strode back to his camp. I could see the offense he had taken as if it were an illness that had stiffened his every limb.

An unknown archer from the Achaean camp felt the insult to his lord most keenly. He shot an arrow into the Trojan camp, and a soldier fell dead. His friend avenged him, and a general engagement was soon underway. Hector had no choice but to give the order to attack. So ended the last chance for peace.

I retired from the walls, for the third time a Queen — and for the second Queen of Troy.

XIX

Deiphobus Triumphant

I married Deiphobus.

He burned his eunuch outfits along with Paris's too ornate ones. He had made for himself robes of state befitting the dignity of a King. Now he did openly what before he had done in secret. He met with Hector to discuss strategy, retired Priam to a wing of the palace, and took over his role in ceremony as well as in substance. He received foreign chieftains who were vassals of Troy and persuaded the Hittite King to open a supply line for food as well as send all his troops.

Hermione did not understand how he gained his power and delighted in Deiphobus's newfound status. He spoiled her with gifts and let her sit on his lap while he received foreign embassies in the throne room.

Paris had ignored her, and now she was openly princess of the realm, loving the color and the pageantry of court. Deiphobus presented her with his entire bird collection upon assuming the throne, for he said he would have no time for it.

At twelve she was careless and left the cages open to allow her pets to fly about the throne room. If a green parrot landed on the prostrate backside of a monarch, she laughed, nor did Deiphobus permit anyone to reprimand her. I tried, but he gainsaid me, "I want her to have nothing but happiness all her days. I wish it were as easy to make you happy as to make your daughter laugh." He adopted her as well as the twins and seemed to show no preference among my children and his own, except that the heirs of his body were to succeed him. He held an investiture ceremony for Little Deiphobus.

I was busy distributing whatever food Deiphobus could obtain from his allies behind the lines or could spare from Hector's troops. My people had no means of getting it for themselves. I had just gotten back from the lower town one evening at dusk. So tired was I, I did not go in to supper but went straight to my room. My maids helped me undress, and I thought to sleep.

But when I closed my eyes, my mind raced ahead of me to the next morning. I was thinking through all the royal duties I had to perform. I did not even hear the door open and did not know he was there until I felt Deiphobus's hand on my forehead. "You are tired and need to sleep," he said. He bent over and kissed my lips.

Though he had barely brushed my skin, I felt anger start up burning like fire. How dare he come near me after the base deed he had done, this fratricide! "Go away!" I commanded. "Go away!" He kissed my lips lightly again and again, and between kisses I complained of his foul behavior.

He kept on kissing me now on my eyelids, now my cheeks, and now my lips. Soon he was covering my body with kisses. I tried my very best to feel nothing. So hard did I try, my complaints changed to mere sounds void of sense.

I felt the by now familiar response that I so hated welling up. I was tired and lonely with the singular life I led. I could not deny my body its release. It ruled me and had its way. The worst of it was when I thought it almost over and he applied the best of his art. He prolonged my agony as wave after wave of shame washed over me, nor could I get away from him. I was thinking, "Yes, yes, I am so like you after all. We are both evil, scheming, creeping creatures of the night. I am as guilty as you. We both murdered Paris."

Afterwards he lay beside me stroking my body. I bit back a retort about how every time I made love to him I found one more reason to contemn him and admire Menelaus. I had an idea. It was worthy of Deiphobus himself but just what I needed at the moment. I was already so far gone in sin that one more offense hardly mattered. Besides, it was in the service of the Goddess.

"There is one thing you could do to make me happier," I fought back the excitement in my voice.

"You know I seek to please you."

It was a pretty speech for Deiphobus, but I did not listen — then. I could hardly wait to spill out my plan. "I would have you learn to trust me," I said.

"That is a hard thing for me."

"I would be left alone when I am tending to the needs of my people. I would not be followed about by guards. It insults my honor for them to think that Inanna cannot stand alone against the sky."

He paused and considered. "Very well," he said, and I was surprised he consented so easily.

But I knew he still did not trust me. Suspicion was his nature. It was only that I had softened his heart with lovemaking and made him drunk with Eros. I must flaunt this power if I were to make my plan successful. Odysseus could not even come to me if I were guarded. So when he left my room that night, it was I who kissed him and with that sealed my fate.

Night after night I did my penance, and soon I

asked and was granted other boons of my new King. I gathered all my Spartan women about me and installed them in my service, buying them back from their owners. They still remembered and revered me as their Goddess on Earth. They would do anything for me and keep their tongues to themselves.

They became my spies. I sent them among the people disguised as ordinary citizens, for by now they could speak the common vernacular. They were to report any person high or low who disobeyed my ban on human sacrifice. I told my people Inanna was no longer pleased by it. If anyone was caught offering a child to the Goddess of Death, no matter how desperate the conditions under siege, she would be hanged. Inanna would throw her body to the dogs, and it would be left unburied and without rites.

Now this was the worst fate of all both for the Trojans and for the Achaeans. If a body is not buried, the soul cannot rest after death. It is condemned not to live and not to die. It cannot pass to the Underworld. Instead, it haunts the living. People would promise anything just to have one handful of dust poured over their corpses.

I held audience freely now. I razed the People's Shrine and built a new temple not profaned with innocent blood. As I sat on my dais, the people would come to me and confess their ills. I would dispense justice and settle disputes. If anyone had a private matter, I would take him to a back room where his enemies could not hear.

The Goddess moved me, and I obeyed.

The new Sea People allies of the Achaeans knew nothing of fighting on land except quick raids for rapine and booty. So they stayed off shore and became the supply line, stretching to Agamemnon's newly conquered territories in Asia Minor. They enabled the Achaeans to sit in a foreign land and fight day after day with no end in sight.

Surprisingly, after their easy victories in Asia Minor and at sea, the Achaeans' luck deserted them. Hector and his allies were fighting for their homeland, and surely that gave them the advantage, that one last measure of devotion. Hector was defending a walled city that was impregnable as long as its supply line continued and could not be taken by direct assault as long as anyone remained on its ramparts.

But that alone could not account for the Achaeans' failure. Hector had advanced his front line as far as the Achaean trench and had several times penetrated into Achaean lines almost to the point where he could put the ships to the torch.

As I learned later and now suspected, the blame fell on Agamemnon. He continued to call himself King of Kings, but his chiefs no longer obeyed him. Achilles took himself apart and refused to fight. His men sat idle beside their ships. Other lesser kings, his vassals, followed him. Achilles nursed a grievance against Agamemnon for stealing away his concubine Briseis.

Agamemnon had started a new custom. When the women captives were taken, he walked among them and pointed to the most beautiful. They would be rounded up, and he would taste each one on successive nights, sometimes more than one a night. Only then would he decide which ones to keep and which to distribute among the other chiefs. No chieftain wanted a woman who wore the badge of another.

Deiphobus saw that the Achaean host was at its weakest point and decided to add what trickery he could to Hector's clash of arms. He did it in secret so that I did not know, for he suspected that I would contemn his means. I was born a Spartan and thought it not right unless a man confronted another openly when he meant to kill him.

Deiphobus had almost daily reports by runner of events transpiring in Boghazkeuy, the Hittite capital. The news from that city was bad, but he invented a way to turn it to his own advantage. He sent a secret missive to the Hittite King, so confidential that the runner who took it was later put to death. The Hittite King, in great grief, was only too happy to comply. He ordered a merchant with his caravan of goods to proceed to Troy. I saw the man entering the city gates when I was about my business in the lower town but thought nothing of it. Many men owned such ugly, scarred faces. Nor did I stop to wonder why he traveled alone or why he left his caravan well outside the city in the hills while he paid his call on Deiphobus.

Deiphobus named the merchant his envoy with credentials to negotiate for the Achaeans' surrender. Hector's lines fell back while the merchant and his caravan advanced across the field into the Achaean camp, announcing themselves by a staff with the head of Hermes.

Agamemnon was overjoyed that the merchant had brought such sumptuous gifts just for considering surrender. Solemnly the merchant and his family handed out brightly colored blankets and silks. No one wondered that day why the merchant's family consisted exclusively of women behind veils.

This merchant had been strictly instructed to pander to Agamemnon. So when Agamemnon said that his brother Menelaus deserved no gifts, he received none. Agamemnon intended to dishonor Menelaus for insulting him. Menelaus had confronted his brother before the assembled host and said with an unflinching gaze: "You make war on a disabled ship peopled by Trojan fishermen, a woman, a girl, and one eunuch and claim a one-half share of all the shields and swords captured in battle with the Trojan navy."

Agamemnon felt the mood of the assembly and the cold eyes of the chiefs fixed on him. He was cornered. Yet he would put a brave face on it. "Is not that woman called Helen our chiefest enemy? She must die by your own sentence," Agamemnon sought to be clever.

"Enemy or not she is still only a woman. And since I am her husband, she is mine to kill, not yours whether you are High King of Mycenae or not. In your haste you would have sunk my daughter Hermione to the bottom with the rest, and she is innocent of wrong-doing."

Whisperings had spread even among the troops that their chief was overreaching himself. It was said that he wanted to set himself up as another Priam, another Bull of Heaven, to lord it over them like an Asiatic emperor over his slaves. Agamemnon acted as if he had to answer to no one.

Agamemnon was happy when his brother took offense at his insult and retired to his own ship. Odysseus seconded Menelaus and left the assembly immediately. Achilles still refused to break his oath and sat by his oars with his men. The favorites of Agamemnon delighted in their gifts and waved the scarves about in the air, little suspecting that they would soon turn into their death shrouds.

Agamemnon, of course, graciously declined the offer to surrender, and the merchant just as politely retired. The Hittite disappeared quickly back into the hills from whence he had come. No one ever saw him again.

It was but days we had to wait before the dawn brought us the sounds of lamentation from the Achaean camp. Menelaus, Odysseus, and Achilles swiftly put out to sea beyond their companions. Their allies, the Sea Peoples, who never docked longer than it took them to put the supplies ashore, took fright, sailed out beyond the horizon, and were seen no more. Hector at first thought to take advantage of the confusion to mount a surprise attack. But when he marched out to battle, he got no farther than halfway across the field before he saw what was the matter.

Plague ruled. Men were sweating in fever, and their faces were erupting into tiny red pustule beads. Some god was wroth with them and did battle all alone.

Hector's men fled in a rout. The gates of the city could not open swiftly enough to hide them. They tried to climb the walls and seek protection even as kittens return to their mothers when frightened. Only those Trojan soldiers who had suffered this plague before and bore its scars felt safe enough to leave the city, pour oil into the trenches, and set them aflame. Day and night the fires were kept burning to purify the noxious vapors in the air and ward off evil spirits.

Day and night I kept a vigil in my shrine praying to the Goddess. The people fell to their knees with me. Nor would I lift my ban on human sacrifice. Yet so strong was the fright that a few of my subjects could not resist their panic. They disobeyed me, and I had no choice but to order their hanging. They had to be more afraid of me than of the plague, or all would be chaos. In all matters I let the will of the Goddess flow through me.

Sunset after sunset went by, and still Troy was spared the Goddess's wrath. Plague had often visited here, I was told, starting in the most crowded and humble quarters of the city. Often people feared more to live than to die, so disfigured were they. They did not want to stalk the streets as monsters.

Safe from the plague we remained, but people began to come to me begging food. The supply from Deiphobus was running low, and I had to devise a system of rations. I did not like to talk to him more than I had to. Yet this time I had to consult him in the light of day instead of merely at night when I did my penance and paid for my freedom.

He was sitting in his aviary playing his cithara while Hermione ran about persuading the parrots and the mynas to perch on her fingers and talk. It was strange these days to find him so idle. He was usually followed by a crowd of men seeking audiences or was busy receiving envoys. "Why all of a sudden have the Hittites stopped supplying us with food?" I asked.

"For the same reason that the Achaeans are laid low," he said and would not have explained himself.

"Have they rebelled and become our enemies?"

"They have more than they can do to keep themselves alive right now," he said. "They too are stricken with the plague." Deiphobus gave me his usual defiant look, daring me to criticize him.

"They are stricken with the plague and you invited one of their merchants to sue for peace with the Achaeans? You had the Hittite give them blankets and scarves that those who died had used?" I had wondered about those negotiations. Even then I had questioned how Deiphobus expected them to surrender so easily.

"I thought you were on our side at last," Deiphobus said with a bitter twist to his lips as if he had just tasted the lees of the wine.

All I could think of was his baseness. "You are no man. You are an evil spirit!" I burst into tears. I would say more, but I could not or I might ruin my plan to bring

Odysseus to me.

I took myself apart and kept to my room for several sunrises. I prayed for the people who were born in the same land I was. I thought especially of my own dear lord. This was merely the latest of the afflictions I had brought upon him.

We had to endure our isolation from the rest of the world and our famine through the cold season. The people were digging deep into their pithoi for food. The soldiers ate their fill first and then gave us what was left over. I kept for myself only what was necessary and gave the rest to the children. All food tasted bitter in my mouth.

Everyone in the palace lived on rations. Even Deiphobus looked haggard and tired. He had never sported much flesh and now grew thin. It was just as well that Paris was dead. He could not have survived.

Then I noticed that my portions began to increase. I looked to see if the Hittite merchants had returned, but the market stalls were empty. Hermione was eating well as were all the children, but everyone else's allotment remained the same. No doubt Deiphobus was playing favorites to preserve his family, and this was very bad policy. I upbraided him.

"It is impossible that anyone should even notice let alone resent it," he averted his eyes. I did not have time to guess what he was up to. Only much later when the Fates were about ready to cut off the cloth of his life did I learn. He had taken from his King's share of the rations to give to us. He was starving himself.

To his dying day I do not think I ever did understand him.

Early in the planting season of the tenth cycle of

the seasons since my capture, I was leaving the shrine late one night. People were gathered in the street. All were gazing up in horror and pointing. In the distance I heard Cassandra wailing doom. A great ball of fire trailing a tail of flame blazed across the skies. It looked like the Goddess combing out her long golden tresses, each strand of which is a thread of fate. So bright was the apparition it dimmed the other stars. Never had I seen anything to compare. But it was a portent just like the day the sky grew black in Sparta and swallowed up the sun. I felt the familiar chill. The Goddess was speaking.

I gave voice to her words even as they came to me. "Trojans, you have nothing to be frightened of. True, such sights portend some awful event. But the King who shall fall will be Agamemnon, King of the Achaeans. You will be saved."

So they were comforted when night after night the omen reappeared.

The Achaeans must have assumed the omen portended victory. Odysseus, Menelaus, and Achilles sailed back and rejoined those of the Achaeans who still survived, although their Sea People allies had disappeared for good. I heard later Achilles was so angered by the devastation that he took to the field despite Agamemnon.

Almost everyone without exception who comes into contact with the plague is stricken, but not Agamemnon. Miraculously, he was spared without a blemish, and he preened himself. He thought the gods had marked him out for a special fate. At that, they had.

Achilles rallied the remaining Achaeans and led them against Troy's walls by surprise. Hector barely had time to advance to meet him. Achilles killed Hector and dragged his body tied to his chariot back and forth in front of the city as if it were Hector who had brought the plague.

Leaderless for the time, Hector's soldiers fled back within the walls.

We had some good luck. The Hittite merchants returned, and our supply lines were reopened. But to our surprise it was only for the few sunrises needed to replenish our stores. The next time Achilles took to the field he drove all before him, broke through our lines, and ringed the city around, stationing men for a siege.

He intended to starve us out, and men whispered this was the end. They pointed at me and scoffed, for the first time doubting my powers. This was not as I predicted. I questioned myself. How had I offended? "Please, Goddess," I prayed, "if I have sinned, make me alone suffer. Let me atone. Don't lead my people off into slavery a second time."

Help came from the most unexpected quarter. I had so despaired that for two sunrises I had not dared show myself in the lower town. It was not out of fear but shame that I acted, hiding myself in my room. Suddenly I sensed that someone stood behind me in the shadows. I could feel that it was Deiphobus. He stood there in silence for a moment and was gone on cat's feet.

I don't know how long I sat there alone with my thoughts before I heard cheering. I ran out of the palace and saw crowds gathered near the city walls. The army was ringed around the ramparts, jumping up and down flinging their spears into the air. The people in the lower town had caught the infection too. They leaped into the air and cried for joy. I could not imagine what sudden reversal of fortune was upon us.

I ordered my litter-bearers to take me at once to the watchtower. A warrior came through the gate dressed in Hector's armor. I opened my mouth to scream. But then I realized from the limp that it was none other than

Deiphobus.

He had not been reared to arms. He had no practice with any weapon other than his cithara which he had often wielded as one. The only spare time he had been given to learn was the plague season and the time since the death of Hector, and that was hardly enough. It was impossible that a cripple should do battle.

The people of the lower town had small reason to love him and had feared him all their lives as some sort of loathsome spirit. Yet they cheered him, raised him up on their shoulders, and carried him around. They chanted, "Achilles-Killer, Achilles-Killer, Achilles-Killer!" For the first time he seemed a man and a King to them. This may have been the supreme moment of Deiphobus's life. He caught sight of me, and at once the look of triumph in his eyes was subdued and veiled with caution.

I could not believe what I heard. I climbed the watchtower. "Mother," Hermione said out of breath. She had scampered there despite my warnings to stay away. "Deiphobus has saved us. Look!" She drew me to the ramparts. Even then Trojan soldiers and their allies, crazed with happiness and exultant confidence, were lowering themselves from the walls and pouring out the gate, chasing the Achaeans back to their ships.

I saw Odysseus in his boar's helmet and Menelaus wielding his lion and griffin shield fighting off a band of wild Trojan warriors who tried to leap upon them as they dragged the corpse of Achilles back to their lines. Someone had killed Achilles and demoralized the Achaeans, that was certain. But how could it be Deiphobus?

"Look, mother," Hermione said, "there's Hermione. There I am." She looked proud with her nose in the air.

My daughter was pointing to the ground at

Achilles's feet where lay a crumpled pile of silks that had been a girl. I took her by the shoulders and shook her, "Hermione, are you crazed? What are you speaking of?"

"Haven't you heard, mother?" Hermione stared at me in disbelief. "She was a prostitute of the town who murdered another prostitute. She was hiding out from the kin of the murdered girl who had sworn revenge. Deiphobus offered her an honorable and an easy death, quicker than the one that was pursuing her."

I still could not understand. I could not make out even the form of the trampled girl now. Her own blood was mingling with the crimson of her silks.

Hermione tried to be patient. "Deiphobus asked to meet with Achilles to hand me over. He said he did not want me to be killed in the fighting. Menelaus was only too eager to get me back. Deiphobus stepped out with the prostitute donned in heavy veils. They walked up to Achilles in stately procession. She was a good actress to the very end. Deiphobus handed her over and returned alone almost as far as the Skaian Gate. Then he turned and shot Achilles dead with the bow and arrow concealed under his flowing robes of state." She jumped up and down and clapped her hands.

I was horrified. "Hermione, how could you do this to your father?"

She looked at me quizzically. "I just told you. Father shot Achilles!" she stomped her foot.

A crowd headed for me. They pulled me down from the ramparts and lifted me high onto their shoulders too. Deiphobus had restored my flock to me, but I could not thank him. That was his misfortune.

It was not until it was too late that Deiphobus had what he wanted from me. Now it is my misfortune. Forgive me, now that I am so close to the end of my days myself, my thoughts are peopled with the dead. Almost everyone I once knew is now gone to the Other Shore. They say even the noble Odysseus sailed away from Ithaca and never returned. But my mind is drifting.

XX

The Plot To Save The People Of Troy

One day as I was giving audience in my shrine I pointed to a shopkeeper and his neighbor to step forth and voice their grievances. These two seemed about to kill each other. I asked what was the matter that they had been disturbing the peace quarreling with each other and keeping their neighbors awake at night.

"Goddess," the aggrieved party stepped forward, "he will be making eyes at my wife."

I knew my people were on the mend when they could worry about anything other than their bellies.

At that moment there was an uproar. The people waiting to be heard were jeering and throwing pebbles at a beggar. His clothes were made of burlap, his robe as well as his hood, and he had mud smeared all over his face. He wore no shoes, the poorest of the poor. He barely hobbled along and without his cane could make no progress at all. The crowd jostled him from side to side.

The people shouted, "Go away! You are bad luck! We've had enough of that." No one offered him an alm.

"This will cease at once!" I rose to my feet. "May the Goddess smite you all if you have no better manners. He has more right to the attention of the Goddess than you do because his need is greater." I thought I had taught my people to show better charity to beggars. They were the protected of Zeus, god of the homeless wanderer.

They grumbled a little and then fell silent. I motioned to the beggar to follow me into the inner room where I received those I especially wished to favor.

The beggar threw down his stick. Age vanished from his limbs. He shoved back his hood with one swift motion. There stood Odysseus, straight as a warrior.

It had been so long since I cried that I had almost forgotten how. I opened my arms and ran to him.

"Meet me in this very room at the hour of the raven at the end of the second watch," he held me away from him. "Bring no one with you and no light or I shall depart at once, and you will never see me again. I shall signal my presence with two knocks on the door. You alone shall let me in and tell me at once and without hesitation why I should still trust you. Tell me what you will give me to prove yourself. If I am satisfied, we shall have further conversation. If not, you have seen your last of me. Do you understand?"

I could only nod "yes", for my tears would not let me speak. I did not want him to go, and I stumbled after him, but he was soon through the door.

For awhile I stayed to compose myself. I had to conceal that I had been crying. Thank the Goddess that I kept a supply of ceremonial paints in this back room. I painted around my eyes in blue, the angry mood of Inanna. If I scared my people, they deserved it.

Soon afterwards I dismissed the assembly. I had much to occupy my mind. It was best not to try to divine Odysseus's intentions. I must follow his directions exactly.

I avoided Deiphobus. I told him I had to run an errand of mercy to the family of a dead woman. That should be believable, for I had often done the like before.

He did not question me.

If I came alone, Odysseus knew he could trust me. I could not imagine what else was required. He was a pirate King and never rich. Yet it seemed to demean his honor to offer him money or jewels. Nor would that prove that I could be trusted. Yet he insisted that I tell him what I would give him, and that puzzled me.

Perhaps he wanted a base from within the city that he could operate from. Maybe I should find him a house suitable to the station of a beggar. At least I should offer it. The only problem with that was that there was no place within the city that was not now crowded with people, and he should not have privacy to work in. It would be dangerous, but danger was Odysseus's element.

I kept my appointment. I stood alone in the dark in the back rom of the shrine and waited. At every sound I started and checked the door, but no one was there. Perhaps this was a test of patience too.

When the knock came, it came unmistakably. Two sharp raps. With my stomach in my throat I hesitated a moment to compose myself and threw the door wide open. I waited for him to say something, then I remembered that it was I who was to speak first. "That you may trust me, I offer you a house or any kind of base of operations that you may choose."

To my shock he said nothing but took one step towards me. "I am sorry that you take offense. Perhaps you need money or weapons?"

He took another step towards me, and I fell back. Now I was becoming frightened. Something had gone very wrong. "Please tell me what you want, and it is yours," I pleaded. "I shall give you anything you name."

Still he was advancing towards me, forcing me back. With a bitter taste of irony, I saw why he wanted me

The Plot To Save The People Of Troy

to come alone and in the dark. That was what he meant by trusting. My experience with Deiphobus should have alerted me to this trap. "Very well," I said, "if that is what you want, I offer you myself."

A hand grasped my neck and shoved me backwards against the wall. In a flash I thought, "This is not Odysseus but some murderer who has killed him first and now plans to take me." I tried to free myself and squeezed the wrist of that hand, but it was like squeezing iron. He stepped into a shaft of moonlight falling through the light well. Menelaus!

My gasp turned into a moan. He stood before me disguised in a hooded cloak similar to the one Odysseus wore, his face besmeared with mud. Every angle and line in his expression stood rigid in judgment upon me, his faithless wife, and that judgment was utter condemnation.

This was an execution, not a trial. They planned to murder me, and the war would be over. There was no dignity in such an uneven struggle. I had failed. Somehow I had displeased the Goddess.

I dropped my hand and my head and awaited death. Deiphobus had not neglected to inform me again and again how Menelaus had sworn to kill me. And Menelaus was a man of his word.

I heard Odysseus's anxious voice in the doorway, "Remember, you promised to spare her tonight."

No longer could even I imagine what was going on. Did they plan to capture me and take me back to the Achaean camp to stand trial? Was that Odysseus's idea of playing fair? He had broken his promise to help save my people. The trickster had triumphed again.

"If I had not sworn by the River Styx to let you breathe yet a little while longer, I should make you a shade before you could say a word," said Menelaus. "Go, creature who was once my wife," he pushed me away. "Peddle your wares and trade your body however your lusts direct you. Odysseus says he has some use for you. I think you are long past any honest use, but we have no choice."

"And...I...have...some...little use for Odysseus," I put my hand to my throat. I tried to control my voice, but it would always be breaking off in sobs. I would not cheapen my thoughts with words. Besides, we were past words — Menelaus and I.

"Go ahead, wretch," said Menelaus, "make deals with Odysseus for your miserable life. But as surely as the sun rises, the next time you meet me you shall die by my hand. You will not wriggle past me or offer me your body."

"I shall do anything to help you take Troy if only you free them from their overlords and do not carry them off as slaves. I am content to die for them if I must...You much mistake me if you think my life sweet."

"We can trust her," Odysseus said.

Menelaus lifted my chin. I could barely see him through my tears. But his countenance was as resolute as I had ever known. He disappeared and waited for Odysseus outside.

I collapsed into Odysseus's arms, which were there before I could ask. I wept as if I knew no other language. The last time Menelaus had touched me he still loved me. I never thought to feel his hands without any warmth or gentleness. When he left for Crete we clung to each other. Our whole wedded life had been one series of good-byes. After ten cycles of the seasons we were still taking our leave of each other, and it still hurt. All the passion he had once cherished for me was changed to loathing. But the Goddess had warned me it must be so.

Odysseus tried his best to comfort me, stroking my

hair. "In my heart I believed in you no matter if you asked to be put off my ship, no matter if the Achaean camp cried with one voice that you had made Hermione conspire to slay Achilles. I persuaded Menelaus that if you did not call for the guards you could be trusted."

I could feel Odysseus's trust without a word from him. It had always been that way with us. The Goddess kept putting him in my path, taunting me with the choice of Menelaus for my husband. Odysseus kissed my forehead and laid his cheek against my head in resignation. He had accepted our fate. We still had our work to do, work which only we two could do together.

Odysseus held me until I was still. Then we planned to meet in this same place every night to plot the overthrow of Troy.

I left the shrine last of all that night. My nerves were so wrought up that I jumped when I heard a rustling sound. I looked up and saw an owl perching on the roof by the light of the ball of fire trailing flames that still stretched across the sky. Now I was not so certain whose victory and whose defeat it was presaging.

Too little had I thought of it anon, but now surely the end was near.

XXI

The Last Days Of Troy

Deiphobus seemed more distant. He complained of feeling weary. He would retire to bed early and alone. Even when I came at my accustomed hour to seduce him — I did not dare omit that now — he patted my cheek, kissed me, and turned me away to my own bed.

Often during a meal I surprised him staring at me. Not as he eyed me during the days of our early acquaintance, with lust and a sense of his own power. Now it was a large-eyed, vacant expression as if the life had been sucked out of him. I said to myself, "His soul is big in his eyes," and that surprised me. Before I had not suspected he owned one. It might get in the way of all his devisings. Once I asked him rather nastily, "Who has died?"

Yes, in those days my tongue still knew spite. Now that salt has turned into bitterness. I eat it and rue it every day of my life and will until I too die, for my burden of guilt over Deiphobus is heavy. Yes, in those days when I thought myself already old in experience, I was still young.

I thought it but lucky chance that he was aging before my eyes, perhaps too ill to notice that I was plotting revolution. The people believed me to be Inanna. My sign was in the ascendant, blazing fire in the sky. Every night it reappeared, and would until Troy fell. For their own good, I commanded them. One by one I called my most faithful followers among the commoners into my room in the shrine. I told them that I had been visited by a dream. On the third day of the new moon at the hour of the owl, they must rise up and do battle with their masters. Hector was dead. Deiphobus had usurped a throne that was never meant to be his. If they did not shun him, the Goddess would show her wrath, and they would surely die.

It was agreed that on the appointed night all those in collusion with me would wear a white armband of cloth tied around their wrists. These alone would be spared death or slavery. All others would meet their fates.

We divided the city into zones. Those who lived nearest the prominent citizens of Troy, who had long ago sold their allegiance to Priam and his sons, were to rise up first. In the stealth of the night they were to sneak to the doors of those very houses and slit the throats of the guards. Then they were to wait for the owners to emerge.

Those who lived nearest the walls had their own duties to kill the guards. Others were assigned to the temples. The palace, I told them, we could safely leave to our allies.

There was the sticking point. For ten cycles of the seasons they had lived in fear of the Achaeans. The Achaeans brought plague, the Achaeans brought famine. How could I expect them to trust their former enemies as friends? Even my powers might not carry so far.

They loved magic and stories, so I took a chance. I prophesied of a sign the Goddess would send them. It would be great and magnificent, far greater than any artist's vision. They would know it because it would rival in magnificence the fire in the sky. From the belly of this giant horse would be born men of bronze to lead them.

The beggar Odysseus became a familiar sight in Troy. Each time he came, he concealed weapons among his robes. I in turn took those weapons from him in my secret room of the shrine and transferred them to my followers. They took the weapons home to hide beneath the floors of their houses in their giant pithoi jars.

When I met with Odysseus at night it was my habit to bathe and anoint him. It was the custom, and he was a wanderer sacred to Zeus. I would have given the task to a maid, but none could I trust, for stripped of all his grime Odysseus showed his noble blood. I would do him the singular honor of being bathed by the Queen of Troy.

We had need of a candle, and Odysseus's embarrassment was plain to see. After I had dried, oiled, and dressed him and was kneeling to put on his sandals, he raised me to my feet and said, "You and I know each other without speaking. I cannot save you from Troy only to have Menelaus kill you."

But I had to bow my head, "As Menelaus wills it, let it be. That is between my lord and me."

The horse was the most famous of all Odysseus's inventions. He told me he dreamt of it one night and woke up knowing the entire plan in full. There was no other way the Achaeans could take Troy except by stealth and cunning, for a frontal assault would require more men than they had left. All hope of that had died with Achilles. Nor did the Achaeans have enough provisions themselves to starve the Trojans out.

Their Sea People allies had never returned. Agamemnon had already received disquieting reports about how the Sea Peoples had turned traitors again and were raiding the mainland, and for themselves, not as vassals of Troy. The Achaeans were impatient to return home to see what was left.

The Last Days Of Troy

At least then when the Achaeans needed courage the most, the Goddess spared them the knowledge of how Aegisthus had made himself the King of the Sea Peoples. Nor did Agamemnon suspect Clytaemnestra when she wrote wishing him good tidings. The King of Kings was always an easy prey to flattery. She asked him to light beacons from island to island and mountaintop to mountaintop, even to the peak of the mount of the Goddess that brooded over Mycenae, to signal his victory. But that is another story.

Even in such desperate straits Odysseus was hard taxed to persuade the Achaeans to adopt his plan.

When they were gathered about their campfire in conference, Agamemnon was the first to object. "Why can't we be satisfied with what we already have?" he asked. "After all, we cannot be greedy. We are all of us rich with spoils and lords of Asia." So spoke the conquering hero.

"Helen is not yet ours," Menelaus at once objected. "Our honor is not yet avenged nor the insult to our house, brother."

"You must wage your private wars yourself," Agamemnon said. "We have given you ten of our best cycles of the seasons and can spare no more."

"If so, Deiphobus triumphs," said Odysseus.

The other chieftains agreed at once with Odysseus. They hated Agamemnon.

"Your wits must be addled by some god," Agamemnon said. "You ask us to risk our lives all on the word of that traitress Helen. I say no!" Here was Agamemnon's strongest argument. My name was lower than anyone's among the Achaean host.

"If I can trust her, so can you all," Menelaus said. "I am more aggrieved and have less reason to trust her than any of you. But I have met with her and know her mind. Still, I will not break my faith with thee. The day we triumph, she will die."

Once more, no one wanted to admit how much more courageous Menelaus was than the rest of them. If he could do battle with the false Goddess Helen, so could they. When it came to a vote, they shouted Agamemnon down. But the High King held onto power in any way he could. He volunteered to help in some capacity, but did not specify which until he heard Odysseus out.

Odysseus's plans were always beyond the imaginations of lesser men, which is why they succeeded. Yet, this plan was so fantastic and risky that he had much to do to convince them that it was their last chance.

The next night Nestor, who was well beyond the years of fighting, put out to sea. He sailed to a nearby island in the Great Sea where the forests were not yet depleted. There his men built a great wooden horse, towering forty handspans into the air. The smithies decorated it with a collar of bronze melted down from the spoils the Achaeans had taken in their many battles along the coast of Asia Minor. They studded the collar with jewels and its eyes with sapphires so that it was the finest horse anyone had ever seen. Then they built a great raft of logs and by night ferried it back to Troy's shores.

That night was the last before the appointed doom of Troy, if the Goddess should will it.

That evening I had much to do at the shrine. I had told the people that the horse, the animal favored by the Goddess, was about to appear. They must urge their fellow citizens to admit the horse to the city and spread the word that the Goddess would bless them if they did. But nothing could be said about the men in bronze that the horse would give birth to or the Goddess would desert them for the rest of their days. I, Inanna, would be put to death by "the powers of darkness". That was another name for Deiphobus, or so I imagined then.

Silently they filed past me, and I handed to each one an armband of white cloth to tie around his wrist tomorrow night. This was my farewell. After Troy fell my work would be completed, and I must go. They would be free to set up their own government, appoint their own King as they had done aeons ago, and find their own Goddess. I would appear to them again in another form.

My people fell to their knees before my throne and kissed the hem of my garment. I laid my hands upon their heads and blessed them. This reminded me much of the last leave-taking of my Spartans on the day before Sparta fell. I hoped for better luck this time. My Spartan women could not keep their eyes dry. They were going home.

As soon as I arrived back at the palace I went straight to my children. I kissed Hermione and lingered long. Then I kissed each of my six sons. Odysseus had promised to bring them back to the Achaean ships. My sons by Deiphobus were in great danger, but Odysseus promised to send them to safety. Perhaps I should never see them again, but at least they would not have their brains bashed out on the battlements of Troy. So much did I trust Odysseus that I had no doubt of their salvation. Yet not even Odysseus could turn back fate.

Little did I suspect that only one of my children would I ever lay eyes on again in this life, for a reason far beyond the powers of Odysseus.

Coward that I was, I wanted to avoid Deiphobus. I imagined myself brave when I told Odysseus, "It will be my lot to kill my third husband."

When I had time to think twice about it, I wanted to surrender that task to Menelaus or Odysseus who would do it gladly. Yet they would also do it brutally with the sword.

I owed the father of my sons better. I would kill him gently using my medicinal arts. I would invite him inside my bedchamber at the last light of day and make love to him to soothe him. I would offer him a cup of wine. Then he would sleep his life away. When they found his corpse, they could do as they wished to the last King of Troy. He would be beyond them.

That night I was walking on the acropolis because I could not sleep. Still the ball of fire trailing a tail of flames lighted up the sky like dusk. I could see Deiphobus approaching me. He held his cithara.

"I see we are fellow night strollers," he said. "Shall I play a tune to lull us both to sleep?" His voice made me shiver. It was queer somehow, very brittle and make believe like an actor.

"No," I said, "I am too tired. I am going to bed."

"And not even a kiss good-night?" he grabbed my arm and stared straight through me with eyes that seemed to rival the ball of fire in intensity.

"No," I pulled away and fled back to my room.

But a little of the old Deiphobus was alive that night. He sang of Medea whom Jason courted to help him gain the Golden Fleece. She risked everything for him, gave everything, including the lives of her father and her brothers. She forswore herself for him and damned herself forever. But when he took her back to Iolkos, he did not remain faithful to her as he had promised with many words of love. She had her terrible revenge. How could I not see that night as I lay awake weeping at the sadness of his melody that Deiphobus would have his?

XXII

Defeat And Triumph

The last day of Troy dawned. I could not seem too anxious even though I knew what sight would greet the townsfolk. I had no idea whether Menelaus would kill me outright or put me on trial and execute me publicly. Odysseus had promised to save me, and I had declined. Today my fate should be complete, my mission accomplished. No mortal should seek to live beyond his allotted span, for that is to mock the gods. All was in the hands of the Great Mother. In that I rested content.

Soon there were shouts of mixed joy and disbelief from the lower town. Everyone was jostling to be the first to climb the battlements and look out. I had to pretend ignorance and surprise as my maids dressed me. Deiphobus and I went by litter. After last night I feared to meet him again, but now his face was inscrutable.

Though we were the rulers, we had to fight our way into the watchtower. There, where the Achaean camp had been, towered the horse, a fearsome and a magnificent wooden giant. He seemed to touch the heavens on that sunny morning.

The fires of the camp burned low, and the tents stood just where the Achaeans left them. Not a man to be seen. We watched and watched for the sign of life that I knew we would never find.

Deiphobus said, "We shall see what goes here," and ordered the gates to be opened. The King and I advanced following the Trojan army, with the nobles and the people behind in solemn procession. We walked among the camp and looked in each tent. Here a cot was crumpled with the form of the last occupant and all but warm from the impress of his body. There were the remnants and scraps of a last meal. Not even the chamber pots had been emptied. At one camp site we found dice and cards, at another a pile of gold talent chips used for gambling. But nowhere on the horizon could anyone see the sign of a ship. All was silence.

Now one person and now the next dared to meet his fellow's eyes and read the message there. One laughed, and the next leaped into the air. A third chortled, and a fourth broke into song. Aprons, sashes, and even money were tossed into the sky, anything a person had on him. This was a day they imagined they would never tire of passing on to their grandchildren if they lived fourscore and ten. I looked around to make certain no one had misunderstood me and worn his white armband too early. No one had.

One neighbor shouted to the next, "The cowards have gone home!" The cry was raised so loud that the gods could hear it on Mount Olympus.

Deiphobus had himself lifted onto the shoulders of the soldiers. He wore the bull's head crown of Priam and looked as much the Bull of Heaven as he ever had. He spread his arms, "Today I give you victory!" He smiled, and now I sometimes think that smile the bravest gesture he ever made.

Everyone gathered around the horse and stood in silence gazing up at it, shielding their eyes from the light blazing from its great bronze collar.

Defeat And Triumph

I wet my lips, "That horse is sacred to the Goddess."

"Bring it inside the walls!" my friends among the people shouted, perhaps a bit too precipitously. They were gazing at it in adoration as a sign from the Goddess. "Take it to the Temple of Inanna!"

Out of nowhere, it seemed, the red-haired Cassandra appeared, her eyes as wild as her appearance. She looked as if she had not slept in days and was buoyed on only by the strength of one emotion. "Stop!" she shouted, and everyone stared at her. "Fools you be, all of you. Can't you smell the deceit and the trickery here? I smell blood. I tell you I smell blood!"

"Cassandra!" Deiphobus reproved her. "You can see for yourself that not a soldier lingers. What danger can there possibly be?"

"Burn the horse! I tell you, burn the horse if you would live yourself to see the next sunrise, brother."

My heart thudded in my chest. I knew Cassandra was a self-styled prophetess, but I did not know she could predict the true. So upset did her forebodings make some of the soldiers, that they shot several arrows upward that stuck in the belly of the beast before Deiphobus raised his hand.

Deiphobus's face was hardened into stone. "Take her away!" he shouted. "Cowards all," he glared at them, "what harm can this horse do us if we leave it outside the walls to see if it is cursed or blessed?"

This too I had not foreseen and did not know what to say. I dared not advise against caution, or Deiphobus might suspect me.

Then out of the marshes ran a youth all bespattered with mud and his clothes torn. He looked wild but just as eager to reach us. I was proud of him. I had helped to school him along with Odysseus. He did not even forget to throw himself at Deiphobus's feet. The guards began to close in around him, but again the King held up his hands. "Let us hear what this last Achaean has to say for himself," Deiphobus said. He took the youth aside and questioned him closely a long while.

My heart thudded so hard I thought I would die. "Peace," I told myself. "Soon you too will have your rest."

The Bull of Heaven put his arm around the youth's shoulders, "We owe this youth our gratitude. If not for him, we would be eternally cursed by the Goddess. The Achaeans asked their prophet what they must do to return home in safety. She told them that since they had sailed in blood, sacrificing a princess to speed them to Troy, they must sacrifice a youth to appease her on their return. This poor boy was the one they selected. He hid himself in the marshes. Meanwhile, to please the Goddess, they had built an image to her hoping to draw her favor. They left it here on the dock, thinking that we would fear and shun it, perhaps burn it. Then we would draw the wrath of the Goddess down upon Troy."

Here the people gasped.

"The Achaeans made their departure as mysterious as possible to frighten us and make us afraid of the horse. They hoped we would not draw it into the city and gain the favor of the Goddess in addition to having won the war," Deiphobus continued. "As a further obstacle, they built it forty handspans high and gave it no wheels. But we shall overcome their silly devisings. We shall draw it not only into the lower town but up the road to the acropolis, even to the very sanctuary of Inanna herself!" He pointed towards heaven in a dramatic gesture.

"Perhaps this escaped Achaean lies," I said to deflect suspicion from myself. But Deiphobus only looked at me sadly.

That day was a hot one, and many people died hoisting the great horse onto a wheeled platform by means of ropes and pushing and pulling it up the hill to the temple. I wept that they should make such a sacrifice. Surely the new Troy would be built on their blood. Nor did I dare picture how hot it must be inside the belly of the horse for Odysseus, Menelaus, Ajax, and the other chieftains despite the air holes drilled in the top. I walked along beside the procession to give the people courage, and strangely so did Deiphobus for whom walking any great distance was difficult. But I could not begrudge him his last great spectacle.

That evening Deiphobus proclaimed such a celebration as the world has never seen and is not likely in these latter days to see again. Great amphoras from the wine magazine of the palace were hoisted out and given freely to all comers. The commoners were allowed to walk about on the acropolis at will, as was not permitted except at the times of the festivals. If Deiphobus kept up like this, he would become the most popular monarch ever.

The kitchen slaves were busy all day preparing a banquet. In the evening air this too was served on tables. The fishermen contributed their catch, the first in many moons, which the cooks cut up into a stew that smelled of onions and garlic. Pomegranates, olives, and nuts of all kinds flowed freely. No longer was there any need to hoard.

As it grew dark there was music. People clapped their hands and kept time. Man danced with man and woman with woman, woman with man, and even man with dog so happy was everyone. They did not even look to see who their partner was. Torches lighted the night sky. The women hung garlands of flowers around the horse's neck, ears, and tail. The Achaean youth who had told all was the guest of honor. They hoisted him up onto the back of the horse and showered him with money. Few could throw forty handspans, but they were too drunk to care and just tossed money into the skies wherever it landed. Soon the hooves of the horse were buried in piles of gold.

The dancers linked hands, and holding torches circled around the beast. Each boy in town proved himself by climbing the horse and sitting astride its back. The dancers formed a human chain and wove their way in and out the legs of the horse endlessly singing paeans.

Even the soldiers of Troy were rolling on the ground and in the bushes with their favorite wenches. They had no need to post guard tonight.

Deiphobus took a goblet of wine and drank it down. He pressed my arm, "Come, let us take a walk." I had no reason to deny him that. Besides, soon I had to start thinking about what I did not want to ponder. It was almost time. Soon everyone would be retiring to bed or sleeping where he fell never to wake again.

We strolled around the horse, and already the crowds were beginning to thin. I did not know what to say, so I said nothing. Perhaps this would be the last night I would ever see too, so I tried to gaze at the stars. I said to myself, "Soon I shall walk along your silver rays to join you, brothers."

"Helen...." Deiphobus sighed like the name of a lost child.

That restored me to myself. "Come," I whispered. "Come, let's to bed. We have much reason to celebrate." I tried to put promise in my voice, as much as I had heart for.

"Not we, my dearest," Deiphobus said, "not we. Perhaps Odysseus, Menelaus, and the rest up there in the belly of the beast."

I died on my feet, for I swear to this day my heart stopped beating. He knew everything and had been scoffing at me. He had not acted until now, until the Achaeans were trapped. Now he would give the order, and his soldiers would shoot fire arrows into the horse. He had turned all our tricks on us and defeated even Odysseus.

But Deiphobus did not give me time to react. Already he was drawing me after himself into the palace. We were in his room. "Come, Helen, do not look so shocked. And please, at the last, don't insult me by taking me for a fool," he said tiredly. He had taken off his last mask.

He made me sit down. "Don't think this is not difficult for me," he said. "My life was sweeter to me than to most men who walk under the sun because I had to fight so hard for it. I thought I had gained everything a man could want, even your heart, Helen. Then one night I caught you with Odysseus and Menelaus. At first I thought to kill you at once without explanation," he reminisced like a man fourscore and twenty who had resigned himself to his fate.

"So it was you!" I croaked. I remembered the rustling I heard at the shrine the first night I met Odysseus and Deiphobus's innocent evening strolls.

"Yes," he said. "I brooded on it and kept to my own bed. I could not bear to again feel your lying arms around me. But it was my doom to love you even though I knew your treachery. My life without you, my dream, was nothing. You are my soul, the beauty and the life I always wanted to feel and could not. So I decided to punish you by giving you your wish."

"Punish me?" I said. I was as simple as a child and had to be led.

"Yes, punish you. I shall die even as you wish, and you too shall die even as you seem to wish by the hands of that unworthy Menelaus. I can make you see your error and know your heart no other way. But better to be wise once before we die than to live long and foolishly."

I felt him on the verge of something I could not bear to hear.

He took my hands in his. Mine were cold and his warm. "Darling, your innocence is your beauty. In your heart you can still believe in the goodness of other men although you have met little but cruelty. You die in vain, for the Achaeans will burn Troy from the palace down to the smallest shanty. I have my spies, remember? Your people will be massacred for their pains in rebellion. Your women and children will be chained together and taken as slaves. You cannot guarantee their freedom no matter what the Achaeans promised you."

"No!" I nearly screamed, but he put his hand over my mouth. Then I was choking back sobs. How could the Goddess abandon me so? I felt all alone. The only other living presence was Deiphobus. The rest of the world had vanished.

"Oh, why couldn't you see in time through your hate for me that it was I, not Menelaus, not Odysseus, who could deny you nothing? I gave you freedom to walk among your people once you found your power over them. Before that I only feared for your safety. If you had told me it pleased you to feed them all from gold bowls I would have consented. I would have built them palaces. And now, because you have distrusted me, you have given these people who trusted you over to death."

"Goddess!," I wept. "Speak to me, Goddess!" But

Defeat And Triumph

she kept her silence.

"You should have spoken to me, not your Goddess, Helen. And don't think it gives me any pleasure to see you hurting so," he kissed my hands. "Now," he said, and for the first time I could see he was crying too, "I believe you are to seduce me and then do me unto death."

I reached out and touched his cheek. He kissed my fingers as they brushed by, "For me, you are the only Goddess." Polyphemus had indeed done something noble.

His need for me was so great it howled out like a storm in the wilderness. And like the Goddess shedding her warming rays on mankind when moved to sympathy, I gave him all I had and kept nothing back. I tried to make up in a little time what not even a lifetime could do. No shame did I feel as our bodies wove in and out of each other like the linked dancers carrying torches as they whirled around the horse. Always the horse, like a shadow falling on us and dooming us. And this, the last flicker of light before the long darkness.

His fingers touched me with an awe that was almost religious, the way the old women of Sparta used to grasp the hem of my garments. I felt the same tremulousness and fear mixed with a deep, abiding trust. At the moment of culmination he seemed to experience a mystical union with that which was greater than himself.

"You have forgiven me," I said. "No other man would have done so."

"One does not hold the Goddess to account for her deeds," he said. "She does as she pleases with her worshippers."

Never had anyone worshipped me so, but never had I felt less like a Goddess, more human, or more frail. Inside me, where the Goddess used to lodge, was all

Deiphobus or nothing.

Already even as we lay together for the last time I could hear screaming from the lower town. So soon had the chiefs lowered themselves from the belly of the horse when the city slept in a drunken stupor and opened the Skaian Gates. So soon had they signaled Agamemnon and the rest of the Achaean fleet as they sailed towards shore from the island where they had been hiding. So soon did the sober Achaeans sneak into Troy.

Deiphobus could hear them too. "Good-bye, my life, my love," he said. "We shall see each other once more before the long darkness, but never again like this. There are a few necessities a King must attend to before they reach the palace."

In my mind's eye I could see it all happening even as he left me. I had put the storm into motion, but it had a life of its own. The Achaeans gathered in groups outside the homes of the town notables and the soldiers who had carelessly flung down their armor the night before. The Achaeans pounded on their doors. "Come out, you fools!" they shouted. "Meet your doom!"

The Trojans woke with a start from their drunken stupor. They fumbled about in the dark trying to find their swords. But no sooner did they step outside their doors, than they were struck dead without knowing what happened. Their wives and their daughters cowered in dark corners, but the Achaeans were hungry for them. The conquerors dragged them out onto the streets to be lined up in chains.

Those wearing white armbands joined in the fray against their fellow Trojans even as I had instructed them. But when it was clear which way the battle would go, not even their armbands protected them. Achaeans who had long hated them stabbed them in their backs, and they fell

Defeat And Triumph

to the earth, their cries of betrayal rising up to me. I felt each one of them like a pain in my vitals. Yet I was powerless.

Soon I heard a great crashing sound. The doors of the palace were rammed and forced. The cries of Priam's harem as they fled about the palace rose to the heavens. Soldiers pounded on the roof, shouting to each other. I could hear the swoosh of Trojan arrows trying in desperation to find their marks, but they were chopping and pounding with unmatched fury at something. It seemed as if the whole remnant of the army were throwing itself against a wall. They groaned with the effort.

Then I heard a sharp cracking and ripping of wood. The building trembled as what felt like a great tree tumbled down onto the roof and over the side onto the ground. The walls shook and the mirror cracked. Brushes and combs slid off the dresser. I fell to the floor and imagined the roof crashing in on me, but it was only an illusion. They must be trying to tear the palace apart so that the Achaeans could not capture it. I heard the cries of men being crushed and buried underneath the rubble. Then a moment of silence, followed by the pleas of survivors.

I knew. In their last spasm of denial the Trojans chopped down the watchtower that stood on top of the palace and tumbled it down upon the Achaean horde below forcing the doors. Soon the tramp of feet signaled reinforcements rushing up to the palace gates. Now the Trojans' last hope was finished.

I dragged myself to my feet, although I could hardly stand. My legs were wobbly as I pulled myself to the door by holding onto the bedpost and each chair and chest. The amphora with the wine had fallen over onto the floor and cracked. Wine oozed out of it, a purple stain on the floor.

I struggled out of the room, staggering as if in a drunken stupor. In the aviary the birds flew about in a panic. Their cages had fallen or been jogged open, and many parrots lay dead on the floor. Others flew against the walls and injured themselves. I saw one lying on the ground struggling. One of its wings was broken, and with the other it was beating itself about in a circle.

"I have done this," I said to myself as I fell to my knees in front of the poor creature.

Before I left the aviary for the last time, for now I see it only in my dreams, I noticed that Helen and her cage were nowhere to be seen. "Deiphobus would not let her suffer long," I told myself. Yet even now as I write, who would have thought it, but Helen sits perched on my shoulder watching me, older than us all.

I made my way to the throne room where Priam and his hundred wives awaited their fate. The women lay kicking and screaming, rolling about on the floor. They tore their hair and scratched their faces, ripping their silken robes. They were raised to be soft and delicate like so many parrots to grace a harem, and not this. They felt in their vitals what lay before them. Those who survived the mass rapes would be put into chains and fetters while they were still bleeding and too sore to walk, they whose hands had never known anything rougher than the texture of fine linen. They would be marched down to the ships, torn from the only home they ever knew, and taken as booty to a foreign land to work as slaves. They who knew nothing but the arts of allurement would carry water, scrub halls, and work like donkeys until they died.

Those who saw me only cried harder, begging me to save them. They rushed for me, held onto my long robes, and I had to fight them back and slap them senseless to get them to be quiet.

Defeat And Triumph

"Aren't you afraid to die?" one of them said.

I smiled bitterly. "They will not dare touch me. Only Menelaus may do me to death."

Into the room rushed a pack of Trojan soldiers carrying two youths. They lay them down in front of me. I imagined I saw the bodies of my two slain brothers, those dear corpses from long ago. So alike were they! But no, they were the bodies of my twins, Castor and Pollux the Younger, only eleven cycles of the seasons but already men. Their eyes were still open, and they breathed. But their wounds bespoke death.

"They heard the clatter of arms, grabbed their own swords, and joined the fray on the roof," said an officer. "They were shot by arrows before we could stop them."

I touched their foreheads and kissed them each good-bye as I had done long ago with my brothers. Odysseus had failed to save them, the sons of Menelaus, his heirs to the throne of Sparta. Menelaus had made war to regain them, but in their hearts they knew no other home but Troy, no other father but Deiphobus. I could not control their destinies. When they were born, I thought it was to godlike deeds so greater than mortal did they appear. Now they had fulfilled that wish in a way that showed the hand of the Sisters. Such a glorious feat for such little men.

I stayed to close their eyes. I dared not think what had happened to my other sons by Deiphobus.

Now we all heard a great crash and screaming. The doors to the palace had been forced. Soon they were at the doors of the throne room. Priam, whom I had assumed to be blissfully unaware of all that transpired around him, had at the last staggered to his feet. Some glimmer of his past state awoke him to courage. "We shall fight them!" he shouted and started for the door, Hecuba and Hector's widow Andromache trying to stop him.

"I will meet them on my feet," I said and stood up, no longer afraid. They had done their worst, and now I understood how it had always been with Deiphobus.

At that moment the doors to the throne room gave way, and in burst a horde of soldiers, drunk with triumph. They grabbed Hecuba and Andromache and trampled Priam where he stood. I recognized the Spartans in the lead. The women clutched me as if I could protect them. I tore my way through the crowd of women and leaped in front as the soldiers rushed towards us. "Stop, you cowards!" I yelled at them in their own language. "I who was once your Goddess on Earth curse you to the end of your days!"

A few in front who heard me stopped in terror, recognizing me. Others ran closer, looked back to see what had happened to their comrades, and slowed down in uncertainty.

"Who is that?" one too young to remember me shouted to his comrades.

"That is Queen Helen, the Goddess on Earth," a veteran said. "Menelaus forbade any of us to even touch her on pain of instant death."

"Stop!" I cried at the soldier who was ripping the clothes from one of my women — for my women they had become, the last of my people. I grabbed the sword of a Spartan too scared to prevent me. When the Achaean did not heed, I saw only red as I plunged the sword into his back. Before he died, he knew me. To this day a few of these Trojan women still serve me, although we are all old. One dips my pen in the inkwell for me and smiles.

I needed only one example before the others started to cower before me. "Get back!" I shouted, poking the sword at them and jabbing them. "Is this what you call victory to trample an old man to death, to rape women? Does it make you happy to burn a great city and pillage its temples? Will the gods thank you for this? The Goddess does not mean for this to be!" Suddenly I knew. She had not failed us, but men had.

Two men were pushing through the crowd of terror-stricken soldiers. I knew them before I saw Menelaus and Odysseus with their bloodied swords. "Well," I shouted, "here we greet the conquering heroes, the two chiefest of the cowards!" I laughed bitterly. "They who promised me they would save my people have lied to me, yeah, even broken their sacred oaths. They have massacred them. But, know you, the Goddess will be revenged. If you will kill me, come and take me! Let he who is man enough try."

Menelaus stared at me as I presumed greatly, "I told you that the next time you saw me you would meet your death."

"Then meet your fate first!" I pointed to the corpses of our two sons. "Look what you have done."

He had not expected the plan to save them to fail. He knelt beside them and lifted their lifeless hands. Then he wept as if each sob were wrenched out of him. But I could not pity him.

"Helen," Odysseus said, and he did not seem surprised, "it was Agamemnon who failed us. He pretended to agree to our plan. But when he had the men alone at sea he told them that the spoils of Troy and its women should be theirs. He promised that he would take no booty and his share should be theirs. He has done this out of spite because we chiefs would not follow him."

I held the rein of my sanity even a little longer. "Odysseus, I charge you on pain of your life," I said, "to see that these my last people, my women, be spared their degradation. You shall answer for their lives and their spotless honor."

He nodded his assent and charged his Ithacans to obey.

"Do you dare to make deals with us?" Menelaus said, even as he strove to master his grief.

"Do you dare to call yourself a man? Agamemnon! His name is a thorn in my heart. Is not one of you," I shouted to the multitude, "man enough to free yourselves of this tyrant? Do you fear him? Well, I do not!" Feeling my hands grasp hard my sword, I broke through the crowd which parted in fear before me and ran out of the doors.

I could feel that Menelaus pursued me without even looking. But he was heavy with bronze armor and weapons, and I was light of foot and ran like the wind. I needed not my strength because I planned not to live out the day. The soldiers were busy at their plundering and butchering and looked not for me, the accursed Helen.

As if a prayer were answered, I spotted Agamemnon more quickly than imagination could wish. There he flaunted himself for all to see at the foot of the blazing Temple of Inanna beside the horse. His soldiers formed a ring around it. On the roof at the very pinnacle stood Cassandra, her red hair flying about her. I might have guessed she would never desert her temple. She would die with it. In her hand she held the sacred image of Inanna in gold which had stood on the altar. Soon the roof would collapse, and she would die with her goddess.

"Conqueror," she screamed to Agamemnon, "if you dare to take me, you will trespass against the Goddess. She will pursue you, hunt you down, and you will die like an animal in a net entangled in your own evil doings," she prophesied more true than she was ever to know. For my sister struck Cassandra down before she ever saw the corpse of her lord and conqueror.

Cassandra leaped off the roof to her death, but there were too many soldiers ringed about to accomplish her wish. Agamemnon had ordered them to catch her, for he would have her. They brought her struggling to him. He grabbed her by the hair, pulled her head back, and kissed her, and his men laughed. She scratched his face just like a wildcat.

At that moment I reached him. I drew my hand back to strike and forever stop his vain boasting, but fate reached out. I was not allowed to deliver the blow that awaited him at the hand of my sister. Menelaus grabbed me around the waist and pulled me back just in time, and my sword merely grazed Agamemnon. But it was enough to make him jump back and face me. I spat in the face of this King of Kings.

"Is this the royal whore, still alive?" Agamemnon taunted Menelaus.

"Look to your own oaths, brother," said Menelaus. "You have broken the most sacred oath you swore by the River Styx not to harm the Trojans that helped us." He turned around and dragged me after him.

I broke free. "Go ahead and obey your brother as you have always done. Kill me. I am not afraid to die. See, I will even help you," I ripped open my dress at the breast. "I die at the hand of a coward who will not even see justice done."

"He will be punished," Menelaus said through his teeth.

"Then let me live to see it. I ask no more. That is only fair," I said, "since you broke your bargain with me."

He struggled with himself. He looked as if he would lunge at me, and I closed my eyes to meet my fate. I heard his sharp intake of breath followed by the sound of his sword clanking back into its sheath. He yanked me to him and gave me his cloak to cover my nakedness. The last I ever saw of the city in which I spent ten cycles of the seasons, I saw slung over his shoulder. I looked on my people in chains, white armbands or not, and called to them, "You shall be avenged!"

As we hurried out the gates, I saw my people being led out by the shipmasters while the soldiers of the Achaeans danced drunk in the streets. They had adorned themselves with the gold bracelets and pearls of the houses they had pillaged. One had tied around his neck the girdle of a maiden.

But only the last of the stragglers remained. By the time we reached the ships, all of Troy smoked and blazed like a giant volcano.

Menelaus took me to his tent. There were Priam's women that Odysseus had saved. They greeted me with tears. There sat Atossa richly robed, much older with gold rings dangling from her ears. On her lap sat her little son and Menelaus's. She did not rise when she saw me nor did she look surprised. She glanced once towards Menelaus, and her gaze spoke of resignation. He met her look, and I did not want to witness what passed between them. She rose and left the tent, placing her son in my lap. Her eyes were two wells of tears.

The next day we found Atossa's body. She hanged herself. We burned her corpse, laid her ashes in an urn, and buried her before we set sail from Troy's shores.

I raised Megapenthes to manhood, and several cycles of the seasons ago Menelaus married him in grand style. It was the same day that Hermione married her cousin Orestes from Mycenae. But of course Atossa's son could never rule Sparta.

Defeat And Triumph

That evening the Achaeans were banqueting and gorging themselves. They made merry and danced with each other, singing bawdy Egyptian songs. I remembered from last night (or was it another life?) the sounds of merrymaking in the doomed Troy.

The singing of "When You Embrace Me" stopped. There was the sound of scuffling and cries of astonishment. Nothing, I thought, was left to surprise me when I heard Menelaus's voice saying, "Why, Hermione...."

I leaped to my feet and fled out of my tent. There stood the daughter I thought never to see again. Deiphobus, disguised in a plain cloak, led her by the hand. She carried Helen in her gold cage and Deiphobus's cithara. Deiphobus had promised I would see him once more.

Menelaus ordered the guards to stand back. He approached the child who had been his favorite with outstretched arms, caring naught for Deiphobus. But she spat at him and threw her arms for comfort around Deiphobus's neck.

I did not stop to take notice of the shocked expression on Menelaus's face. I flew to them and threw my arms around both. "Hermione," Deiphobus said, stooping down to speak to her, "this King is your father. You must go with him, do him honor all the days of his life, and be a staff in his old age even as you would have been to me."

I did not turn away to hide my tears. I could not be ashamed of them.

Hermione wept, "You are my father, and I will have no other." She clung to him as if her life depended upon it.

Deiphobus forced her away from him and turned to Menelaus. "You must vow to me by the River Styx that you will deal gently with her no matter what she says, or I shall not release her to you." Swiftly he flashed a knife and held it to her throat. Everyone gasped and backed away except me. Strangely, his action neither surprised nor shocked me. "Swear it, or I shall put her out of her pain even as I did to my own sons so you barbarians should not bash out their brains against the battlements of Troy. Swear it, for Helen is here by her own will while Hermione is not."

So that is what happened to the last sons I ever knew! I could not weep for them, for they were lucky to escape so easily. But to this day my womb has remained barren in sorrow or perhaps as the penalty I must pay to the Goddess.

I waited for Menelaus to trade harsh words with him, but he surprised me. He said gravely, "I swear by the River Styx, I who have never broken an oath but one, that I shall not harm my daughter Hermione. She is entitled to think of me as she will."

Still the soldiers had to drag Hermione off to her tent as she howled, "Father!" with strangling cries that were terrible to hear. I tried to comfort her, but she shook me off. To this day she calls Menelaus by his title and the memory of Deiphobus "father". And when she is alone she plays Deiphobus's cithara. To this day, he sings his songs of loss and sorrow through her, and his voice haunts me still.

As soon as Hermione was separated from him, Deiphobus had no defense. The curs fell upon and disarmed him. I could not protect him who had been King, although I was mortal enough to try. "Fools," I said, "without him you would never have taken Troy!"

But Deiphobus's eyes met mine. His manhood could no more stand to have revealed the sacrifice he had made for me than he could bear the catcalls of "eunuch". It was the hardest thing I ever did, but I swallowed my words. I let him die with dignity.

Never to this day have I told Menelaus our secret, and he and I now understand each other. But I think he has guessed how great was the love his rival bore. Neither have we spoken of Atossa, and Menelaus built a magnificent tomb in memory of her. The Spartans call it the "Menelaion".

"Name the manner of your death," Menelaus said to Deiphobus when Agamemnon tried to intervene, for he had heard the commotion. This was unlooked for clemency. I had imagined unspeakable tortures. Yet, though I did not guess it, Menelaus was already looking towards the future I did not think of. Even Deiphobus was shocked, he who was never surprised at anything.

"I leave Helen in better hands than I imagined," he said. "Very well then, take me to the place of execution." His face was impassive.

I thought nothing had yet happened when Menelaus called me. Deiphobus was lying in a cot in a tent. He bled from the wrist he had been allowed to slit. This was an honor indeed, perhaps a tribute to the man who loved me as much as Menelaus. Each had given me what was dearest to him. One gave up a kingdom, the other forswore himself. They understood each other.

He put his arm about me. I wept on his breast.

"I die content," he said.

"I shall follow soon."

He smiled, "Do you think I would consent to leave you if I thought Menelaus would kill you? No," the flicker of a smile played about his lips. "I would have killed him the first night if he had tried. For if he meant to do it, he would have done his work then."

I stayed to close his eyes. Long after he was dead, I sat with him so he would not be alone, he who had been alone so much of his life. Menelaus finally put his hand on my shoulder to lead me back to his tent. He had not begrudged me this vigil.

No one could sleep that night. Agamemnon was raging about the camp drunk and brawling. He hurled a knife into the fire. "She should be dead ere now!" he pointed at me. "I am King here."

There comes a point when every man has had enough. Menelaus could bear more than most. But his time was now. "You should be dead ere now," Menelaus said.

Odysseus sensed danger and tried to check my lord. This time Menelaus said, "No man shall stop me." He drew his sword and Agamemnon drew his. I sat down with Odysseus to see justice done, and he touched my hand to give me courage.

Agamemnon was no Paris and fought like a maddened bull. The brothers raged at each other like two men who have a lifetime of grievances to settle. Now one triumphed and now the other. Both took wounds. They sweated and grunted it out most of the night. The world was splitting atwain.

Odysseus whispered to me, "If Agamemnon should win, I will defend you. I shall take you back to Ithaca. I will not permit that cur to kill you."

"But he won't win."

Menelaus fought with more than his own strength. Right was on his side and the Goddess, as I was beginning to feel. Finally Menelaus knocked him down, and the King of Kings did not rise again. Menelaus picked up the sword

Defeat And Triumph

he had thrown down long ago and pointed it at his brother's heart. "Renounce your claims over us," he said so that the whole army, which was by now gathered around, could hear. "Admit that you are no longer High King of Mycenae, for you do not deserve it. When you reach home, proclaim your son Orestes to stand in your stead. You shall give up your ill-gotten spoils and women to be divided evenly among all but me. I do not wish to profit from the disgrace of my own house."

Agamemnon was loath to obey, but he loved his own life more than his honor. He agreed, perhaps with the thought that he would make war later to gain all back. But that later he was never to see.

"And one more matter," with his foot Menelaus pushed him back to the ground when he attempted to rise. "You shall not speak against my wife and Queen. I was wrong," he said, now turning to face the entire army, "and I freely admit it as any man who fears the Goddess should do. This woman does not deserve death and censure but the highest praise."

He took me by the hand and raised me to my feet, as at the very same moment Odysseus let go my other hand. The Goddess was nearer to me than ever before. She filled my whole soul, and said, "This, Helen, is my last gift to thee. Take it and be content. You have earned it."

"This woman, look at her well, shall never cover her face in shame again the way women in our country do. She shall walk in the light of day. If woman could be goddess, it is surely she. She is no traitor but Goddess on Earth or Inanna, however men may call her. She loves us all, all mankind. She gave us victory and would have given victory to the innocent commoners of Troy also who had no part in this quarrel if it were not for this cur," he pointed towards Agamemnon. Agamemnon took that opportunity to sneak away into the shadows.

Menelaus was not content until the whole army took his signal and kneeled to me, gazing upon my face by the dying embers of the campfires. The Goddess glowed through me and irradiated my face. I could feel the divine force.

It was almost morning. That was the last I ever saw of Odysseus. He slipped away to set sail first of all, for his journey was the longest. He looked at me one last time while all heads were bowed, and we said good-bye with our eyes.

"Helen would bring peace where there was war, and now that we are threatened at home by the Sea Peoples we need her wisdom and strength to defend ourselves and rebuild a nation," said Menelaus. "I for one shall follow her all the days of my life if she will have me."

With that my husband, Menelaus, King of Sparta, son of Atreus, knelt in the dust and handed me the sword of the House of Atreus with double lions on its hilt as if I alone were the victor.

I knelt beside him, enfolded his head in my arms, and kissed him. We held each other and knew each other for the first time. The glow of the Goddess and the peace that she brings passed from one to the other. It was a sacred moment. No one spoke. The Goddess had taken him away, and now the Goddess had given him back to me. Blessed be the name of the Goddess.

About the Author

Linda Cargill has been interested in ancient history and myths since the eleventh grade when she first read James Michener's *The Source* and Mary Renault's *The King Must Die* and *The Bull from the Sea*. She visited Greece one year later in 1973. She first pursued her interest as an archaeology major at Bryn Mawr College (until she decided her interest lay more in mythology than in the technical specialty itself), and then as a literature major at Bryn Mawr, Duke, and the University of Virginia. She read everything she could find about ancient Greece and the Greek myths, but was dismayed at how male-oriented the stories were.

The usual picture of Helen is of a flippant, flirtatious queen, or, even worse, of a sexy siren who elopes with Paris and starts the Trojan War. But the author's research showed that there were variants to the usual myth, in fact as many variants as there were ancient writers. So she chose the one that was the most sympathetic to Helen and added a few plot twists of her own, as any ancient writer felt at liberty to do.

This is the author's first novel. She has written book reviews, published an article in *Cat Fancy Magazine,* won an honorable mention in the *Atlantic* short story contest, and placed in the National Writers Book Contest in 1986 for *To Follow the Goddess.*

She currently lives in Virginia with her husband, her son Kenny, and her three cats— Monkey, Happy, and Grumpy —where she is busily at work on a trilogy about the women of the Caesars.

Order Form

Mail Orders Only:

>Cheops Books
>977 Seminole Trail
>Suite 179
>Charlottesville, Virginia 22901.

    Please send me _____ copies of the novel To Follow the Goddess at $9.95 each. I understand that I may return any book for a full refund — for any reason, no questions asked. If your book is damaged in transit, we will replace it free of charge.

____ Please add me to your mailing list to receive notices of future publications.

Please Print:

Name:
_____

Address:
_____

City: _____ State: _____
_____ Zip: _____

Sales Tax:
    Please add 4.5% for any book(s) shipped to a Virginia address.

Shipping:
    Book Rate: $2.00 for the first book and $.75 for each additional book. (Surface shipping may take 3 to 4 weeks.)
    Air mail: $3.50 per book. Federal Express 2 day air $11.50.

    If requested, all books will be autographed by the author.

____ Please autograph.